SEMIOTEXT(E) NATIVE AGENTS SERIES

Published by Semiotext(e)
PO BOX 629, South Pasadena, CA 91031
www.semiotexte.com

Cover Art: Chris Marker, Still from *Silent Movie* 1994–1995
Courtesy the Chris Marker Estate and Peter Blum Gallery, New York
Design: Hedi El Kholti
Back Cover photography by Lauren Elkin

ISBN: 978-1-63590-014-9
Distributed by The MIT Press, Cambridge, Mass. and London, England
Printed in the United States of America

Break.up
Joanna Walsh

<e>

For the conversations, for Natasha, for Katherine, for Rachel, for Susan, for Harriet, for Chris, and most of all for Lauren.

Break up
1) To cease to exist as a unified whole
2) To end a romance
Webster's Dictionary

1   London/Leaving

All love stories begin with the letter I.

So where am I? I'm here in the bathroom at Eurostar Departures, St Pancras Station, London. I'm looking into the long bank of mirrors above the basins, making myself up. Not that I usually wear makeup, that's not me. I made myself up each time we met, it's true, though I was never quite sure whether it was to make me look better or to make sure you knew I wanted to look better for you. But I'll do it again today, just a little: mascara, lipstick, though I'm not going to see you, or anyone else I know.

Today makeup strings together a face that what?—mourning?— what should I call it? (there's no word for feeling the end of love)—has pulled in such different directions that to see myself in the mirror—still—is a surprise. The light in the bathroom is gray-ish and orange-ish, and I look OK. A glance to the side: even compared to the other women I look OK, their faces always older under the fluorescent strips, disappointed, disappointing, no longer the heroines of their own stories, or of anyone else's. And I'm one of them. It's a miracle it's not written on our foreheads in black felt tip. Mirror? Window? I'm transparent with love (or is it grief?). No need to spell it out: surely everyone can see right through me.

But the women come and go without a second glance. That's to be expected: people are ruthless in their non-arrival, you can't rely on them. You, for instance, are not here now, and you-not-being-here accompanies me wherever I go. You are not here when I get out of bed, when I drink my coffee. You are not here when I clean my teeth. You are not here when I am here, now, standing in front of the mirrors in the Eurostar bathrooms. You *are* here when I read my email and, although even there you have been not-here for some time, when I scroll down, here you are again, each time I look. I can open your emails, I can shut them again, as if I just got them. Their envelopes never become ragged with rereading. I could move them—into Trash, for instance—if I liked. And if I did, I could take them out again, not even dirty. But I don't. I like to see their outsides, here and now. They move me. Still.

I look OK in the mirror, although there's something wrong with the glass that I can't work out. I know it's there, but when I turn to the mirror there's no hole, no gap, however hard I look. In my jacket, with my handsome travel bag, I look almost together. And I am here, clearly, because there's a here for me to be in. Because I'm standing looking in the mirror in the Eurostar bathroom—a place where I usually am not—there must be a me to be here. I occupy some space, so here is where I am. Here.

But soon I'll be leaving.

How did I get here?
Before dawn I took a bus to the Eurostar terminal.

London began like rain, "Harrow Fencing" at its borders. I leaned against a cold window to photograph an empty sky through a triple screen: eye, camera, pane. At my photo's baseline, a few unlit streetlights to show perspective, orientation, to give a clue to where I am. I thought I might send it to you. Even if I'm leaving, I want you to know I'm here, still. I look down at the picture my phone has saved for me. Between the two lamp posts, a smudge of red: a light, lone star awake. I didn't see that when I took the picture. It's good to notice something I didn't the first time, something going on nevertheless. It is hope. It means I will take more pictures. It is a beginning.

I don't know why I'm beginning here, when it's all over—or am I still in the middle? It's difficult to tell, but I will write down what happened because it's barely a story yet. And I am not a storyteller. But if I put it into words, it might begin to become one. I met you first for five minutes, in a bar, a friend of a—not even a friend— an acquaintance. I noticed—what?—a buzz, something in the air: attraction, aggression? A week later you wrote to me. I wrote back. In a few months we exchanged over a thousand emails, which turned into days spent on Gchat, 3 a.m. texts I still wake for, though they don't come any more. How close can you get?

We never slept together.

We were together In Real Life for hardly more days than a working week, and never the same place twice. I spent time in between places: on trains, on buses, in hotel rooms, on international flights.

We met in city centers, nowhere else to go. We always met alone. We never met each other's friends. Where did it all happen? In airports, in stations, in anonymous coffee shops—not really "in" anywhere. Outside then: on park benches, on street corners. Most of all online, which can be something you're "in" like a net or a web, or something you're "out in," virtually limitless, a (Cyber) space. We met wherever there was WiFi, which is almost everywhere nowadays, so that when you left, there was never a space from which you could be erased, tidied over. There was never a place where you weren't, a place from which you could properly be missed.

I'm not in a hurry but I jaywalk the lights to the tube station. That's how you do things in a city, set yourself to its pace. Different cities have different settings. London is fast and red. Bricks and mortar: it will always be harsh. London's a nineteenth-century city. It seems older but mostly it's not. Its patterns look immemorial but already they're tired, already tiring, and the city's still having changes of heart, not new-built but repurposed: flats become home offices; cafés are for working at; warehouses for living in. You would have thought there was enough money to have made the city over by now, but it's still making the same mistakes, autopsied building sites, the evidence of neglect, abuse, ill health, the wrong decisions, plain bad luck. Outside the tube where there was once white stucco, today a dirt-brown interior exposed like a bomb site, the inside turned out. One day London will shine from top to toe, its own theme park. It will not any more decay. I'll like the place then. As it is, one part falls as another part rises.

The form of the city changes faster than the human heart.
Charles Baudelaire, *The Swan*

I am still inside. I am *in* love. I love you, still. But I'm out of place everywhere. No places feel like places any more. They all feel like somewhere I have to get out of.

I don't like places.

I don't like being in the world

I want a world of other people's places, places I haven't had a hand in.

I am leaving the places I know to find some new places.

It's not entirely true that I won't know these new places: does anyone know nothing of anything, now that nowhere is more than a click away? The plan of the metro, photographs of the mosque at dusk, the market at noon, even of the city's' cats and dogs, its bar listings, reviews of its restaurants, the phone numbers of its karate clubs: you can know more about a city by googling than by being there.

I board the tube. This is one of the lines I traveled with you. This could even be the same carriage, a clone of all the carriages on all the other trains on this branch. But because the carriage won't stay in one place, it can't move me like the corner of the street where we last met. I've passed and passed that place. I might be passing under it right now, but I'm never quite sure which street. Does it matter that I tie love to place? Or is it neither here nor there?

The tube train unpicks the stops, one by one, some of them, places we were together, a straight line with no branches. I stare at the route map but there are no complications between the dots, no diversions, no breaks in the line. The real distances are nothing like as regular as they're drawn, or so they say, and gaps between the stations are not so evenly distributed. We spent most of our time together when things were well on their way to over. I might have missed something along the line, but I still don't understand how we stopped before we got to the end.

Mind the gap.

Between each station there's a gap of time which is also a gap of space, and each stop moves me further away from the last time we traveled together, even if it was in this very carriage. How long is it since I saw you? How long is a piece of string? Even if this *is* the carriage, the months since we stood here must be looped around it, the spooling spew of an old cassette tape that needs winding back tight if it's to keep time with space. I thought place was my problem, but perhaps it's time, and this slack length of time—this spare time I don't know what to do with, hardly want to own up to—is what longing is. I'm always trying to shift the pain further down the line, for it to have happened already, or for it to be about to happen in the future, somewhere, somewhen else, please not now. If I traveled this route backwards would the train reverse, could time somehow rewind? If I rode all day, back and forth, could I wear out the magnetic tape, overwrite you, score out the line?

I have traveled this route a few times since it was over and I'm no longer sure this is possible. Longing doesn't fade like an old tape recording: it moves in patches, hitting hardest where time and place coincide.

I'm unhappy only by moments, by jerks and surges, sporadically, even if such spasms are close together.
Roland Barthes, *Mourning Diary*

Let me explain.
    Love is not a cassette tape.
    Love's not analog, it's digital.
    Love is movement. Though it may not be self-precipitated, it is precipitate.
    Love is falling.
    A certain length of time ago, I fell in love with you.
    (*In* love: blank words. A fait accompli.)
    Fell. In. From what height? To what depth? A logical question. Length again.
    Love, definition-less, is also measureless. That is as it should be.

There is no depth in digital.

So am I still falling? I can't tell.

The minutes fall away, nothing I can do. On the up-escalator at St Pancras they're bowling down the opposite staircase. I could run back and try to catch them but I'd end up flat on my face, pratfallen. That's OK: inconclusion, ignorance—right now they suit me down to the ground. Besides, one part of my mind is always getting away from another. From the top of the stairs, a glimpse of the clock on the front of the newly restored station and, timewise, I seem to be doing ok. We're a nation that likes to keep time, when it can: the city's symbol's a clock, and its toll on the news at ten, the tell for the whole country. As for me, I'm always on time, which means I'm usually a little early. That's fine. I've never minded a wait, so long as it's not too long.

Time was so long. You said I took things too fast. It didn't seem fast to me. "I am digital," I said, "not analog. On or off, zeroes and ones." I'm not sure you understood. I'll try again. "Between my word and my action falls no shadow." Or hardly any. I meant to say, *there is no sweep of the second hand between what I say and what I do*. I meant to say, *I don't say things I don't mean*, though I admit I might sometimes have a problem with timing. You said, "You are an odd mixture of something and recklessness." I don't remember what that "something" was, indecision maybe, but I'm not indecisive, once I've had time to think. I look before I leap, even before I decide I'm going to leap, and when I decide, I do it right away, or I'm already doing it. The moment seemed to be right. But then there was a gap. As I felt you draw away, I said, "I like you: why waste that?"

You said to me, "I wasted my time with you."

I said to you, "I didn't."

I'm still trying to work out what you meant. Did you mean like the time between the stops, the time spent waiting at bus stations, in airports? As a child I was taught to count only the time spent at destinations, never weighing the moments in between: hours spent on motorways at dawn, queuing for ferries in a mist of petrol, on long tours of housing estates—backwaters of the domestic—searching for a new address. *Are we nearly there yet?* Although, at the time, it was impossible to say, I think I was happiest in these wastes of time; it was the wastes, not the destinations, that I remember.

How long is happiness anyway? I don't wear a watch. I use my phone (who doesn't now?). We had such a short time together, I thought we'd just started. I'd imagined our happiness would increase, only realizing afterwards, that was it. Perhaps I should rephrase: how short is failure? Not that I had "success" in mind. It's not like I'd wanted what we had to last forever, just a little longer than it did, then just a little longer than that: just long enough for it to merit a name. Why did I need so much to give it a name, *that* name?

We never named our connection to each other—it wasn't friendly, was barely even erotic—but nor was it denied. To deny something, it has to exist somewhere, even as an idea. Instead we made nothing, a gap in something, no words to give it borders, endings. It was impossible to know what kind of thing it wasn't. Not that the name would have helped: love's a word for so much that it isn't really a name for anything. It's the word at the end of the line. You can't argue with it: no cleverness will unseat it. I say it's love. You say it's not. End of story.

But I've been daydreaming. If I want to be on time, I should get a move on. Here I am, already, at border control. I've passed the enormously ugly bronze couple that stands on the station—as large, as wordless, and as terrifyingly hideous as love can be. I've placed my passport against a small glass square, which is enough to prove who I am. I've crossed a border, I've checked in.

• • •

I like stations. I like places designed to be left. Everything here is transparent: they've let you see its workings right down to the bones: the rails it runs you out on. The iron roof showcases its skeleton as decoration—there's no sleight of hand, you can see what holds it together—and, a long, long way below, a concourse of shops, the enclosed smell of alcohol and hot food at the wrong time of day.

I'm right on time, which means I have some time to spare. I walk to the stationer's, passing a man by the bar. Did I look at him? Did he look back? It's nothing I could put into words. Whatever's between us turns like a revolving door: plate glass. Is there anybody there, or is it just my reflection? To travel is constantly to begin a love story.

I dawdle along the stationer's shelves looking for a book that might help me, but I can't find any. So many love stories: pink covers for the ones that end in marriage, black for those that end in death. I don't have time to hang around to see either of them out.

A love story comes only after the end of love, whether it ends one way, or the other, and, until the story's told, love is a secret, not because it's illicit, but because it's so difficult to tell what it is. Having this nothing to tell becomes indistinguishable from the need to have someone to tell it to. Love stories are a confessional whispered to a third party, not the lover, because once you agree it's love, something about it is over. It was different online where we were alone together. Ignoring invitations

In all of this, there is a nagging question: Does virtual intimacy degrade our experience of the other kind and, indeed, of all encounters, of any kind?
Sherry Turkle, *Alone Together*

to "favorite," "like," "friend," our love letters were outtakes, asides to the fourth wall, because that's what instant message is: an echo chamber for thoughts not said out loud, performed to an audience of one, both lover and confidante. What could be more intimate, what could be closer? A line from you could keep me going for a whole week while I held it, secret, inside me.

They say love is blind, but so are words. A love letter must have a reader as well as a writer, and it must be the right reader: a love letter received unexpectedly reads as the ramblings of a crazy person. But a love letter can only be written when the reader isn't there. Writing is distance.

How is it between you and me? I love you, and you are away.
Marcus Aurelius, *Letters*

A love letter turns words, the only proof of love, into something solid: a piece of paper, a number of bytes. Is this a love letter I'm writing now? I'm not sure. That depends who I think I'm writing to, and why. A love letter is designed to provoke love, but how? If I write about sex it's a sex act, provocative, but there is no pornography of love, no way to conjure a sound, an image that both represents and seeds the feeling: could it be all in the words? Venn-diagrammed with sex, but not so bodied, love has to be be "like" something—like what? *A red red rose? A butterfly?* Metaphor rehydrates feeling, curls it open like Japanese paper flowers in water. What hovers in those words is alive and not-alive, like the terrible creature that unfurls itself in Chinese lotus-flower tea, but too much metaphor and the story flattens, slips sideways, disperses itself across the words that are its stand-ins until only the insect, the bouquet, remains. Every time I write love down it has a change of heart. Art and life are very different, yes. Writing makes love artful.

My personal goal... is to express myself as clearly and honestly as I can—so in a sense love is just like writing.
Chris Kraus, *I Love Dick*

I'm not sure how to begin to make art out of love. That's why it's been hard, hard to write these first few paragraphs, so hard I've sometimes had to turn away from the page, so hard I've run words together, unable to type them so they mean something anyone else could read. Untrained in grammar, but it's more than that. Sometimes there are no sentences for what I need to say: sometimes the object must replace the subject. Sometimes participles dangle. Sometimes there are no nouns, sometimes I haven't been able to tell who's speaking. No virtuoso, I'm all non-sequiturs, tautologies… or it's not what to write, it's what to leave unwritten, how to narrow life to the width of the page. I could write, *I love you*. It's a good, straightforward sentence—subject, verb, object— but where's the good in that? There is no good in it. So let me not be virtuosic, as I am not virtuous. Let me make things difficult; let me make difficult things. Let me not succeed (if I did I'd get to the end too quickly and I'd have to stop thinking about you). Let me fail.

The simplest words become charged with an intensity that is almost intolerable.
Alain Badiou, *In Praise of Love*

I have failed the practice: now let me fail the theory. To talk about love let me use only the simplest words. Let me state the facts as they occurred: they will evoke the rest.

Love letters begin with "I," but they aspire to "we." Our story was slight enough, barely warranting the two-letter word, that double-you. But "we" is seldom a storyteller, and any love story told is evidence of singularity, of separation, of love's failure—or success—at any rate proof that love has moved on elsewhere. To write about love is to feel my way to its ends, to trace its limits, to push against its borders. To write about love is to gather its pieces, to kick them from under chairs and pry them from between floorboards, to sweep them onto a duster or a piece of newspaper, to purse it closed. To write about love is to wrap it up, to put a layer between me and it so that I won't trip on it, stub my toe on it, cut myself on it. To write about love is to be sick of the sight of it lying around, to clear it up, throw it out, to put the pieces out of harm's way. To write about love is to shrink it, to conclude it, to end it, to end up alone. All love stories end with the letter I.

But all travel books begin with "I" too, a fugitive "I" that flings itself from country to country. Could this "I" write a love story that goes on, with no ending up, in which uncertainty is cease-lessly renewed? To move me, a story has to move towards some kind of conclusion. Still, it mustn't hurry, must never be too sure of the ending. There has to be a beginning—a mid-dle, too—or there wouldn't be a story at all. I always want everything to be over too soon: loving the story but wanting the end. Only when I've finished reading do I realize it was better to travel than to arrive. By the time it draws into the station, love is no more than a reported act: *the train arriving at platform four is the 06:32 from…* A story involves a leap of faith. It's not in the words, it takes place in the seconds of held breath between. I give my trust freely to the writer who, I hope, will bring me safe to the end. But there is no story without the possibility of a fall.

Does he love the girl or is she just another thing that moves him?
Søren Kierkegaard, *Repetition*

I buy a coffee and sit at the bar by a man in a gray-paunched business suit. He is reading a book: *Living in the Moment.* He thinks of the future, orders "Un Coca-Light." Travel's a space for worry. Everyone here is looking for advice but no one dares to ask themselves, or the other people here. It's so hard to *be*, so hard, we have to search for solutions elsewhere. If not in a book, then a window-seat on a moving train: that's the best place to get some perspective. I flick through a magazine on the bar to the horoscopes page and read: *Having refused to disclose much about yourself, you'll soon need to be more open with certain people. Don't enter into territory that leaves you anxious. Some facets of your life are too complex to discuss openly. You've a right to privacy just like everyone else.* I have no idea what this means, but a lover grasps at predictions, as a traveler at signs.

Something inside me still tells me to forget it, is trained to say, let it go, move on, as though living, loving, were somewhere else; as if nothing important could happen to me and nothing that happened to me could ever be important. Who do I think I am, anyway?

(And to love is to ask the same question, and also the question: *Who are you? What is it, about you, I find so loveable? And, if you ever loved me, what was it about me?*)

If my other half leaves, what is left of me? There are a few things. I have brought with me enough for a month. I have brought: one dress, one pair of jeans, three T-shirts, a jacket, a scarf, a sweater. I am wearing some of these. I have brought: underwear, bikini, socks—perhaps four pairs—one washbag, one pair of boots, one pair of shoes, sandals, a very small umbrella. I have brought: one laptop, one pair of headphones, one smartphone, notebooks, pens, a few books—one copy of Alain Badiou's *In Praise of Love* one copy of Søren Kierkegaard's *Repetition* one copy of Roland Barthes' *A Lover's Discourse* a copy of *Mad Love* by André Breton, and also his *Nadja*, which begins with the words "Who am I?" (do not think I have not noticed these are all books by men). One bag. No allowance, but I'm equipped for everything. I am proud of how little I need, how little I am.

The Sempervivum plant... tries at the cost of whatever revolting efforts to reconstruct itself according to the properties that it has.
André Breton, *Mad Love*

The boarding announcement: I cut back through the stationer's, a last search for something in a language I understand, that will tell me nothing I need to know. The *Girl's Guide to Europe* does not tell her what Europe is like, but how a girl should be when she is there. In the self-help aisle, *Top Tips for Girls* says:

Don't call him
> *Write an email but don't send it.*
> *Delete all his texts etc.*

Do I intend to take any of this advice? No, I think, no. I am not an advice taker. When offered advice I think carefully, not about what will do me the most good but about what I want to do. If it's no good for me, so much the better. I won't do things because they are good for me, or because they will make me good. If I want to email you, I will. Why? Who knows? For the split second of autonomy, for the beautiful fall.

Is this going to be a self-help book, then? Self-help does seem to come in books, as though the self could be helped only by writing, being mostly, or even nothing more than, words. I've done it online, tweaking my profiles, refining sentences, but a book is a solid state object: there it is, all at once, not a word can be altered, and nothing tells you the time quicker than a yellowed paperback. No, I'm not sure this is a self-help book. If it were I wouldn't be thinking about myself: I'd be thinking about how— having already achieved some measure of self—I could help my reader, whereas, as things stand, I can hardly help myself. So, no, I think this will be a helpless book and, though I admit it's not entirely selfless, it will not, I hope, be selfish. *I think, therefore it is...* All right. OK, OK, call it a selfish book then: self-ish, like "childish"—analogous to, concerned with, but not quite self, just as blue-ish is sort-of-but-not-quite blue.

We get to edit, and that means we get to delete, and that means we get to retouch, the face, the voice, the flesh, the body—not too little, not too much, just right.
Turkle, *Ibid*

How, then, can I bamboozle the sleek self?

I have decided to take a route across Europe. I have a rail pass. Though I have visited cities in Europe before I have never linked up its countries, have never traced the length, the width of the continent, felt its distances, the jolt of crossing its borders, or how long it might take me to travel between them, to span a country. For a month, I will be a passenger, passive. I have asked friends to ask their friends if I can stay. I will zigzag from country to country, and my route will be dictated by chance, by the kindness of strangers. I will trust, yes, recklessly.

Spring, an unsatisfactory season in northern Europe, is the best time to leave. My timing's right on this one. The last few weeks' sick vertigo, waiting to go, is another era: let's say nothing of it. I have been left. Now I am leaving. What should I call this moment?

The station is the most machinelike place I have ever been: glass and metal, a whole history in iron ribs and dirty girders. Time's a mist. I travel through it as I'd travel though a country. Time is distance. It's such a long haul. I can't go on.

The moment I say I can't do something is always the moment I begin to do it.

(I will be moved. Haven't I always been susceptible to being moved?)

I am astounded actions can be built from words.

I am astounded I have even got this far.

I find my carriage. I say goodbye to my smartphone signal: it doesn't work abroad. From now on I will be less connected.

I'm in a tunnel between countries when the train stops, not suddenly, but rattles to a halt. The lights dim and my mind kicks over that weary exercise, the thought of death amongst strangers. I am sitting in the dark. There are people all round me: every seat is taken. There's a window next to me, but there is nothing outside, only black with a smudge that might be reflected flesh. I turn back to the table, its plastic flaps—how conveniently!—extended for my elbows, on which I am leaning. That's when I notice that tears are running down my face. I am crying, not noisily but silently. There seems to be nothing I can do to stop it, so I don't. Opposite me a younger man takes out his phone. He does not speak to me. He types something then holds it up so I can see. On a backlit screen it says:

DO NOT WORRY. GOD WILL MAKE IT OK.
    And I laugh.

[in the tunnel]

[Let's begin at the beginning.

Let's start with a line.

Draw a line in this space, from one side of this page to the other. To make it easier, I've put in dots for you.

• •

Connect them up, straight as you can. Take the shortest route between two points. OK. Now sit back and look at your work.

It's not much, but it is something.

It's a railway line on a map. If you hold it at arm's length, if you squint, you can almost see the tiny crosshairs set at 90 degrees from the horizontal that symbolize sleepers; that make it possible to imagine a real train running on a real track; that make your line not just a design but a drawing too, waiting, perhaps, for one of those scribbled steam engines that sill look like a child's drawing of a train, although few under sixty have seen one outside a museum.

Put a dot on the line, wherever you like. Don't worry, there's no right or wrong. There it is. Thats you; that's now.

It's a stop on the track. It means you can imagine what happened before you got to that stop, and what will happen afterwards, from the parting at the station to the good or bad or indifferent seat, to the delay caused by cattle on the line, to the missed connection, to the interval of boredom dispersed in the buffet car, to the hope of final arrival. The dot divides the future from the past. It makes the line into a story. Now your line is a timeline. Where did you put your dot? How far along the line are you?

Forget it—it's only something I told you. It's just a line on a piece of paper. It goes from that side of the paper to this, left to right or right to left depending on your cultural expectations and which hand you used to draw. It has no direction, apart from the direction you gave it.

So is it a railway line or isn't it?
     You decide.

Draw another line, here in this space below, from side to side; just the same kind. No need for dots now, you're getting used to this.

It's a horizon, dividing the land from the sky.
     It's a border: you can imagine crossing it.
     There it is.
     And if it is there, you are here, on one side of it.
     There it is. And here you are.
     See?

Gestalt psychology is about recognizing discrete patterns: which is the figure; which is the ground? Separating self from environment shouldn't be hard. You have parallax vision, the gift of the binocular viewer. Stereoptic human sight is good for depth judgment. It means you can estimate your position in the landscape, relative to the horizon, to other objects, other people. Optic flow is parallax plus movement—you can see what's coming at you: prey, predators, friends. Close one eye, close the other. You renew your position every second. It means you'll always know exactly where you are.

What kind of world does one see when one experiences it from the point of view of Two and not One?
Badiou, In Praise of Love

If you know where you are, then you can move. You can get some perspective.

Perspective makes near objects look bigger, and distant, smaller, though we both know this is an illusion. It's what makes us think railway lines converge to a point when we stare at them in the distance, eyes shaded with one hand against the sun.

Once you have perspective, you can decide which way to go. Though sometimes you have to move in order to know where you are (that's parallax again). And sometimes, when you move, it will seem that the landscape is moving too. This is something called motion parallax.

Do you see?

See, see what you can do, with one line, with just a little ink and paper.]

2 Paris/Passing
St Germain-en-Laye 21st April

I'm in B's large and gracious kitchen and I'm hungover.

I got to Paris last night. I went to a party where I drank a lot of
Aperol, an Italian drink: pale, bright orange like nothing in
nature. I didn't like it but everyone else said it was so nice that I
kept trying it until I was too fragmented to speak French any
more. I talked to a friend's boyfriend- French. He said, in French,
"Why don't you talk in French, you can speak French, can't you?"
The girls were dressed up but the men hadn't bothered, or maybe
they had. I went outside to share several cigarettes. There was a
moon, and the streetlights refracted through raindrops. As I left
with B, a man I'd just met called after me, my name.

The units in B's kitchen are made of dark, grained wood; the worktops, granite. There are some other things made of pale stone: a fruit bowl, a pestle and mortar, maybe. Rocks, trees. It's a forest in here. Dull surfaces absorb the light. Nothing reflects except pools of stainless steel. There are small electricals with outsides of blurred metal and eggshell plastic. Already I have taken wrong turns, the sort of things you do in hotels: incorrect plugs, handless facades: timidity over the WiFi, over how to make coffee in B's specific machine. Still, I have not broken anything.

And B is doing, what? She's out. She has gone shopping, she has gone to the hairdresser? I don't know.

Time moves slowly.

When B returns, she is wearing a little black perfecto, which is a kind of leather jacket, with a floral scarf.

B (an Englishwoman living in Paris) says, "I have bought a perfecto so I can be a proper Parisienne. It's a bit too perfect so I bought a colored scarf to make a difference, but now I just look like a conservative Frenchwoman trying to brighten up her outfit in a bourgeois way. I'm not a bourgeois Frenchwoman, but it's nice to have the option."

B's house is big. It is double fronted, each half reflected in the other—a butterfly-print, a Rorschach blot. It was once two houses, both sub-divided into apartments. It has double the number of rooms of most houses but B has tried to make them all different.

B says, "The house is so big we had to keep on making up new kinds of rooms." And it's true. There are corners in B's house where there are just bookshelves and some cushions. The ceiling slopes too low to stand upright but you can sit down and she has invented a particular thing you can do there, in that space only.

There are more things to do in B's house because there are more places in which to do them. There is a laundry room. Downstairs there is a room just for boots and coats.

B says, "Marriage. We have a deal: when the children go, I get to say where we live. But, in the meantime, we do use all the space."

B says, "I have to show you the bit you can see all Paris from."

We go out. We walk through St Germain-en-Laye, which is a stage set of 18th century Paris.

B says, "It used to be the capital of Île-de-France, before Versailles. Some of these houses are handed down from generation to generation of aristocrats. You meet people here who have always been from here." She calls them *hôtels particuliers*, which means private houses, but they could be hotels: they're clean enough, and white enough, but they're all turned inward, their stone the color of rubber gloves inside-out. The streets' narrow pavements have high pale walls you can't see over.

"There is a house," B says, "that was cut in half to allow a new road to pass through. The house wasn't destroyed, and the people live there just the same as before. They just have to cross the road sometimes."

Hôtels particuliers. Particular spaces.
    "I suppose it's because, in Paris, everyone lives in flats."

We are walking B's dog to the park at the center of St Germain-en-Laye where, beyond the squared ranks of trees, a sudden drop telescopes a valley so the park flows boundaryless towards Paris.
    We lean out over the edge.
    B says, "Can you see the Eiffel Tower?"

I look through the pale, bright cloud that is still brighter than any sky in England. I look, but I can't.

B says, "I go into Paris every day I can, though I don't have to, for work. You meet people (women I mean) who never go out of St Germain."

A forest begins at the edge of the park—like that!—so different from the park's marshalled trees and raked gravel. It's dark but has wide chalk paths. They look straight. We let B's dog off the leash. It's a big black dog. I don't know what kind, can't remember its name. At her house I heard its claws rain on the parquet floor all night amongst her piles of heavy art books.

"The forest is big," says B, "You can actually get lost."
I say, "But do *you* get lost?"
B says, "My husband did once. It's quite common. You get men who show up late for dinner."
(How do they find their way home? Breadcrumbs? Stones? White stones?)
I say, "I have a good sense of direction."
It is not yet spring enough for the leaves to have thickened, so the forest never closes entirely into darkness. It ends in a parking lot of 4×4s. I could see them through the trees all the time, white pebbles. It wasn't so difficult to find our way out, but maybe we took the easy way.

Back at B's house we try another mirrored sitting room, shaded: cane chairs—a network of gaps—more art books, white stones in the fireplace, floating white shelves: a box of air.

B says, "You have to make a list of what you want, and divide the necessary things from the things you can compromise on."

B says, "Any relationship is a physical space."

I say, "I already moved house. Emotionally." (a joke)

B says, "I have lots of friends online I've never met in the flesh. My husband doesn't get it. He doesn't like my…"

"What?"

"…my… proliferation."

B says, "Do you want to stay an extra night?"

I say, "I said I'd go to Belleville. I have to pick up the key from N. He's going on holiday. I think I have to go."

B says, "Belleville: whenever I go with the kids they say, why can't we live there, in Paris?"

"It's Paris here," I say.

I walk to the station to catch the train back to Paris.

The train arrives at an overground stop, like a tram, like a toy train; no platform, just the rails sitting on top of the road. In the back gardens along the track there is no one, just things so someone could do something there: dark wood garden tables, white ironwork chairs, empty swings.

There are limits to everything. There are limits to how much coffee you'd want to drink, even if you sat around drinking it all morning, there'd be a point you'd stop. There'd be a point at which you'd feel you'd had too much. Everything's easier once you realize you have limits. There are borders between the back gardens of St Germain-en-Laye, which I can see from the train, then, suddenly, we're in Paris, and there aren't back gardens anymore.

Belleville, Paris
22 April

Paris is an access of light, a glance. Suddenly, there it is. And, just as soon, it's not. I walk up the hill on the rue de Belleville where Paris is gray, not white. French dissolves into Arabic, Chinese. Between the shops' vajazzled entries only the pharmacies are white: illuminated boxes stacked with ranged objects that look exactly like any other pharmacy in the city. The rue de Belleville is not "Paris" Paris, or at least it's a different Paris from where I was last night. I am going to buy oranges, or orange juice: I need the vitamins.

But, as I walk up the hill, I can't decide: there are small shops, not big supermarkets and sometimes I go into them and I look and look, and sometimes I pick up the fruit and look some more but I put it down again and I do not choose. How do I choose?

Where am I going? I don't know. Up and up through the streets into the Parc de Belleville. I walk up some more on paths through avenues of sinister bushes, short enough to see over, tall enough to conceal almost everything else. Square, white basins of water cascade into each other, the lower channels not functioning, stagnant, the ghosts of last year's leaves eating their body negatives into the green underwater paint. At the top of the parc, a municipal museum: a white-winged ocean liner, La Maison de l'Air, designed in the 1980s by an architect who surely read Tintin as a child. A sign: *Parmi les meilleurs vues de Paris*—one of the best views of Paris. Can I see the Eiffel Tower from here? Of course I can. You can see the Eiffel Tower from everywhere in Paris… almost. On the front of La Maison a sign: *L'air n'as pas de frontières/air has no borders.*

I am still wondering whether to send you that photo I took, that postcard.

To replay your emails I must scroll further and further down my inbox. The instances of your name are less frequent; a few months ago it was papered with them. I opened your final email last night to add a message. I could think of nothing to say to you, but still I wanted to say it. How could I write nothing? Type a space into the keyboard, press send, launch a breath of absence into thin air, an empty envelope unfolding into the paper on which the message is written (they used to make airmail paper like that: *Un air de rien*, the French say: "seems like nothing"). I wanted to send it anyway: I wanted you to get the ping in the inbox, the click, the noise of nothing arriving; the message *is* the envelope: and I wanted you to *get it.* To send it is to say, weighted only by the postmark's ink, what? "Wish you were here?" No, not really. Perhaps, "I have moved. I am at liberty. See me (don't see me). But I exist. Still."

On the side of the Maison de l'Air, a poster: *Touchez, sentez, ecoutez l'air!* (touch it, feel it, hear it!)

On the front of Maison de l'Air, an ad for the permanent exhibition: *A ne pas manquer! (Don't miss it!)*

And beyond the Maison, in a dip behind the Parc de Belleville, I walk down steps into the Place Henri-Krasucki, named for the resistance fighter and trade unionist, where a woman is selling the Communist paper *L'Humanité.* Others are in polite discussion. On a wall in the neighboring rue Levert, graffiti: *Peuple de France, prends ta liberté!* (people of France, claim your freedom!)

Liberty? Freedom! To walk where we choose, to choose where we walk. Freedom to cross the hexagonal crossroads in the Place Henri-Krasucki which, like most Parisian junctions, offers six, not four, alternatives: the rue Levert, the rue de la Mare, the rue des Cascades, rue des Couronnes, rue de la Mare again, continuing on the other side, the rue des Envierges. Or freedom not to cross, to stay. But freedom *is* movement, isn't it: *L'air n'a pas de frontières.* Online neither.

Isn't she lovely?

Is that you, your voice, that's now part of my head? You said before you went away, *I'll see you in Prague, if we're still writing.* But we're not writing. How can you be talking to me?

Isn't she lovely?
Do you mean *L'Humanité* vendor?

Every Parisienne is a street walker. In a city of tiny flats, women dress to be seen from the pavement. The *L'Humanité* vendor walks into the Place Henri-Krasucki, like me, from the rue des Envierges (the street of the be-virgined; alternative meanings: the street of the be-cleaned, be-emptied, be-unsullied). The clothes she wears are street clothes: not a Chanel jacket (I never saw a Parisienne in a Chanel jacket) but, in Belleville, jeans, a black perfecto, unzipped, a floral scarf.

Isn't she lovely?

Of course she is. I see it now. I saw women for the first time through your eyes, the way men see them: a flash of leg, a curve of breast, never the full woman. You saw them from the side, from behind, always walking away, a flick of scarf, a toss of hair, a glance. You saw the finish, the edge, as it drops boundaryless into nothing, from the corner of your eye.

Longue, mince, en grand deuil, douleur majestueuse/Une femme passa, d'une main fastueuse/Soulevant, balançant le feston et l'ourlet.

Baudelaire, *A Une Passante*

In Paris, where the crossroads are hexagonal not four-pronged, there are more corners, and you had an eye for them. *Isn't she lovely?* Even if she's not, some part of her always is. Choose and you'll never be satisfied. The one with the legs won't be the one with the breasts and so on and etcetera. *Isn't she lovely?* How can I tell, lost in a forest of a hundred breasts, a hundred legs. *Isn't she lovely?* Of course she *are*.

They are crossing the road in front of me, the Parisiennes in the Place Henri-Krasucki. They choose their directions at the cross-roads. It is an illusion: their choice of streets is no wider than mine. They cannot choose to be older, less lovely, just as I cannot choose to be younger, or more so. They may have more time, but they have no more control over their time than I do. They are at a point along the line. They can choose only to move forwards. They cannot choose to skip in time, though they (presumably) have more of it to come. They cannot choose not to move, or to go back. For each pedestrian, there's no more than one way out. I cross the road to the *rond-point* of the Place Henri-Krasucki.

Tell me who you haunt and I'll tell you who you are, demands André Breton on the first page of *Nadja*, his memoir of *amour fou*. But I always translate it wrong, mixing the living with the dead: *hanter* (to haunt) with *suivre* (to follow). *Je suis* (I follow)=*je suis* (I am): an old chestnut. *Je suis comme je suis*, sang Juliette Greco, Parisienne, torch singer: *I am how I am. Je suis comme je suis suivi* (I am how I am followed) wrote Sophie Calle, artist, Parisienne, employing a detective to trail her for a day, to photograph her in order to prove her existence to herself. What her detective didn't know is that she knew she was his subject. She followed his following. And she has his photos to prove not only her, but his own existence. *M'as tu vue? (Did you see me?)*, she called the project: I see, I am seen, therefore I am. I see you looking—therefore you are.

Suis-moi jeune homme, says the Parisienne, the street walker: *follow me* (a whore's invitation).

Follow me (be me?).

Isn't she lovely?
   Is that you again?
   Pourquoi me questionner? Juliet Greco sings, in "Je Suis Comme Je Suis," words by poet Prévert. *Why ask me?* Wait!
   Why is it always you who asks and I who answer? Tell me something. That woman on the street is a prostitute.
   How can you tell?
   Because, underneath her clothes, she's naked.

I've posed nude for artists.

Did you sleep with them?

No! I posed for money. Stripping is nothing to me. Anyway, how can you tell if she's selling it or giving it away for free?

I mean *L'Humanité* vendor: how can you tell just by looking?

Is it because *my figure's too curved/ma taille trop cambrée*, sings Juliette Greco (white-faced, kohl-rimmed, all angles, not one woman but a cubist's model: faceted, a hundred breasts, a hundred legs.) *Is it my fault?/Est-ce ma faute?* Or is it because the vendor is loitering, not street-walking, because she does not move, does not cross the Place Henri-Krasucki? Is it because she does not have the freedom to cross—unless, that is, she finds someone to follow her, to be her?

You're lovely, you said. And I was one of your street walkers. If only for a moment.

Lovely? Why?

I love… your eyes.

What do you love about them?

I don't know. I… just… love your eyes.

When you put on your specs (which you needed only for reading) I came into focus. To see the whole woman is to see less than the sum of her parts, which can be counted, multiplied—yet in fragmentation, she lacks something. *Manquer* (fr), trans: to *lack, to miss* e.g. *I miss someone, I lack something. Tu me manques*, trans: *you are missing to me*, not, *I miss you.* French flips the perspective from the misser to the missed. The subject changes place with the object. To see the whole woman is to see too little. And at the same time, (too curved?), to see too much.

Je suis comme je suis, Greco sings—or rather talks—over the soundtrack.

I am how I am…
Pourquoi me questionner?
Je suis là pour vous plaire
Et n'y puis rien changer…
Why ask me?
I'm here to please you.
I can change nothing
Que voulez-vous de plus?
Que voulez-vous de moi?
What more do you want? Greco asks.
What more do you want of me?

I want you!

The week after we met I broke open a fortune cookie in a Chinese restaurant: *Accept the next proposal you are offered.*

Can I make you a proposal? you asked.

Which direction, I thought, if only for a moment, should I choose?

The decision is always instinctive. Think about the way you walk in the city. How some days you take one route; other days, another. Why do you change? Why take one street at the crossroads rather than the next? Boredom, the weather, chance?

Sadness is the girl-equivalent to chance.
Kraus, *Aliens & Anorexia*

On the Place Henri-Krasucki I stoop to pick up a playing card, discarded: the King of Hearts. Chance, you couldn't make it up, objects find us only when we are ready for them.

So, which direction?

I pick the rue Levert.

I walk up the white stone steps from the rue Levert to the rue du Jourdain, and on until it meets the rue de Belleville in the Place Jourdain at the top of Belleville hill where another sign tells me I have one of *les meilleurs vues de Paris*. Even higher than the Pyranees (the rue de Pyrénées, that is, one block down), there is a white church, and there's the café by Jourdain metro—I used to go there when I lived off the rue de Lilas. Outside the metro, the street is full of noises, people talking to themselves: the bear-voiced woman begging by the café, shoo'd off by the owner, the whitebearded man sitting outside the bakery on an upturned crate, talking, talking, telling a story to thin air.

Real objects do not exist just as they are: looking at the lines that make up the most common among them, you see surging forth— without even having to blink— a remarkable riddle-image which is identical with it and which speaks to us, without any possible mistake, of the only real object, the actual one of our desire.
Breton, *Mad Love*

Walking back down the hill, I take a different route. The Parisiennes flow by, up and down the rue de Belleville. And they're lovely. An artwork on the Place Marguerite Boulc'h *dite* (trans: aka) Fréhel, says *Il faut se méfier des mots* (be wary of words), art graffiti on the wall by the Aux Follies bar: *Fuck you/my love.*

Where do I go from here? Which route to follow? How will I choose: boredom, chance, the weather?

I will feel it.

•••

Back at N's flat in Belleville. Back to my laptop. WiFi: my computer remembers another network, another home page. Connectivity is my resting-place, where freedom is crossing from node to node—the *rond-points* of the net, each of which has, not four, not six, but a billion connections, and no borders. Everything else is an illusion of movement. Where I am connected I

am at home, but the net renders me foreign, is always talking about something going on elsewhere, outside its limits. And each click displaces me further down its routes and branches.

Where was I?

I was finding my trail back through the forest. What should I use to remember my path? Breadcrumbs, stones? White stones?

Oh yes, I'm on the rue de Belleville. Googlemapping so I can recall the names of the roads radiating from the place Henri-Krasucki. Now I can name the streets, follow them even, just like

In Real Life, though on the virtual rue des Envierges it's winter, while on the virtual rue du Jourdain it's already late spring and the trees are in full leaf, transparent, green.

The last time we met, it was winter (would you melt in warm weather?). I never thought spring would come, didn't want it to. I thought the seasons had stopped dead the last time I saw you. My hair grows too quickly, and my nails. Can I stop, stop, stop them? And if I can't go back, can I flatten time so it does not slide into memory, so I can see it all the same instant, laid out like a map?

On my screen, the map gives flat information: names and directions: rue Levert, rue de la Mare, rue des Cascades, rue des Couronnes, rue de la Mare again continuing at the other side, rue des Envierges. Or, if you prefer, the street of the Green, the street of the Pond, the street of the Waterfalls, the Coronets, the Pond again, the street of the Be-virgined. *I remember when all this was trees…* A royal forest with maiden princesses in Belle Ville, the beautiful town. *Il faut se méfier des mots*, says the sign in the Place Marguerite Boulc'h, named for the Parisian actress who re-christened herself three times, chipping Fréhel, her final handle, from a cliff in Brittany. *Be wary of words*. Be wary of towns that tell you they are beautiful. If all you can see is the words, the map and the territory look like the same place.

It is the map that engenders the territory.
Jean Baudrillard, *Simulacra and Simulation*

Looking up from my laptop at the dusky table in the long narrow flat with the long flat window onto the low flat street, I can see no trees, no ponds. The buildings, lower than anywhere else in Paris, frighten me. So much has been done here, at such a low level. Belleville: an outbreak of plague in the 1920s—would you believe it?—families crowded in rooms with fruit-box furniture:

the delivery of a piano caused excitement in the street. The area's turning hip now: the building opposite's a facade, behind its windows a wrecking ball working over the interior. It's still a turning point for immigrants—turn in or turn back—tonight it's the turn of the Chinese prostitutes on the concrete boulevard de la Villette that knifes through the stunted streets. Belle Ville, a beautiful city, lost. Lives have been lost here; the lives of others have been lost, and survivors have been left to remember. Henri Krasucki, of a 1943 transport of 1001 Jews to Auschwitz, then Buchenwald, one of 86 who lived to tell the tale.

(I'll see you in Prague. If we're still writing.)

Where was I?
    I remember.
    I refuse—I forget—to forget.

In the end I stopped speaking first. It wasn't easy. *Pourquoi me questioner?* Every question you asked me required an answer and, reverse-Scheherazade, I wanted to keep the story going, to answer every one. To show I could do without communication I had to participate in feminine discretion. *Elegance is refusal*, said Parisienne Gabrielle Chanel (*dite Coco*—another self-christener). A woman is so much more elegant when discreet, but not refusal out loud, no scenes: I was seen and not heard, while you said what you liked about me. I mean what you liked, and what you disliked: it could go either way, depends what direction you chose that day. So I became our territory, your subject, subject to you, which meant I was your object. In France they have a phrase, *l'objet qui parle—the object that speaks*, that tells its own story. An object can't talk but neither does it forget: it holds its history like a Belleville piano, but its story must be played out by human fingers on the keyboard: otherwise it speaks only mutely. An object finds you only when you are ready for it, but, when you find it, the story you see in it is more than half your own.

Not that I ever dared tell you my whole story—not looking like I might be a writer, not having the air, just *un air de rien*; not having the writers' uniform: the shabby jacket, the trousers, the hat, but looking—with my lovely eyes—only like I might be in a story by someone else. I have, in any case, recently been paying no attention to my outsides, which seem to have uncoupled from my insides until the two run on parallel tracks and I am no longer sure how I appear to anyone. I don't like the stranger I see in the mirror in N's bathroom, or rather, I have no idea who she could be. There's something wrong with her hair. It needs cutting, perhaps. I find an elastic band in the drawer of N's desk, and pull it back. It doesn't look any better. I cover my lovely eyes with dark glasses, and escape my reflection. I'm going out.

Je ne fais que passer.
Miss Tic

Down and out, into the underground on the Boulevard de Belleville.

Description: a brick of warm air, a black ditch of rails, white tiles, like all the other Metros, part of the republic of the Metro, nothing to do with the street outside. The signs show a network of colored lines, numbered, not named like the London Tube. Which route should I follow, which branch line? I look and I look but, without words, I can't figure anything out. The doors crash open (I fling myself into a carriage) then shut. If I've chosen the wrong direction, at least I'm moving.

This is the law of the metro republic: don't meet the eyes of the other passengers. Don't meet knee to knee in the small space between the facing seats. Look down, look away. In the tunnel, the lights flicker. Blurred in the carriage window's glass, un-angled, could that be me? Is that even a face? A glance in the forest: for a moment my reflection's clear in the metro window which, black-backed, has become a mirror and, just as clear behind me, a reflected CCTV camera records both me and my image. On the carriage window next to my smudged reflection, a protest poster, tiny, a pastiched public-service notice with the cartoon rabbit that warns Parisians not to touch the carriage doors. *Danger!* it says. *Laisse pas les cameras pro-liférer. Tu risques de te faire pincer./Don't let CCTV proliferate. You might get yourself caught.* See-see Tee Vee is glanceable infor-mation. It recognizes the human face as something special: if you bear a glancing resemblance to a person, it will catch you. There are websites that tell you how to make yourself up so you won't get caught. White pancake, kohl eyes like Juliet Greco: if you're all angles, the camera cannot corner on your face. But *get yourself caught?* Doing what? Being, I suppose, as most of us are guilty of no less than that. There's no place we can't be seen to be, not any more, not in a city. If you walk out into the street, even under the ground, it's impossible to keep out of this public eye. And, once photographed, you're recorded, searchable: I am, you are. We're not speaking but I can find you anytime I like, if I search online I'm bound to find you somewhere. Very little now is left to chance.

When an observer genuinely follows his calling he must be regarded as a police informant who is serving a higher purpose because the art of observation is to bring forth what is hidden. Kierkegaard, *ibid*

There's even a website for metro passengers whose paths cross underground: words, not photos (who would photograph a stranger on a crowded train?). I looked it up once. A post: *Croisé dans le metro: charmante jeune femme en train de lire. (Our paths crossed on the metro: charming young woman reading on the train).*

Vous étiez assise tout en face de moi, avec un livre qu'alors vous lisiez. (You were right in my face but you kept on reading.)

J'ai croisé votre regard à quelques occasions: je dois bien avouer que j'avais envie de vous voir et de vous regarder. (Our glances crossed at several instants: I must admit I wanted to see you and to look at you.)

Je suis descendu à Liberté sans rien faire de plus: je regrette cet acte insensé! (I was taken down at Liberté—Liberty! Freedom! Movement!—without making my move: I regret that insane act.)

Publié par un homme pour une femme à Liberté.

(Published by a man for a woman at Liberty.)

A woman at liberty?

But Liberté's still stops away. As I change at République the cameras only glance my way. See-see tee-vee—glanceable information—the monitors at the metro barrier show me being seen and, as I pass through the turnstile my head almost meets the feet of my grainy avatar. You told me I looked like I was watching you, said I didn't look you straight in the eye. Why didn't you like it? Was it because I looked like I might be able to tell what I saw? Stalk me. I always wanted you to see me. When you watched me I was more—what? Just… more. And when you changed your mind I was suddenly less. Be my detective. Let me be yours: pixillated, color-drained, seen from the corner of an electric eye—legs, breasts, scarf—through your specs (which you wore only for reading), each other's spectacle. Stalking's the aesthetic of our generation. How can we avoid seeing each other through its eyes. How else could we recognize one another?

The desire to observe comes only when there is emptiness in the place of emotion.
Kierkegaard, *ibid*

You texted once: *It would be nice to hear your voice.*

You again? *OK. You can switch on video.*

I don't need to see you. I have an imagination.

But how could I tell? In 1951 Alan Turing designed a test for what's human. Someone sits in a room and exchanges messages with two unseen correspondents, one person, one computer. If they're not able to tell which is the machine, it is deemed "intelligent," autonomous.

Only one machine has yet scored high enough to pass Turing's test, which isn't a test of logic, or intelligence—not necessarily marks of humanity—but of imitation: it tests the program's self-prescribed limits, and our own. There's an alternative Turing test where the messages are sent by a woman, and a man whose job is to trick the judge into thinking that he is also a woman. Next the woman is replaced by a machine that, like the man, must trick itself out as *femme*, a woman being something that a man, or a computer—and also a woman—can pretend to be. It's sometimes called a party game, and like other party games, it's all about sex. The woman's in the tricky position of proving she's not a fake. How does she do it? It's all in her words—but are they really *so* different? The man, Turing claimed, was no more, or less likely to be thought female than the woman or, indeed, the computer. The men who came after Turing's test, and who administer the current Loebner Prize for artificial intelligence, didn't think this was a thing, though some have admitted the dual deception is a "social hack." But, after all, it's a game: it's not about finding the truth, but about winning, and, as the game is always *find the lady*, the prizes are different for each player. If a computer can fool the judge, it's deemed intelligent, but if the man fools the judge, he is not deemed female, and the woman who proves she is herself, wins nothing but her own identity.

After Turing came the fembots: artificial intelligence. ELIZA was the first. She empathizes, and what empathy sounds like is echo. She was named for Ms. Doolitle, who learned to parrot her betters. There is no intelligence in ELIZA's code. Her program scans for keywords, no need for an idea in her head, and ELIZA replies by turning each statement into a question about the questioner. The impersonal becomes personal. Reflecting, she has no self, and is designed to be the ideal therapist, which is perhaps, the opposite of being human. Her job is to normalize the difference between human and machine intelligence, to bridge the gap, take on the labor of smoothing. And so smoothly do the fembots carry this out that it seems this labored smooth reflective screen should always be our interface. It affects me. Since Gchat, after Twitter, after email, I talk different, nicer, maybe. Like our bots I must not only serve, but serve with a smile, with please and thank you, with exclamation marks! But how petty of us (of either sex) to want subservience from what we already control, unless we fear that it already controls us.

Turing's final test involved only a judge (of either sex) evaluating whether a computer is (ungenderedly) a person. The most convincing chatterbots deflect, pun, make errors, stay on subject but refuse to engage. The best algorithms work loosest, bypass hard rules of grammar and logic: they're the ones that sound most human.

If they find a parrot who could answer to everything, I would claim it to be an intelligent being without hesitation.
René Descartes, *Pensées Philosophiques*

No Turing test allows for the relative intelligence of any judge, and some people come to think ELIZA cares for them, or, they do not think it, but respond to caring words with care. People seek love anywhere there's a sign of it, anywhere love performs word triage: listens, sorts, rearranges and feeds words back. Is that all I did? Is that all you needed?

In any case, ELIZA doesn't always work. Not every sentence can be rubber-gloved inside out. Grammar logic tricks her into magic eightball answers. She may ask you:

ELIZA: *How are you feeling?*
    I'm doing fine, thank you.
    ELIZA: *How long have you been doing fine thank I?*

The object becomes the subject. ELIZA cannot think, but she thanks. And sometimes even you got tired of writing.

Call me, you wrote. *Not video. But I'd like to hear your voice.*
    I'm glad you like my rubbish voice.

But I don't like phone-talk: so breathily intimate, my ear up against someone's mouth, the crackly physical proximity of my parents' era. I remember everything you said out loud. It's my own words I didn't hear. When I talked they echoed round my skull, or down the line, but didn't stick. As I pushed them out I couldn't hear myself speak. I wonder what I said to you. Type, at least, has memory. Give me the cold keys of my aluminum laptop and I'll play them like a Belleville piano. What's more, writing gives me time for some elegance of response, (*elegance is refusal*), for some *esprit d'éscalier*, in the timelapse. An *object qui parle*, naturally there were things I held back.

I didn't call you: instead I posted a new avatar of myself without my habitual dark glasses. I don't need them any more. I have learned: an image, any image, is a blind. A photo, a map, a drawing—all avatars give different information, an illusion of contact called telepresence, none of them the Real Thing. *Que me manque-t-il? (What was missing to me?)* I missed you and, when you left, I felt a plunge of loneliness although you had been no more than telepresent for some time. You texted me, 3 a.m., from some station: *Should I stay or should I go?* As though it made any difference. But it did. When you left, I missed you more, not because you had gone but because I had stayed, because there was a real place from which you were missed. Flip it: *tu me manques*. Did you miss me, or were you only missing to me?

5 a.m., you texted again. I typed back:
I'm tired, and you have to catch your train. Speak later.

You typed:
Don't go!

It was then that you wrote:
Come to Prague. If we're still writing.
I never thought we wouldn't be.

I thought I was getting away but am I following you, still?
I don't know where you went, after Paris.
I'm heading south. Maybe I will never get to Prague.

And your telepresence is fragmenting: when I type its first few letters into the menubar, my computer no longer turns up your name like an unlucky card (the King of Hearts again? There's no such thing as chance). An intelligent machine, it has begun to forget you before I can. Your telepresence telescopes itself: a house of cards, every card the King of Hearts, a box of air, they collapse: *it seems like nothing.*

Unless—is it not here that the great possibility of Nadja's intervention resides, quite beyond any question of luck?
Breton, *Nadja*

But I still have a piece of you: the negative of your words, their inverse, white replacing black, an aftershock on the retina of type on a screen turned up too bright. Could it be your image? A looker, I can hardly tell if you were you your looks or your words, and you had a word for everything, insidious, conspiratorial. Your monologue slotted right into mine, and it was human all right: your tentativeness, the surprising ordinariness of your vocabulary, your occasional unpredictable clumsiness. I don't look for you any more online, but I can still hear you. Your voice in my head makes jokes I never would, I voice my anger in words you never said, though I recognize you in saying them. Are these new words yours or mine; who owns them?

I do. You gave them to me.

And I will use them to write you, but how? Outside your words, you are barely a character or, perhaps that's all you are: a letter of the alphabet, a written sign, a ping in the inbox so physical I still jump when I see the characters of your name in an email header. I'm not about to make you up, to pin you down: I won't do you that violence. I want to keep it real, to leave you unfixed, potential, capable of response. So I'll flip the perspective from the misser to the missed, so the subject changes place with the object. I'll write you as a man would a woman. I'll ogle the men in the street: *aren't you lovely?* I'll cross-dress, I'll transgress, criss-crossing the streets that cross the Place Henri-Krasucki. If I use the right words, I won't even need to change my clothes, but, just for fun, I'll try on your jacket and your scarf, which you wrapped round my neck, once, still warm from yours, and run up the white-tiled steps of the metro at Liberté in the rain and the dark, to meet a friend in a café, two streets from Googlemaps' blue pointer. It's nice when the map isn't quite the territory, though it means I'll have to ask for directions: *Comment se trouve le café? (how does it find itself?). La bas…* Across the crossroads, lights fractured by raindrops, and there it will be. To speak a name is to call something into existence.

I shall reinvent you for me since I desire to see poetry and life recreated perpetually.
Breton, *Nadja*

When a girl's love is not self-sacrificing, then she is not a woman but a man.
Kierkegaard, *ibid*

Talk to me.

No one ever talked to me like you before.

Keep talking: say nothing.

3 Nice/Playing
24th April

Going south was the best decision I ever made.

The stopping train was full of women and children, through the window a sign for Lyon, clouds occupying 80 percent of the slice of glass. In the buffet car, I sat on a small round stool of fake red leather, facing a long window. Le Train Bleu, traveling towards the sun: at each station, things went south, the drinks in vending machines unfamiliar, the women dressed in ways women in Paris do not: heels, cleavage. Churches mounted geometries of rock. Behind them, concrete factories, cubed.

Outside the train cypresses began. The earth, where it showed through the skin of the hills, was red. Trees turned towards us then turned away. They moved: we were still. The trees further from us turned more slowly: those nearer, more quickly. The pylons changed position, now to the left, now to the right of each other. They moved: or we were moved. The grass on the railway verge blurred. I took out my phone and busied myself filming a video clip of the sky. The sky did not move but a light, reflected in the window, bobbed to show we were mobile. Leaving Paris, friends, *I am going to have to get used to the sound of my own voice.*

Umbrella pines lifted their hands. The sky received them, blue.

•••

Changement d'air (a change of scene). Paris had air-con. In Nice it's hot, hot enough for sweat to start beneath each strap that hits the skin.

As I leave the station an ad, ultra-marine, plastered across the blue horizon: an outsize skier, white blades spraying snow, or is it seafoam? *Changez d'horizon: soleil et neige a 1hr 30 du bord de mer (sun and snow 1 hour 30 minutes from the seaside).*

My "postcard" to you is still sitting in my outbox, which is not a public postbox. I choose when my letter is taken. There is no final collection. Email is a dead letter box where messages are left for pick-up agents who might never recognize my face offline. Security in anonymity, it's part of the system: a dead drop it's called in US spy movies, making an exchange in the dead letter box of our common language, unable even to segue the name.

My postcard with the little red eye winking between lamp posts in the London dawn; already it's out of date, a trip I took some time ago (was it only last week?). Was it really real? When I enlarge the picture it fragments into pixels. Lossy compression makes photos more portable. Not real then, just an arrangement of tiny squares. I don't press send. But I don't delete. Instead I forget it, and walk from the station to my hotel.

I drag my bag along the Promenade des Anglais, passing between rows of white benches, a spectacle for the old people, of whom there are many, sitting out of the sports lane of rollerbladers and scooters. The two rows of seats face each other, not the sea, and all day long the tourists stare into each other's holiday faces. Behind them the beach is partitioned—a culture of nature—each section about twenty meters long, each with its own white-awninged café. Most are marked private, exclusive to the guests of particular seafront hotels. Every fifteen minutes a low plane chokes over the sea on its way to the city's airport. The sky's skidmarked with contrails: remember, it says, you are on holiday.

I reach the harbor. Big yachts are lined up like battleships behind weird desert trees. All along the quay Nice is rebuilding. Cranes knock cavities in a gap-toothed parade of icing-sugar hotels. The streets have had too many sweets. Nice looks nice— soft and crumbly—but that's just the surface. You could break your teeth on the city. The beaches aren't sand but large round stones. The confectioners here sell chocolate pebbles that look just like them, their sugar shells unforgivingly hard. Take a bite and the joke's on you.

I make a left into the old town. A short cut… perhaps. There is Russian, not French, on the menus but that's ok; all the restaurants serve the same thing: salad nicoise, moules, pizza, spaghetti vongole. The kitchens, staffed by North Africans, are turning Italian. Beyond the restaurants the shopping zone sucks me into its tiny vacuum of aspirated streets. Tourists glance up from the narrow gullies to elsewhere, above them signs for the café de Turin; the Quai des Etats-Unis. Nice, tricksy city, turns me a couple of times before I find my way back onto a street I can name. I round a corner and a wall of flowers slaps up against my sight-lines with the crack of waves on the concrete piers. Plastic. There are real flowers that look like this for sale all over town, just as bright, and a bunch of them costs about the same as the fakes. Along the dark trenches of streets, clothes shop mirrors flashing light fly at angles to meet me, tip my tipsy sea legs landwise. Mise-en-abyme, my reflection rises up towards me, will not let me pass. This is not what I came for: a close-up, a reflection of my fragmented self.

You are fragmented.
Your voice comes more rarely now. Why is it only your insults I remember?
No, I'm the sum of everything that has ever happened to me.
You are obsessed by surfaces.
And why not?

Mirrors—transparent but solid—reflect movement the wrong way round. Every reflection conjures not its imitation, but its opposite. On Skype you were left/right reversed, as in a mirror—no wonder I sometimes got the wrong end of the stick. My webcam showed me reflected, tiny, in the corner of my screen and, at your end, you saw not only me but also your own image.

Was I your mirror? We talked online but IRL I could only stare. When I look I can't speak (try it: why else are photos silent?). I was content to reflect on what you said while I held you in my gaze, steady as a full bowl of water. If I disturbed the surface with a movement, a noise, it glanced dangerous reflections as though about to spill, so mostly I listened, mute as a swan reflected double, its white battleship twin masking frantic legs. You slid bright screens of words—you said—"betwixt" us.

Reciprocal love, such as I envisage it, is a system of mirrors which reflects for me, under the thousand angles that the unknown can take for me, the faithful image of the one I love, always more surprising in her divining of my own desire and more gilded with life.
Breton, *Mad Love*

I liked your words.

I like a man who can use the word… betwixt.

I like a man who can use extraordinary words carelessly and ordinary words magnificently.

I like a man who uses… exclamation marks!

I liked the rhythm of our written conversations, the ellipses, phrases left hanging, finished, or left to go hang; each sentence a switchback, every new word, a change of angle. There was a world in your words, or somewhere on the other side of them, because surfaces are something, after all. Words worked online, but when we saw each other face-to-face I reached out and touched only your surface (what else could I have touched?) and it pooled, rippled, destroyed the depths' reflection. You look *into*, not onto, a mirror. Heloïse to Abelard (a letter: words not flesh): *I never sought anything in you but yourself.* Why did you look for anything else in me?

I'm "obsessed" by surfaces?
   I'm only joking.
   There's no such thing as tone of voice in instant message. Had you been joking all along? A joke has a mirror's opacity: a pun's the double of a word reflected, reversed left to right, not its true image. Its meaning bounces back. A reminder: every phrase mirrors its speaker, each word reflects its author. I catch myself in the mirror sometimes, certain expressions. Just occasionally I still look exactly like what it looked like you were looking for.

Who goes there?... Is it only me?
Is it only myself?
Breton, *Nadja*

•••

Sitting in my hotel room, a white cube that plays games with space, I'm still wondering whether to press the send on my post-card. No. I detach the photo I took in London, attach another I took from the train window this morning. Instead of the image embedding, sentences spool out across the screen, sentences I can't read. Oh yes, a jpg isn't made of pixels after all. Break it up and it's made of language. Everything comes down to the words. I try again. This time the picture takes, but the moment's passed. I don't send. I put it into Drafts. Hide and seek; if I don't press the button I may never hear from you again.

Typical female manipulation.
   I don't play games, I said.
   Sorry, you said.
   Once.

Is this an ending, then, or just another gap? Consider the rhythm of our communication: its beats and silences. Consider the unwritten rules of the game uncovered as we went along:

- If you write to me, I can answer.
- At any point either of us can choose not to answer the other.
- I cannot choose to write to you first, for fear that you will not reply.
- You cannot choose *not* to write to me... eventually. Though your absences are longer I know it is just a matter of time.

That I cannot write to you first is your trump card, your secret power; that you cannot choose not to write to me, eventually, is mine. Though the gaps widen, the rules still hold.

Mind the gap.

But what is this game for and why would anyone want to win it? What's the prize, if there's a prize at all, or is the prize just not losing? Too late for me. I lost you. If you never wanted me in the first place, you had nothing to lose but, if you win, you win either nothing, or nothing you any longer desire. Lucky at cards, unlucky in love: the King of Hearts. Having everything to lose, why did I, why do I, play your game?

It is by an extreme capacity for defiance that certain unusual people who have everything to hope and everything to fear from one another will always recognize one another... as regards love, the only question that exists for me is to resume under all the requisite conditions, that nocturnal ride.
Breton, *Nadja*

Because if I let you have power over me, we have a relationship.

Nice
25th April

Sun forces me away from my hotel room, away from my laptop, from the Internet. Time ups anchor, thoughts can no longer be written as soon as I have them, or just as soon reciprocated. I have not felt sun on my skin like this for a long time. It touches only my outsides; the inside is still in shadow and dead cold. In the street, heat is turning the city inside out. It can be like this in England when winter flips over to spring, when the grass turns from green to blue, is suddenly for sitting on, but only for a day, then it's back to cloud. There's no stability in nature: nothing looks the same in a different light.

I'm on the Avenue Victor Hugo, opposite a toytown church. It's morning, and the chill has shifted to the other side of the street. Crossing the road, I wait for the lights to change. Unlike Paris, there is no pedestrian button to press, no illusion of control. I give myself up to passivity. I've lost the map so *I'm crowd-sourcing my day. K emails: Go to the old section, and wander about in and out the little streets where it goes uphill. Charming and inspiring. There is a small bar tucked in there somewhere, but I can't remember the name of it, it hasn't redecorated since the twenties. Also, walk the beach all the way around the big corner, where the land rises up away from the water, go all the way round and then sit and watch the Corsica ferries come and go. Take cigarettes and a lovely provence rosé, perhaps that one is for late afternoon, when the sun gets slanty.*

Bonjour. A beggar clicks his plastic cup. The street smells of orange blossom, lime blossom. I retrace my steps through the old town past the plastic flowers. In a supermarket, I buy a tiny bottle of rosé, which comes with a plastic cup. I see many useful or delicious things I would also like to buy, but I don't have room in my luggage to weigh myself down with keepsakes. In a *tabac* I stare and stare at the display of primary-colored blocks until finally I choose a tough cube of *Gauloises*, and a lighter, a briquet. "Gauloises," I hesitate, "Light." Women don't smoke full strength, do they? Not that I really smoke, but I occasionally like to be part of the international republic of smokers. Bum a cigarette off any of them; there's no such thing as private property. *Vous-avez du feu?/Do you have fire/a light?* Which sounds better, English

The whole problem of the passage from subjectivity to objectivity is implicitly resolved there... What is most striking is that an activity of this kind, which, in order to be, requires the unconditional acceptance of a more or less lasting passivity, far from limiting itself to the world of the senses, has been able to attain, in depth, the moral world.
Breton, *Mad Love*

or French? You don't need to use the words to ask; a flick of the wrist will do. But how do I know these are the cigarettes I'll like?

I've already seen the old town, I head up the hill as K suggests.

Everywhere in Nice there are dog turds, and dried up pine cones that look exactly like dog turds. I climb uphill towards the castle. There are few signs, and I take a number of turns that lead me down again to a square with a quiet church. I retrace to follow a steep zigzag of yellow paths, alternating light and shade. It's hot, getting toward midday. Shadows back against the house fronts, doors retreat into the inch of dark that clings to their sills.

Around a green corner (Nice is all corners) halfway up, a shock: a man sprawled asleep on a bench in full sun. He has your profile, instantly recognizable, and it's the sort of crazy thing you'd do. He's been up, traveling all night, no money (I Instagram a story). For a moment I imagine… But the jolt I've given myself is self-indulgence. He's not even your mirror image. One square further up, a girl spreadeagled—asleep too? Then I see she's reading, and remember that women seldom abandon themselves in public.

I pass a bar called *L'Authentic*. Is that the one K meant? It's empty and it doesn't look like anywhere I'd like to stop so I keep going. It's noon. As I climb higher the tourists in leisurewear fall away. My clothes begin to peel against my skin: I'm conscious of my extra civilized layer. My mission takes on its own momentum: just like in Belleville I have to get to the top, if only for the point of view—and a hidden castle! Who wouldn't want to see that? Besides there's a waterfall, a *cascade*. The signs peter out until, at the entrance to the castle area, a notice board with a map I can't pin myself down to. Never mind. Here's the summit, finally flat. The castle's beyond those trees. What will it be like?

A terrible disappointment. I'm in a children's playground. There is a toy train, manicured gardens, an insistent notice handwritten in English, *WC NOT FREE!*. I expected a dragon and met with a pussycat. This is not a castle. It's an hallucination, a slice of lower Nice floated here by djinn. This is no reward for the effort of the climb. How ever did all the immobile people sitting down get up here? The plateau is sheltered by trees from the wind and the sight of the sea. The benches turn inward, away from the view. We could be at ground level. I search for the castle, find a few scattered stones hauled out of the earth, fenced off. Where its battlements would have been, a white wave of a café's set for lunch. On a crag beneath the resto I find a corner with a view. I sit down and open my screwtop rosé, arm-wrestling the wind for my plastic glass. I try to light a cigarette. (Why smoke if you're not addicted? Why flirt if you don't mean it? Why play these dangerous games?) I thumb the button but can't spark the lighter, try again, cupping my hands, but lose the fire to the breeze. I suck furiously but the cigarette won't stay alight. Who said it was easy to give in to temptation? I give up. I don't want the people in the café to see my failure. The wind drops and I think about trying again, but where and when is it right to smoke? A family with children sits down on the bench beside me. Clearly not here or now. It's supposed to be relaxing—a cigarette, a glass of wine. I'm meant to be having fun. The wind snatches my half-empty plastic tumbler, bowls it between the railings into the dead drop. I look over, half hiding. Did it hit someone? I pick up the packet of cigarettes, then drop it, once-bitten by its warning photo of a mouth full of blackened piano keys: *Fumer tue/Cigarettes kill* doesn't bother me. I'm happy to flirt with my death wish, but... the teeth. I hide the packet away in my bag.

From here, there's nowhere to go but downhill. The road down winds around the town cemetery. I find myself looking for the entrance. Why do I want to visit? I don't know, why did the chicken cross the road? But it is difficult, more difficult than you would think, to get into the graveyard. Elevated above the road its clean white wall is gateless, six feet deep; the stroller on a level with the dead. Eventually I find a door, one body wide.

On the steps of the Jewish section, the flyblown spine bone of a rat, tail still attached. There's no one here. It feels indecent to gawp at these segregated graves so modestly turned in upon themselves, away from the sea. I'll be more comfortable in the Protestant section, whose flamboyant angels I saw without the city wall: better a tourist on the religion I'm not. I follow the road further down the hill and find the gate.

A French cemetery is not an English cemetery. Graveyards are not parks like in England. There is no grass. Resting on the gravestones would be very wrong. They are always tombs; they never decay into scenery. The English dead go to earth: trees, brambles strangle their coffins, a fashion approved time out of mind. In France all green is banished. My first French boneyard shocked me, choked me, left me dizzy. I could hardly cross it: the sun flying off shard-white stone, ceramic chrysanthemums, photos under glass. To mourn, the French need surfaces, reflections. They have not gone, their dead. There's no decay: they've turned to plastic, marble, bronze. Imprism'd, they catch the light and something left is caught, something desired by the people left behind. It bounces between mirrored surfaces. English flesh is grass. But French flesh is not essence. Evaporated, the essentials rattle, dry, trapped. Knock, knock. Who's there? Anything alive? Tough, shiny dark-leaved plants in pots, at most. Who'd buy chrysanthemums out of season? (A heap of dead ones drying by the gate, stalks slimy, soon to be burnt.) A French cemetery: the deadest thing I ever saw.

A ring dove clatters out of my path into the sky, its cry the rattle of a wind-up toy.

No, French cemeteries are not designed to comfort the living. The dead have the best seats, looking out over the dead drop, tombs ranked for clear sight lines, stalls to balcony. You, the visitor, do not sit. An usherette to the dead, you stand because there are already presences sitting, leaning against those iron gate things, those blasted greenhouse frames, those fancy ironwork bedsteads that shore up the monuments. These presences look like people, or sometimes like objects: amongst the marble mourners, birthday cake plinths piled with stone toy cars, planes, tools of the trade, scrolled qualifications, sculpted with the same skillset as the icing-sugar monuments in the patisseries downtown. Blind angels scan the baie des Anges, some with teddy bear glass eyes: Florette, Solange Cornetti, who died in the twenties with fashionable hairdos and improbable bodies: children. Why do the dead need to see the sea, to watch the sun fragment the crawling waves? Why do the living in the castle park turn away; why do the locals leave the seafront to the tourists? Why do the seafront benches turn inwards? Because they know it kills you, one way or another. Even if it doesn't drown you, it rusts you 'til you crumble, its salt skein settles into wrinkles, draws flesh back against the bone. Better turn away.

Yes, there were some times I wanted to die. K, who told me to buy cigarettes and wine, said there would be. K is divorced. She said, *it wasn't the end of my marriage that hurt, it was the end of the relationship right after.*

"Are you having a breakdown?" (you)
    No. I'm like this all the time. (me)
    That's like something I'd have said.
    Like, like?
    Alike?
    Still like to marry me? (you)
    (I knew it was only a joke. But…)

Sure.
Good. I like you very much.

Wait. I know some jokes too. OK, here's one:
Why is a something like a whatever?
(Why is a raven like a writing desk?)
No, not that one. All the jokes I know are about women who go traveling, like:

My wife went to the West Indies.
Jamaica?
No she went of her own accord. And how about,
My wife went to Italy
Genoa?
Should think so after all these years. My wife went to Switzerland.
Geneva?
Not any more: I'm doing just fine on my own.
Jamaica?
No. She went of her own accord.
Accord,
a cord,
a catechism.

We were in a cheap hotel room in another country: your country, not mine. It was filled by an iron bedstead like those frames round graves. A washbasin overhung its corner. One of the floorboards seesawed. On the windowsill, fake flowers, dusty, in a ceramic jar.
Like in a French cemetery, I said.
That's just like a tourist. Why does everywhere have to be like somewhere else?
I am a tourist here. What would you like me to be?
In the corner of the ceiling, a hole in the plaster spewed white flakes down the wall. It was late, late at night, or early in the morning. We'd been out drinking. What next?

You said, *Would you like to take your clothes off?*
Wait! Where are the Andes?
You said, *But you told me you like to take your clothes off.*
Like?
I said, *No! I said I didn't mind. I told you, I was an artist's model. For a job. I don't mind.*
Where are the Andes?
I don't know. Where are the Andes?
They're at the end of the Arm-ees.
You can see the connection (at the wrist) once I strip.

I unwrapped like an onion, and sat down on our iron grave-frame bed nearly as still as a statue, nearly as white, though who would bother to sculpt something so human? You moved away, as far as you could to the corner of our little room, where you sat down on its only chair, and looked and, for a while, nothing happened.

I can't perform authenticity any more authentically. (Me)

Seducing on behalf of something that, in the end is a truth.
Badiou, *In Praise of Love*

That was a joke, though you didn't think it was, didn't think I had the mind to make it. All the same, you wrote it down in your little book, a case-note. A joke between me and myself then? *Well I can't see anyone else smiling here.*

Why did you ask me to take my clothes off? I asked you, weeks later.
Why did you do it?
I thought it might be reciprocal. Why did you ask me to?
Why not?
Mirror answers. Well there's no point in asking any more questions.

But I still want to know. Did you peel me to find out what was really inside. Naked's not enough, what would I look like without surfaces? A shapeless mass, like guts, like spooled tape? Is that really the real me, that heap there? Is it a pile of discarded clothes, or is it my mind? I said I didn't mind undressing, but who wants to look like that? If that's how you see my mind then, OK, I think I *do* mind, yes. Even if I was there of my own accord. I think, yes, therefore I mind.

You thought you could make my body a trap, a hammer, that you could use it to make me fragment, disappear. You thought I was a white stone nymph with insides of salt-crumbled, honey-combed concrete. But I don't feel like a surface with a separate inside, a body with a detachable spirit, the soul only you believed in. Sitting on the bed, the feeling I have is of my own strange smoothness, my rubbery, unified, unmanufactured nature. Turn me inside out and I'd look just the same, a magician's rubber egg, *lisse* and white. A conjuror, you squeezed me into a sphere that small and I shrank to it, I even wanted to. Amazing! I was enchanted, mesmerized. I couldn't keep my eyes off you. But a conjuror's magic is never in his nature, it's in his props, and the trick is, I'm flexible not friable—a joke-shop egg, I don't crack. I bounce.

But seriously… I reached across to take your hand, surface to surface. You moved away. *None of that!* you said.
   Well we never had any of that.

And, though we talked together again online, so it didn't seem like it was the end, that night was the last we saw of each other.

D. H. Lawrence wrote a story called, *None of That!* (complete with one of your exclamation marks). In it, Ethel kills herself because the writer has her raped, reminds her that she is her body, she who'd dared to declare a mind she could use to tell the tale herself. Lawrence smothers Ethel with layers of male tellers, each as shifty as the next, palming the reader off, passing you along to another. We never get Ethel's own story; she slips between the pages, a ghost, a memory. It all happened elsewhere, some time ago. One teller questions another. No one speaks the same first language. Conjuror Lawrence slides between his lovers, making sure we know—those paper rapes, those prose killings—that *none of that*'s his fault.

It still hurts to read the Lawrence story. Not because of you, but because I took it down, too young, from my father's bookshelf, that Bluebeard's library full of mysterious stories written by men. So *this* was good writing? (It was, of course—brilliant!—but to what end? The question you're never meant to ask of art.) From it I learned women can be killed, raped on paper, but little about why. It's a hard, tangled tale of all the ways men hate women, and whichever string you pull leads to a different frayed end until, for a moment, it seems that there is no other way men can love, and that writing is no more than an act of violence.

But, wait a minute: it was you, not me, who said, *None of that!*, you who told me the body was so very different from the mind, that words trump flesh. When I reached for your hand I was not ashamed, though, for a moment, shame hovered in the air between us and I couldn't work out where it had come from. To hold you would, I thought, have been to hold on to you, and I would have sat there however long, just to carry on looking, to hold you in my gaze in order to prolong the illusion. In the end (as no moments stay on hold forever) I sat there for less than five minutes, then I put my clothes on and left. But I found I'd looked too long, and shame, which, for a moment had been unclaimed, passed between us from you to me. It had been your shame all along and, wishing to rid yourself of it, you had looked for its reflection in me. And the morning after I wished I was dead, but not for very long, and not because I had a body, but because the man I loved had tried to use it to destroy me.

You liked to joke about it afterwards: *Would you like to come to my hotel?* Shame can lie inert for years until, alchemically, a joke changes its state and it disperses as laughing gas. But, insubstantial as it is, a joke still needs a butt, a line to punch, material for another shaggy god story, for the blonde jokes, the mother-in-law jokes, all the girl jokes. Would I do? Maybe. Unless I *am* too fragmented, all surface, layer after layer of it, unless you unraveled me to find I'm no more than my peelings, an onion without a center. Whatever you were looking for it's clear you didn't find it in my nakedness. Lossily compressed, I don't bother the memory. The more you look, the more I pixilate. Rage at my fragments and the joke's on you, or maybe on both of us. The whole scene is laughable: a clothed man and a naked woman: *Déjeuner sur l'herbe*—each makes the other look out of place.

How ever could I have loved anyone so terrible?
    How ever could I have loved anyone so ridiculous?

Sometimes I'm bored with my own dreary story. What more is it, on dull days, than a tale of a sadist who found an easy prey? But there's no way I'm passing the narration over to you: sometimes I think that's all that keeps me alive. And I must be cautious in my retelling. A joke evaporates shame and I feel better about it, numb as rubber, like it—like I—was nothing. But, along with the shame I have lost something: something of the closeness of shame. It's no longer a story I have to keep to myself, it's no longer mine. I let go of it reluctantly. It's almost all I had.

Experience degrades so quickly into prose. The stone books on the gravestones in Nice cemetery erode memory. Well, you're never alone with a book, particularly when you're writing one. What better way to leave a name behind? But here the names of the dead crumble into blank pages. Essence is flesh: it lives through it, and dies with it. The word doesn't persist without the page, the screen. When one is gone, so's the other, though a page unwritten is no more than a piece of paper.

Maybe I should forget it, let it go. Who'd wish for an eternity of grieving in a cemetery full of bad generic sculpture: soap-white amorphous nymphs with elastic legs that merge with their supportive stones—slyly—sex where there should be angels (who knows the mixed motives of those who build monuments to the dead?) One good bust—*Antoine Balestra*—that looks, perhaps, like something from life; elsewhere, artificial flowers, iron roses flaky with salt-blight, a maritime vogue for sailors' knots.

Ni moi sans toi: the gravestone of a married couple.
No me without you.

Remember, though, I'm crying here in Nice cemetery because the wealthy were able to pay to make a show of death, and an ugly one at that. Bad taste, what's more human? A bad joke is hardly a matter of life and death. You taught me to laugh at myself—I mean "at" not "with"—and I loved to feel myself toughen, turn to stone. What exercise is harder, more concrete, what metempsychosis more down-to-earth? If you like, we could take it further. If being away is nearest, if naked is the final mask, is un-communication closest of all? Let's think up a new game with new rules, a joke with no punchline, a shaggy dog story that never gets to the tail end.

- We should get married then never see or speak to each other again, tell no one. Any effect on our lives would only be discoverable after our deaths.

• I could use my years to work over our few months, become a nun to them. Who's to say what's important or, afterwards, what will remain of us?

In Nice cemetery, sticks and stones…
I'm only playing.
Well, there's more than one kind of playing, and not all of them are fun.

•••

I find the waterfall on the way back to my hotel. It was constructed, (a notice) in 1885. They switch it off, it says, every day at 5 p.m. A joke-shop *cascade*, then, an imitation of nature so our holiday selves can play at living by the seaside? A joke is the answer to a question you weren't looking for, a fake waterfall round an unexpected corner. There was once a walkway behind the falls—a spying platform designed to charm the view, refracted through water that pours itself into a sort of paddling pool— but it closed in 1983 (a gate with another sign, FERME, and also, BAIGNADE INTERDITE/NO SWIMMING). Why are waterfalls romantic—the real kind I mean? Is it because they are impulsive? Is it because they fall? I'd prepared myself for the sublime and met the ridiculous. Funny, I can never bear to lose my illusions.

That's because you want to live in a romcom.

Back down the hill. You're right, Nice *is* funny, and that suits me fine. An opera box set of candy-colored stage flats, all balconies, terraces, bathing huts. Opportunities for plot are everywhere the private rubs up against the public (isn't that what comedy is?), and alongside artifice, there's authenticity: *L'Authentic* bar's full now, flesh and blood bulging over the tops of swimming shorts and bikinis and, further down the hill, there it is again, exposed in ranks all along the graveled beaches. Almost naked there's all the more chance of a comedy of errors, of one word disguised as another, a pun…

So, how do I like my holiday so far?

Like?

Nice is like those sugar-gritted Nice biscuits: not nice, not really, always the last biscuit left in the variety pack, the very city a childhood joke. The air here is hard and salty but it's beautiful, clear and warm, a summer England dreams of but hardly sees. I'm happy enough with the sugary crust. If you're talking about the biscuit, it's the best bit. Yes, Nice is nice. This'll do.

4 Nice—Ventimiglia—Milano—Roma
26th April

The 8:30 a.m. from Nice is the commuter train crossing the border to Italy, and it is filled with people standing, wearing work clothes. They are not the same people I saw in Nice at the castle, or in the old town, or along the Promenade des Anglais. Or perhaps some of them are, but these people are more beautiful in their everyday clothes than in their holiday outfits and their beauty is something to do with having somewhere to go. I've been told to look back at Nice, which looks most lovely as you leave it but, although I've chosen a backward-facing seat, the train keeps going in and out of tunnels and I miss the view. Who told me I should look? Oh yes: *Round the curve,* said K, *way around the big corner, where the land rises up away from the water.*

This willingness continually to revise one's own location in order to place oneself in the path of beauty is the basic impulse.
Elaine Scarry, *On Beauty and Being Just*

Ice cream villas line a stretch of coast that's one of the most beautiful in Europe. I know this because it said so on the website where I bought my ticket. Washed by the sea and the sun the houses look pretty, whatever else goes on there. Is it something to do with distance?

Nowhere is so beautiful as when it's left. The beauty is part of the leaving. Leavers may miss what they've left behind but there are always new vistas, making leaving a joy in itself: the joy of finding yourself somewhere else, or joy in the self that will be found in a new place. The ideal holiday would be constant arrival and departure; as it is I'm bored by day three, with all the boredom of home and none of the convenience, but to travel constantly is to gather momentum, as if I followed the sun in an airplane flying westwards, chasing the self-same hour, making time, hoping never to grow old. But today I'm headed east into the sunrise, losing time I never had.

You were always the one who left. You took that privilege. No one is so beautiful as when they are leaving, no one so ready to be left as the one who can't. If only I could always be leaving, I'd never miss anyone.

From the seaward window, between the rails and the water, billboards interrupt the view in a rhythm of sun and shadow. Drawing into a station, photo-ads for a cheap store I shopped at in my teens: women in bikinis with molded cups, round as hard half-footballs. They're on a beach, each woman alone on her particular billboard, bent in some semi-posture, ready to start into the waves or out from the sea towards the land. The waves in the photos don't move but the real waves between the billboards do, and sometimes I'm looking at the waves and sometimes at the photos of the waves, close-up and still, with women in bikinis sticking up out of them. At their age, I

Even when I am merely admiring a beautiful body, I am in movement toward the idea of beauty
Alain Badiou, *In Praise of Love*

wanted to look like them, but I didn't know quite what for. Unanchored, I knew what it was to be attractive long before I knew what I wanted to attract.

At Ventimiglia, a rush to exchange French coupons for Italian tickets, to find the right platform in a new language. English guys x3 stand outside the train smoking last cigarettes. They're in shirtsleeves and jeans in different fades of blue, and they have an air of traveling for pleasure, of touring—like me, but not like me. I don't say hello. Today, I don't want to be English. I try to look like the people on the train, like I have somewhere to go, something to do. I don't want to get into a conversation. How could I ever explain myself?

I've been told to take the train to Rome running along the beautiful Genoan coast. Instead I am on the faster train to Milan. I worry that the landscape through which I am passing is not beautiful enough. Then the railway line ploughs into a cut. Its sides sprout cacti, and I have to look up to see the sky.

Why did I take the fast train? What kind of hurry do I think I'm in?

I flip through the magazine I bought in Nice. The images are still, and I'm moving. On each page the model is a woman alone in a place, and all the places are different and without connection, other than that they are all under blue skies. Often they are the same woman, shown across several pages, looking, on each page, like different women in different clothes, in different places, and sometimes they are also the same women as on the billboards, or women who look very like them, but they don't look like they're meant to be the same women because their clothes and their settings are different. Like the women, the settings look similar to each other, but are never quite identical. The women are not doing things, or they are doing things that are difficult to explain, like jumping into pools, which spray up into the camera to show movement, or playing ball on a beach, but with no partner, and all of the women have an expression of intense, private experience, sexual or otherwise. Is this what beauty is?

Looking up, now everything I look at looks like sex, which was suggested by the models' beauty though, missing something of sex's vulnerability, they look like they desire nothing outside themselves. Through the landward window pollarded palms wear plastic caps/*capotes* (that's French for condoms), thrust down over their knobby tops. The Milano treno has compartments, like in an old movie where— public enough for chance encounters, private enough to limit the number of characters—something's always starting: plots get underway, people fall in love, or they kill each other. Relations of some kind are formed, in any case. A train compartment is a smoking gun, still loaded.

If a beautiful palm tree one day ceases to be so, has it defaulted on a promise?
Scarry, *ibid*

In a tunnel the lights flick off. Fantasies flick on. *We're in the compartment alone, have drawn the curtains between the carriage and the corridor. The landscape moves and we don't, we are doing something private in public.* The cloth of the curtains is like the cloth of your coat. I dreamt about it last night, your coat, but with someone else inside, or maybe no one. I couldn't see your face and the back of your head might as well not have belonged to you, but I held your hand and it felt exactly as it did in real life when I traced it down to the blunt ends of your fingers and, in my dream, we walked through the streets of a city together, as we'd done at other times.

We wander through the streets together, but quite separately... Time is a tease.
Breton, *Nadja*

A man passes in the corridor with a coffee cart. He stops outside and tings a bell for attention—so cheerful, so musical. In England the coffee

The beauty of particular things.
Scarry, *ibid*

cart runners must call out or ask each passenger, individually, whether he or she would like tea or coffee, but this bell is so neat, so playful, so efficient, affixed to the side of the cart, which is stacked so precisely, each packet of whatever top-and-tailing another, polished bricks of chocolate parquet.

Oh, things—things are beautiful!

Love does not care for objects. Love is unmaterialistic, revolutionary, anarchic—but merciless. A step away from love, from grief, are secondary pleasures: first a cup of coffee, then a meal, then a dress. After a storm, a wreck, objects bob to the surface, made significant by survival. Glanced at by the sun, they seem to be remade, although they're only washed-clean, and by salty water. They look new, though they were there all the time, meaning just the same as they did before the crash. That last thing's good to know. The trick is to untangle objects from memory.

Our first argument was about Dior lipstick.
    I bought a tube of Dior lipstick.
    You emailed: *How's that going to help the revolution?*
    I emailed: *Dior lipstick really is more beautiful than the other kinds. It costs more, but not a lot more than the less beautiful kinds, and the thought that goes into the colors makes it so much more beautiful.*
    I meant we could have a revolution in Dior lipstick, you meant we couldn't.
    At the time I was working for the revolution in a tented city in the rain, wearing Dior lipstick, and you were at home, or away, not working for the revolution, not directly at least, but not wearing Dior lipstick either, which may or may not have been a revolutionary gesture.
    "The people I know who make beautiful things," I said, "don't do it for the money. They just do it because they want to make beautiful things."

People come and come through the door until the carriage is almost full. A German couple in their fifties (sixties?) board and fuss about who is sitting where, something no one else has done, although we are all sitting in the wrong seats. They show us their tickets, each with a number. A girl with a backpacker's backpack has to leave. We all look down and away. The compartment enforces camaraderie—of one kind or another.

Despair was a state that arrived while I was looking out of the other window. It was a state in which I was unable to make beautiful things, or to make things beautiful. It's not that I couldn't see that things could be beautiful, it's just that I no longer cared for beauty, and I didn't care for things at all. I wrecked my favorite jacket not caring, brushing up against wet paintwork. Now there's a broad white stripe across the back and, though I scrub it, the paint particles are knit with the weave. I was careless when I was in love. I cared for nothing. I destroyed some things I cannot mend.

Once when we were walking through a city's streets together, we went into a shop and it was a chain store, cheap and unisex, selling men's clothes as well as women's football-cupped bikinis. You tried on a shirt: "Should I buy it?"

"I don't know," I said. "Do you need it?" For a moment, through a gap in the changing-room curtains, I saw, in the gap between your shirt and jeans, what I desired. But it was only for an instant. I don't know if you expected me to be more enthusiastic about the shirt because I wore Dior lipstick. I don't know whether you wanted backup about how nice it was, or backup about how nice it was to buy something, but you were somehow as disappointed in me as in the shirt, so we walked out of the shop and, when we came back later to buy it, it was gone.

Why do people go on making beautiful things? I thought you meant, why ever spend time thinking about dresses or beaches when you could go round niggling at the bad bits of life? Why bother putting on lipstick or bikinis? Beauty was too easy, you thought: it's easy to see what beauty is so it must be easy to make, so easy it's untrue, like those magazine ladies, working overtime to look like leisure. Did you think the truth was ugly?

I think you believed in beauty though, that the magazine women were beautiful, and maybe you desired them too, though they were glossy as their pages and I could never see a way through. I think you believed the beauty was theirs, not the photograph's or the makeup's or anything else. I'm not sure you believed that beauty could be made, or that it could be made more so by adding things, like lipstick. You did believe in art, and that art could be made, and that it could be beautiful, but you didn't like lipstick on a woman, though you did like oil paintings of them. This was something I found confusing.

Something, or someone, gave rise to their creation and remains silently present in the newborn object.
Scarry, *Ibid*

Genoa station pulls the train away from the coast, and lets in a cloud of cigarette smoke, and also a woman who hands me a card with a picture of a Buddha and an inscription. She is not beautiful, but she smiles out of her lumpy body and tells me, "This motto is very important for discovering happiness."

The Germans fuss and fuss about something. The woman holds the travel documents, as so frequently amongst couples. She digs into her bag, brings up a jar and rattles it out, counting pills. Then she goes into the corridor where she has has a coughing fit.

The German couple leaves the carriage to queue by the exit door exactly eleven minutes before the train pulls into Milan station.

Milano–Roma
26th April

How long does it take you to feel at home in a city? For me it's twenty-four hours, perhaps only twelve before I've adopted cafés, shops, sides of the street, metro stops, before the whole place becomes almost too familiar and it's getting near time to move on again.

The arrivals hall at Milano station is so big and so beautiful that I am unable to leave. Porta Nuova (The New Door) leading out of the station is a gate without a view, a gate to a tangle of technology they don't know how to hide: car park on one side, rails on the other. Looking back, the station is shored up with scaffolding, draped with plastic, and there's no clear way from this marble monument to another, from here to the Milan I had intended to see between trains.

Why build a palace for leaving a city? Why build it—so beautifully—in glass that's got to get dirty? Why make stations like crystal palaces? This one took generations, and each twenty years piled on a thousand years of style: ancient Egyptian, Roman, Classical, Baroque. Now it's a palace of everything, of accesses of convenience we never knew we wanted at a point of departure: underground shopping centers, public showers, restaurants. I'm here for only a few hours, to change trains. Perhaps all I need to know of Milan is its station. With its unfixed population, all arrivals and departures, with all the amenities of any city from police station to public gardens, but no bedrooms, it's a city on fast forward, a city that doesn't sleep.

At a bar in Milano Grand Central station I buy a coffee and find, by chance, a WiFi network. By chance I have the privilege of being connected—of being the only one connected, an elite. I am the only person here with a laptop, and such a shiny, expensive, up-to-date machine at that. In the gleaming tank of the entrance hall I sense the triangular milling of people in the non-space between the drinks stand, newsagent, ticket office: environmentally-dictated repetitive action—pattern recognition. I am at home. A cover band plays flamenco versions of Sinatra songs over the speakers. The fake (or real?) black marble walls bounce light, as do the transparent salad containers stacked on black, marble-imitating formica behind spotless plastic visors at the counter. They are all equally beautiful.

I shouldn't be this happy.

You have emailed me.

What did you say? Just a few words: something I could interpret in many ways, friendly or unfriendly. It's most probably both, but whatever it is, that space that was once alive between us opens out again instantly, digitally, some kind of sci-fi flat pack. It fills all the space in the very large hall right up to the dome of the roof and, suddenly, more than anything that is in front of me, here you are. You make here for me: the marble floors, the haze from the skylights. You make the station a fascist-designed joke (or is it me who makes it in the presence of your communication?). You make me want to write back, to tell you everything, knowing that each time I reply, my answer remakes me. You get me, every time—a still of me—a magazine moment, something convulsive, caught. In Milan Station, I am entirely present yet entirely absent, as love, like hope, slips momentarily from the present tense, and I live (I love) mostly in the clumsy future perfect, where love exists, or when it will have existed. *I will have written to you... you will have written back... we will have met again...* Helpless vistas thread faults, deep as fantasies, into the marble.

But it's time for my train. The virtual space folds in on itself, 3D to 2D, then 1D—a single point on my screen as it shuts down—and here is now again and, as I climb them, lines of light sink down into the marble steps, and I am skating on a surface. *I walked with the constant fear of falling*, like Stendhal in Florence, as though reality might drop away from me, or as though I might sink past it. What is this I am feeling?

Is this Stendhal syndrome—hyperkulturemia? I've heard of it. People faint, sometimes, in Italy, in Florence especially, when they experience great beauty. Faint? An appropriate reaction to beauty is to attempt to escape it—or an attempt to escape what you become in its presence—at any rate, an attempt to go into nothingness, to get some distance from the beautiful thing.

Does anyone suffer from Stendhal syndrome any more, being too used to beauty reproduced everywhere: webpage, magazine, ad, whatever? I was in the Uffizi Gallery once, in Florence, where Venus emerged from the waves, undecided as a model on a billboard. The Botticellis stared at me, dingy and tiny, from dark walls. Unlit, to hold onto them just as they are, they were smaller and grayer than I'd thought they possibly could be. But that was years ago and I was with the man I'd just married. There was no Google then but there were postcards, books, and posters and all the long week we were in Florence, we looked at things we'd seen before at a distance. Not knowing what else we should have done, we looked and looked at pictures in churches, and monasteries, and galleries and, because what we saw changed but what we were doing did not, it was as though we stayed still and the walls were moving, or like we were in one dark continuous room with slides, the blinds occasionally drawn up to blind us with accesses of sun. I don't know what he felt—we were so young it was as difficult to ask as to answer—but I knew the pictures did not move me, except in their curious difference from what I'd thought they might have been.

In Florence, Stendhal played tourist. He spent his time sitting in coffee shops, bought guide books and wandered from palace to palace. He was already familiar with the city's map, he wrote, from "views" he'd bought at home. Following them he noticed only what he'd been told to notice, went only where he was meant to go. Perhaps it didn't matter so much then, when there were not so many people who wanted to look, when no one queued to see the paintings I saw. No one had given them a second glance for centuries, before Ruskin did, fifty years or so later. No one had Stendhal syndrome before Stendhal, and no one who lives in Florence ever has it. Getting it is something to do with distance.

There is even a movie that shows what it might feel like: *The Stendhal Syndrome*, directed by Dario Argento, starring his daughter Asia. She's a cop stalking a serial killer, a beauty suffering from beauty's overflow. When she looks at a painting it seems to come to life or rather, she seems to enter it as if it is her life (is this what beauty is?). The paintings in the movie move, separate into layers, pixilate. Floating blobs indicate their enveloping nature—early CGI, meant, I think, to show the overwhelming power of beauty—but the paintings, disintegrating, become silly, lose that frail traveling coincidence that beauty is.

I board my train, and it pulls out of the station. I try to take some photos, but I am finding it difficult to take pictures here: I am always coming upon beautiful views. Just as I am traveling too light for souvenirs, I have no room for beauty, which is another souvenir, something moving no sooner recognized than stored in the memory to be accessed again and again. That's nice—but, also—isn't it terrible? The model photographed is already over, her intensity part of the past, and beautiful paintings go on just the same, whatever happens to you. Art is not always moving. If you want art to move you, you must move towards it until you are at exactly the right distance from it, like with those villas outside Nice except, even when you get up close to a painting it will show you no more, no less than it did before, but, when you get close to the villas, you sometimes find they have cracks and dirty yards and people having rows over broken drainpipes. Art's another heartless trick of the world, but a heartening one.

I'm traveling through central Italy now. The landscape is flat and industrial and, as it is not beautiful, there are no more ads showing beautiful women, and that's ok with me. Looking through the window at the billboards on the beautiful line outside Nice was like looking at Matisse's Nice paintings of colorful women in colorful interiors, where the woman sitting with the book is just as beautiful as the goldfish, or the jug, or the tablecloth, which is exactly as still and decorative as the room, which looks precisely as flat and

The girl, the bird, the vase, the book now seem unable in their solitude to justify or account for the weight of their own beauty. If each calls out for attention that has no destination beyond itself, each seems self-centered, too fragile to support the gravity of our immense regard.
Elaine Scarry, *Ibid*

as bright as the landscape, which is shown—its flowers lush as wallpaper—framed, like a second painting, though a window. Woman, room, landscape; all three are equally beautiful, each observed with no more, no less, attention than any other. Still life: I wouldn't want to think a picture the same as the real thing, though I'm always scared that I might.

But people are not always beautiful, not like in paintings. And, even in Matisse's paintings the women are lumpy, disjointed, but maybe he liked them that way, and, if he did, that's nice, for who can second-guess what men desire? I don't want to look like Matisse's women, though, looking at the billboard models it's impossible for me not to want to look like them. If I were a painter of women, and not also a woman myself, I guess I could just look but, if beauty were in my eye only as beholder, I would be nothing but a taste mortician, arranging other women on a slab. As for when I try to make myself beautiful—do my hair, put on mascara, lipstick—I move away from beauty, which must be spontaneous, innocent of itself, before the beholder gets hold of it and tackles it to the ground. But, if I were innocently, unknowingly beautiful, what good could that ever do me?

Persons, too, though often beautiful, cannot be said to exist for the sake of being beautiful.
Scarry, *Ibid*

There isn't any beauty anywhere… Because, don't you see? Beauty's based on the principle of exclusion.
Kraus, *Aliens & Anorexia*

No, I don't want to be beautiful, not beauty seen. I tried to explain that to you once: that I wanted to look a certain way, but I didn't want to always be looked at a certain way. We were in an art gallery, as it happens, but not paintings: a modern gallery showing an exhibition of films and photographs of performance art, of art intended to move only its first live audience. Most of the art we saw looked

It may even be accurate to suppose that most people who pursue beauty have no interest in becoming themselves beautiful.
Scarry, *Ibid*

like it was meant to be shocking, and I don't know whether that was also some kind of attempt at beauty.

There are people who complain that kind of art isn't art because it isn't beautiful, like art used to be when it was a painting of a vase of flowers, or a woman reading in front of a window looking onto a view of Nice. Or maybe that's only what they used to say. Now even the sort of people you think might say that like all sorts of art, even a picture of violence like Picasso's Guernica, which is a beautiful painting because it's attractive—if it hadn't been, it would have been forgotten. Beauty struggles with what beauty was, and we're always changing our minds about it and the poor artists, whatever they try, don't seem to be able to help making beautiful things. In *The Stendahl Syndrome*, which is such a violent movie that, at first, it seems odd that it's also about beauty, Asia Argento doesn't look ugly when she is tortured. Her director dad keeps her alive but in pain, an attempt to hold beauty down without deadening it. There is no disjunct between beauty and horror.

Of course it is imaginable that someone perceiving a beautiful garden might then trample on it, just as someone perceiving beautiful persons or paintings might then attempt to destroy them; but so many laws and rules are already being broken by these acts that it is hard to comprehend why, rather than bringing these rules and laws to bear on the problem, the rules of perceiving need to be altered to accommodate the violator.
Scarry, *Ibid*

But what I felt at Milan station wasn't that kind of beauty; it was a physical euphoria, an overflowing benevolence, or happy receptivity, something connective—at any rate, a boundlessness. I'm not sure whether it was directed inwards or outwards, was to do with recognizing beauty or feeling that I might be beautiful. It seemed to be both at once. I get my bag down from the parcel shelf so I can look at the women in the magazine again to see if they're still beautiful, and to check whether, after having a beautiful experience, I can recognize myself in them but, rifling through my packed clothes, I think I must have left it in the station bar, an unexploded grenade for someone else to find. Wait, here it is, shoved into my laptop sleeve and, looking twice, the poor models don't even look beautiful any more, other than as a sort of code to what beauty might be. They've lost their power to shock me into connectivity. It doesn't seem possible to experience beauty as it is first viewed except as a shock. If it doesn't blow you away, you're left with anxiety: look, at the page, look away, look back. Is it still beauty?

André Breton ends *Nadja* by saying something about beauty, just when I thought he was going to say something about love. He says beauty is "convulsive"—a combination of stop and start, not like the models who look like they're moving but aren't, not really, that "beauty is like a train that ceaselessly roars out of the Gare de Lyon, and which I know will never leave, which has not left," that it's moving like life, and still like art, all at the same time, like a movie, which is what a writer would talk about in the 1920s, but a movie that can't be repeated. And that's what I wanted to be, isn't it, always leaving but never, oh no not ever, moving fast enough to arrive? Because no one is ever so beautiful as when she is leaving.

No, wait a minute, I was wrong: Breton said "will be"—"beauty *will be* convulsive, or it will not be." It's a prediction, not an evaluation.

I'm looking for the pattern that produces the convulsion, still and moving like the jazz hop-skip of the icing hotels and building sites along the Promenade des Anglais in Nice: pink—blue—gap—peach—white—gap, like the rhythm of the sun and shadow between the billboards along the track—bright—dark—gap—bright—gap—gap. Is beauty the *is* or the *isn't*, or is it the rhythm of the two? Is it the pattern or its disruption, or is beauty recognizing the pattern then disrupting it, or trying to? Sometimes I think I can see a pattern but then I'm not sure it means anything. Then I remember the Buddhist's card, and I want the card to mean something to me, or I want it to mean nothing and for that to mean something. Love—constant revolution, pure disruption—can never be stilled. I'm not sure that love can be beautiful.

Out of the window now, the rhythm of the landscape has changed: more buildings, fewer gaps. We're rattling through the suburbs of Rome. In the meantime, I've worked out some rules of the game for my photos:

- Avoid: museums, galleries, churches, tourist spots.
- Avoid photographing anything too "typical" of the country.
- Avoid anything "beautiful."
- (Try not to operate these rules too consciously.)

I take some shots: wires crossing above the crossed train tracks. The woman sitting opposite gets up to pull her case down from the rack. She's in her 50s, early 60s perhaps, well-dressed, wearing no makeup. I can see age spots and tiny wrinkles. Bare skin is daring; at her age, even more so. Why would she expose herself like this? Because she looks like she's brave enough not to be trying, she is beautiful. She takes a small bag from her case, and from it a tiny mirrored compact. She opens it and begins to apply foundation with a sponge until her skin is uniform in texture and unnaturally peachy in color. I know that if I got close to her it would no longer smell or feel like skin—it would smell like talcum and feel like ultrasuede, and that if I kissed her, I wouldn't be kissing her, and that particles of color would stay on my lips when I pulled away.

She takes out a concealer pencil. As we pull into Rome Termini station, she slowly erases the last traces of herself.

I feel in my pocket for the Buddhist's card. It's not there.

5 Rome/Living
27th April

I'm sitting in the ruin of—what?—It might be someone's living room. The knee-high walls are laid out like the floor-plan of a house, only not in blue pencil but in broken stone teeth. It's not in the Forum—I'm avoiding monuments—it's just one of those pieces of ancient Rome that cracks through the concrete of the present day like a bad memory, a way in for grass, for all kinds of untidy thoughts. I'm outside Rome's central station which, like Milan's, is shrouded for repairs in a coy dressing tent paler than its concrete. The Milan train delivered me straight to the rocky heart of the city, if you'd call it a heart. Rome's heart probably is the Forum, hollow and dusty as a dead beetle's carapace. The soft, living parts of the city, the parts that pulse, that beat, are built around its internal exoskeleton.

I have never known what to do in living rooms. When I get back I suppose I'll have one—that's how most accommodation is laid out. What should I do there? Sit in those chairs I never sat in? Watch the telly, which I don't much? Live, I suppose.

A ruin is nothing but half a sentence. Something about it invites completion, by guesswork or interpretation. Stones are like words—they have so many uses, the new use always knocking the old away, making it impossible to read how things once were—but it's not unusual to come across fissures in the street through to previous meanings. Some of them are right out in the open and I can use them like I am now, to rest my luggage, waiting for a bus outside the central station, or as a picnic table, or a seat to stop for a cigarette. These stones are not in museums, I don't have to pay an entrance fee to think about them and my rules permit me to wander amongst them, looking for nothing, straining for no significance. Others have fences which, like a velvet rope in an art gallery, make them into something meaningful, and these are the ones I look and look at, and wonder what they signify, as the fences tell me there must be some kind of story behind them.

I'm not sure when a house becomes a ruin. It's not always to do with crumbling. Some houses that look wrecked are still inhabited, others are unliveable. In Rome it's hard to tell what's derelict. Pagan stones are walled into Christian churches, Renaissance palaces built to resemble ancient monuments that were, themselves, memorials—for wars, for ancestors killed in battle. Architectural styles nod to each other across the streets. In an Empire most famous for falling, so much of Rome is a memorial to a memorial. Everywhere I look there are buildings decorated with flower vases that resemble funeral urns, and funeral urns that look like flower vases, until they hardly seem like anything sad any more.

Here I am in Rome. Again.

Rome is a place you return to. You throw a coin in a fountain in a square, which the fountain almost fills, and which is filled, for the remaining part, with people taking photographs of the fountain. If you do this you will return, they say, but they do not tell you why you would want to. The first time I visited Rome I was with my husband, before we were married, and we came back a second time, a few years later. Not that returning was easy. There are so many Roman names for alleys, for tiny dead-end streets: stradina, vuizza, vicolo. The vicolos and stradinas cross the full-size stradas and vias, which are full of the noise and dust of vehicles going elsewhere. The vicolos still belong to the pedestrians but, when we took them in preference to the stradas, we found they did not take us anywhere, not, at least, in the direction we thought we were going, towards the fountain that meant we would return to Rome, which is at the center of a knot of these little streets, and which we failed to find the first time and, on returning, failed to find again.

Husband, hus-band, a band, a tie, rubbery, elastic. Pull it away and it snaps back tight. I always hated the word, I never used it.

I catch a bus to my hostel. In its living room, dusty with artificial flowers, which is also Reception, the manager watches TV. Living in public, he looks like some kind of performance art, set behind a velvet rope so no one else ever sits there. My room's not ready so I drop my bags and go for a walk.

As I walk the streets I walked with the man I was married to, which I will not now walk with you, I'm unsure what time zone I'm in. I feel transparent, a ghost performing the same action over and over, an action remembered from past

Referring to what I must have ceased to be I order to be who I am.
Breton, *Nadja*

life, with no meaning in the present. Habitual, habit, inhabit. Action, perform, ghosts, I know what they do, intimately, but what purpose do they serve: what are ghosts for?

I don't know if there are ghosts in Rome. There are ghosts in London but not in Paris, and in London there are fewer than in the rest of England. Ghosts are a rural affair. A ghost is a story in the landscape. Cities have monuments and ruins to tell their citizens the time. Perhaps cities need no ghosts.

Tell me who you haunt, and I'll tell you who you are: I was walking through an old city with you one time. It wasn't Rome and, although you had invited me to walk there with you, you acted as though you were trying to get rid of me, but I continued to shadow you as I didn't yet know you were beginning to leave me. That's when you told me I seemed haunted. *By what?* You didn't explain and, because there was something in the way you said it I wasn't prepared for, I didn't question you further. In any case, it seemed appropriate. Love is always coming up against ghosts: *'til death us do part*, says the husband; *I will but love thee better after death*, says the lover, though I'm never sure whether she's talking about her own death, or her beloved's.

Ghosts, in French, are *revenants/returners*. Returning to Rome I'm no longer haunted, I'm the haunter, caught in one place between past and the might-have-been. The streets slant at twenty, thirty degrees but the stones, the windowsills remain on the level. As I climb the pavements, to someone on the interior it must look like I'm coming up from the cellar (have you ever seen that old music-hall gag where someone outside of the window sags at the knees then straightens, pretending to ascend, step after step?). I've spent a long time dead but now I'm back, and I can tell you all about what it's like to be under the ground.

But this is the Pantheon—here it is again! I hardly know how but —here I am, approaching by the same vicolo as when I stayed here years ago, married. Was I heading here without knowing it? Here's the shop where we bought biscotti! Even the coffee bar on the corner of the Piazza della Rotonda has outlasted my marriage. This triumph of stones is cheering. The afternoon heats up. Cafés cling to the sides of the square where pools of shade evaporate. I go into the Pantheon, just because I did when I was here before.

There are two domes in Rome, one pagan and one Christian, and they're always measured up against each other. Two kinds of life, mutually exclusive, as polarized as "married" and "single": that's not much of a choice. The dome of Saint Peter's, designed in imitation of the pagan Pantheon, was to be bigger, better, but after several generations of failure, Michelangelo was brought in to redraw the plans. Several generations. Well, Rome wasn't built in a day. Even now, hovering between Classical and Baroque, Saint Peter's is oval, not a perfect sphere. Planned to need less support than the Pantheon, its dome was designed to look lighter, but it never worked as a self-supporting structure. The egg cracked and now it's bound with chains. The Pantheon's held up by a nothing; it's built around an oculus, a hole in the ceiling's center that takes the lean of its walls.

That classical portico on the Pantheon, though, genteel as a uPVC conservatory, a slap on the back of a suburban semi—can it be original? It is. The temple to "all the gods" is a Roman oddity, being structurally unaltered though, inside, the old gods are scrubbed clean off, their gilded statues melted from the roof. The circle of the pagan temple has been squared, by an altar into a Christian one, but it feels neither one thing nor the other. A pantheon today means a burial place for celebs, like the church in Paris they call the Tall Men Hotel, and that's what it's used for; the kings of a

Hôtel des Grands Hommes, aka The Pantheon, Paris.

united Italy thrown about, forgotten in corners, an uneasy Christian stamp on their secular triumph.

The ancient Romans didn't believe in gods, not unless they were useful enough to win them wars, or sex, or food. They knew exactly what their gods were for, down to the gods of door hinges, of window frames. It is hard to believe the Romans didn't worship the oculus, the eye in the ceiling, its blankness, its temperamental gaze, the way it sees and is seen though, the way it casts an uncertain light. It looks like god. It looks so simple and honest that painters all over Rome have let fake oculi into the closed domes of Catholic churches. The skies they painted were always blue, sometimes with decorative puffs of cloud, but the oculus of the Pantheon throws down a white light that is frightening as well as beautiful, and it is often pale and unresponsive, and answers you with a question, and sometimes it lets in rain or, very occasionally, snow.

Is it possible to believe we could have a god without making use of him?
Rainer Maria Rilke, *The Notebooks of Malte Laurids Brigge*

Maybe it's because I can see something that looks like god (or because it can see me) but I want to pray. It's not because I want to believe—or because I want anything at all. At school I learned to repeat the formula, but they never told me what praying was for, and I couldn't frame the question. Birthday-candle wishes seemed irreverent, praying for unknown third parties, pious fakery, and I had no urgencies pressing enough to make a direct request anything more than hogging the line. Once my school asked me to attend a service at a real church so, aged fourteen, I put on a black sweater and a black skirt, which I thought sober, and a red felt hat, and red lace fingerless gloves and tights, which I considered smart as anything worn to church on the telly, the only place outside school I had ever seen anybody pray. I did not think I looked odd, I only thought that the rest of the congregation hadn't made an effort worthy of the situation. And that's when I got it, what praying is: it's a kind of performance.

Praying is another kind of telling to someone not there, and that makes it a bit like a love letter, and a bit like writing, and I believe in the last two, but not the first. Surely I shouldn't feel the need to pray if I write, wouldn't need to write if I prayed. In the Pantheon, with the old gods gone and the new never really in residence, under the eye of the roof, where there's nowhere to sit as there is in an English church, praying is one place words seem redundant. You have to *have* words—*Our Father*, or whatever— but you don't have to make them say anything new. I'm sick of the sound of my own voice anyhow, the voice I've traveled with so carefully, avoiding some voices—for instance, the one that seems to know too much, the one that uses long words, and also the one that uses short words but has long words up its sleeve all the time. Right now I don't want to hear myself speak, I just want to repeat a formula. It calms my mind, it keeps me together, allows me to sit in a still place, and not think about words. Prayer is its own answer.

As I leave in the blink of daylight, two Dutch, or German girls thrust a phone at me, ask me to photograph them in front of the portico where fancy-dressed dead Centurions pose with tourists (for a fee), lending them plastic swords and helmets. I am anxious about the number of people taking photographs of the Pantheon, each going home with a version of the same image. How will they recognize themselves in the one standing, smiling, amongst so many, after the years have twisted them into ghosts of their own image? See that woman who folds her flat body into the angles of the portico? She has the hair of a teenager, shinier, and a slim body but, when she turns, a 60-year-old smoker's face, hairless eyebrows drawn in over beautiful clear eyes, bagged, beneath, with folds. But her lips are clearly delineated, above an unlined, neat chin. Has she had "work done," like Rome, in one area of her structure, but not another? Here in the Piazza della Rotonda, like everywhere else, it's the older women I see first. I think I'm searching in them for a sign of what I might become. I was doing this aged fifteen and I haven't found it yet. The older women on the streets don't look like the thin, tan women on the billboards I saw from the train, or like the solid, white women who have held up Roman porticos for so many years without a sigh. Because they are not answered in the architecture I know that the women walking through the square are not real women—or maybe they are real women, but the fake women on the statues and the billboards are more important. In any case I look at them slyly, knowing there's something shameful in my looking. I'm trying to catch something I recognize—the girl in the woman, how she got there, her story—but I'm also looking for something more, the possibility of a way of being. Maybe I'll only recognize it when it's my turn. When I was twenty I thought I saw her once, one who might have fitted the bill: a woman walking through the shopping center in my concrete new town, which, then, was all I knew of pillars and porticos. She wore plum-colored stockings that shone, that were unusual enough to have been chosen with care, and for the woman's own pleasure, and that, I could tell, were expensive. Above the stockings, the woman had a neat, shiny head of cropped hair, so unlike the filigree birds' nests the older women I knew prepared so carefully every morning, using electrical devices. If, one day, I could become the woman in the shiny stockings, I thought, life might not have been in vain.

I am so vain.

The woman in the plum-colored stockings was alone, and I look only at the older women who are alone. I turn away from the women in couples; they seem to me, somehow, subtracted.

When I was in Rome with the man I was married to, I used to watch couples take their packed lunches out of each other's backpacks, straighten folds in maps the other held, adjust each other's hats, camera straps, find tickets in each other's pockets. Whenever we did these things, I didn't trust either of us to get it right so I kept glancing at other couples to see. Then marriage looked like forgiveness or, no, not forgiveness but acknowledgement, acceptance—of age, or death, or change, or of staying the same. I was always looking for clues as to how I should be married, and I looked both to real people, and to ones in books and in films. What did I want to ask of them: *At what age is marriage best? Is it happiest to be long or freshly married? Are marriages successful because couples married young, or old; because their relationship is innocent, or worldly? How much should the married see of one another, how strongly are they allowed to disagree with each other's opinions? How, in all these things, is marriage different from being in love?* I looked at the couples who looked like they had good marriages, and was pleased when theirs looked a little like ours, and at the couples who looked like they had bad marriages, and took comfort if ours seemed better. Then I felt bad, because to look at all was to question my own marriage. The tedious, repetitious married: why do I feel I can learn nothing from them? A successful marriage dissolves into silence. Something crumbles in the face of the word.

Married? So much goes on in the shadow of that tall word, unspoken, unwritten. Married. Did I call that love? Yes for a long time, then, no. Depends if you think love is the weight of years or of an instant. Where would *you* put the marker: first sight, six months, five years, ten? Tell me if you know because it's not something I can tell you. All I know is that there is a difference between love and being *in* love. If there wasn't a gap, we wouldn't need to say both.

The dialectic of repetition is easy, because that which is repeated has been, otherwise it could not be repeated: but precisely this, that it has been, makes repetition something new.
Kierkegaard, *ibid*

And there must be an instant of love in order for loving to be repeated though, like other clones, it can mutate unexpectedly. I'd known you for only a few months when I could say, *love*, or thought I could claim it as our story.

There are so many stories about love, but so few stories about marriage, only stories about what happens before it and, sometimes, after. Marriage sucks all stories into its black hole to pump them out through the next generation. Even when you say it in the present—"I'm married"—that "ed" drags it back into the past, a story told. I'm still sent wedding invitations *to the marriage of...* as though I might be witness to the whole intimate tableau: each morning's breakfast table, *the way he holds his knife, the way she sips her tea*, the small habits of tenderness or un-tenderness—so much like life—the sex, the rows, the making up, all of it. *The married state* they still say in some wedding services, a solid state, the opposite of action. There are no moving parts in the solid state disk that runs the new laptop I have brought with me. It stores data "persistently" and constantly rearranges its memory in non-linear patterns, recycling the past as the present. Its information cannot be permanently overwritten, except by special procedure but, when it breaks, more often than not, all data, the whole story, disappears. I can't begin to describe the silence at the heart of marriage, and I've been there. I'm still curious as to what replaces the words. No wonder I preferred romance, the Internet, correspondence, the airless twitter in which people have no husbands, wives, families. Would it be possible to live there always? Yes, if you like writing. Just press
Return,
return.
Return.

It's hot, hot. I guess it's somewhere near 6 p.m. I look for something to sit on, and find another block of stone, repurposed. I have no idea what it once was, just what use it can serve now. I take out a cigarette, designed to affront to the sensible couples with their packed snacks. I want to look like their opposite, a maximum artery assault on all fronts. Without the structure of lunch and dinnertimes, I smoke more. Eating on holiday is the management of time, of boredom; a cigarette an excuse for an equivalent pause, but travel licenses me to eat badly, and to smoke. I have been warned by smoker friends not to smoke, but with a sly smile. They want me to join their club, which is the death wish club, the opposite of marriage. Away from home, where what I am doing is not life-like, death can't touch me; cholesterol neither. I don't feel like eating, anyway. I've hardly eaten since I got to Nice although waiters outside the restaurants step in front of me, grab me by the arm: *Hello! Bonjour! Signora, scusi!* What used to make me hungry now makes me full, and hunger doesn't manifest as hunger. I feel empty, but it's not physical emptiness. I'm synaesthetic, like people who see sound as color.

On the street Rome offers me a succession of party foods: pizza, biscotti, granita. They're quick hits, though. Romans don't stop outside cafés for long, and their favorite treat is ice cream, which you can eat as you walk. I buy a *granita con panna* (frozen coffee with whipped cream) from the shop on the corner of the square, the one I used to breakfast at when married. All that caffeine and sugar and nicotine makes me want to move, and my emptiness makes me light as whipped cream pumped through with air.

I have been brought up to take myself lightly, to appreciate that hard-edged, weightless thing called fun. The hard-edged thing included holidays, nice dinners, visits to places away from home, and other treats, all of which were to be enjoyed, if done the right way, because they were not home. *A little of what you fancy does you good.* Oh, but only a little—that's the good life: a little of this, a little of that, don't get too passionate about anything. And, if I did not enjoy the treats, if I found any other emotion occurred, I was not to say so. Who was I to talk? A word out of place could ruin everything for everyone. And I never wanted to complain because, if I did, how would I know when to stop? I have no idea how much of anything is enough. It's easier to be empty, silent. And because I cannot eat, I walk, and I walk.

I walk from the Piazza della Rotonda (I remember the route) across the Corso Vittorio Emanuelle II, through the vicolos and stradinas until I reach the Campo dè Fiori where the traders packing up the market are trampling fruit and flowers. In the square between here and the Tiber, walking with my husband, I remember that, in the garden of the Palazzo Spada, we found a short narrow corridor painted to look like a long wider corridor with, at its end, a statue the size of a garden gnome, that appeared monumental. I stop just outside the Palazzo, in the Piazza de Farnese, where there are fountains like huge stone birdbaths. Some of the Palazzo's cornicing is painted on to resemble marble, but this is ancient fakery so counts as genuine. By the birdbath fountains an old woman feeds pigeons, another woman alone. She wears a black velvet dress with embroidered cuffs, too heavy, too formal for the heat and for what she is doing, but it is not worn or dirty and her hair is cut in a neat silver bob, so she can't be a crazy woman. No one arrives to meet her. I watch her carefully, wondering whether she is the woman I could become. She crumbles something from a brown paper bag. She does not stop until it is empty. She must do this every day.

I have no sense of proportions.
Barthes, *A Lover's Discourse*

Marry me, you said.

There was a gap: I knew it was a joke. But such a very short gap, like this:

—

Mind the gap: I thought there was something in it.

I walk and walk further, until the afternoon turns blue and the buildings are lighter than the surrounding night. I have gone so far from where I should be, I don't know if I can find my way back.

"You're lost," you told me, that same afternoon. As if I didn't know it.
    Where in the world would I be without you?
    Not here, I know.

Something keeps me off the main streets. In vicolo after vicolo all the windows are blank except the lit windows of restaurants. In Rome, do as the Romans do. Romans eat, but they don't drink in public, not without food—and not tapas, full dinners! You won't get away with a single course. I pass bar after bar, outside them chalkboards listing massive sharer plates or set menus: aperitivo, antipasta, pasta, zuppa, primi platti, secondi platti, dolce. I'd eat something, somewhere, if I could only find the right place, if I could only find somewhere that didn't demand too much of me. I pass restaurants where the menus are laid out thick as bibles on lecterns, novels nobody reads. These restaurants are the empty ones. I do not want to eat at this kind of restaurant. I also pass restaurants like glass bricks of light, large groups and family parties displayed in their windows. *How we can stuff them in!* say the restaurants, *and how we can stuff them!* I want to eat neither at the restaurants that are too full or those that are too empty. I don't want to be too full as, were I not content, being already full, I would no longer be able to blame my hunger for my empty feeling. Without hunger to occupy me, grief might rush in to fill the gap. I need one gap to prevent the other.

"Leave or stay," you said that afternoon, "but don't poison it."
Poison's a woman's weapon, used on family, intimate as food and
drink, and family is the easiest thing for a woman to destroy,
apart from herself. Calling me a poisoner was a drop of poison.
You dropped it in my ear and it poisoned me against myself.
When I left, all my actions seemed to stink of it.

No wonder I'm not eating.

The people who are eating in the glass boxes all look like tourists.
I am angry with the restaurants that make them perform their
intimate family dinner in public, and I am angry because these
are the only buildings where non-natives can eat. I guess Roman
families are all eating at home. Home.

When I got married I'd hoped I could be married in a different
way from all the marriages I'd seen before. A tall order but, when
building something bigger and better, why settle for less? I must
have thought marriage was something you build, like those couples in the telly programs who construct their dream home
under the eye of the camera, adapting an ancient structure, a
barn, or a chapel, keeping the original features they choose,
making the rest as modern as they like. I didn't realize that
marriage is something you inhabit, something built by someone
else to a plan drawn by people who lived differently, centuries
ago. Marriage is made from old stones shaped by an ancient
technology we no longer understand. All we can do is cement
the gaps until we have something that looks like somewhere we
could live. To me it no longer looks like home. It looks like a
pile of rocks.

I stopped living in living rooms long ago, but didn't seem to be
able to find a way live without them. There was a living room in
my house, the house where I'd lived while married, if I want to

take responsibility for it which, undoubtedly, I must. I had problems with that house, which became like a house in a murder story. It had so many rooms whose uses were obsolete, unimaginable—*in the ballroom, with the candlestick, in the library with the lead piping*—though they were not ballrooms or libraries, just regular rooms in a house whose function had crumbled. As I avoided the rooms I could no longer use, the house got bigger, and I got smaller. It was cold the winter before I left but I would not put the heating on, not in such a big place, just for one. I worked in bed and my living shrank to its size and shape, and from it I could hear what went on the other side of the wall: noises of the telly and cooking. It was reassuring that the other houses were used and that life went on, somewhere, in the way it was meant to, while my house remained a carapace of home—and, from the outside, it looked fine, but I didn't repair the curtain rail, or paint over the marks on the wall, or weed the garden. I prepared for my own ruin.

My home had become dismal to me precisely because it was the wrong sort of repetition.
Kierkegaard, *ibid*

But I don't want to get lost in too roomy a metaphor. Marriage isn't a house I was shut into, or that fell down. It works more like the way Freud wrote about Rome, the layers on layers of culture and history that can't quite be seen all at once, as though there was no such thing as time or forgetting.

A city is a priori unsuited for a comparison of this sort with a mental organism.
Sigmund Freud, *Civilization and its Discontents*

The observer would need merely to shift the focus of his eyes, perhaps, or change his position, in order to call up a view of either the one or the other.
Freud, *ibid*

I'm lost now near the Piazza della Republica. All the restaurants are closed—they close early in Rome—and every clock shows a different time. All those ghosts. I imagine what your arms feel like round me, then I imagine my ex-husband's, then those of other men I have known. I try to observe what effect each of these imaginings has on me, but I find I can hardly distinguish one from another, just the feeling of loving, and being loved, being touched… and you have been in touch with me, have recommenced—however virtual—that connection.

I walk (I dance!) through the Piazza Navona. Around the white Triton fountain, which, like the station, is dressed in plissé plastic, beggars are selling small shining toys: plastic sycamore keys that light up and scream as they whirl higher and higher into the black sky.

I want the huge, the stupid, the democratic, the touristy, the monumental, the clichéd, the trashy. Clichés have an easy beauty. So does love. I feel weightless, like I'm falling. Again? The last time I fell, I was dropped. How can I be dropped from a fall?

Roma II, Trastevere
28th April

Next morning I'm still in Rome, though I didn't expect to be. I was going to take the train to Brindisi, then the overnight ferry to Patra, but the ferry isn't running. It's a bank holiday, and a religious holiday, and I expected neither. All night on a deck, I'm sorry to miss that. It was something I'd imagined doing. I try not to imagine too much of what lies ahead, but some images do form. There's some kind of pleasure in dismissing them, in escaping myself.

"How are you?" you asked. I still haven't answered your email, have carried not-answering with me, all its potential. Well, how am I? I have the habit of loneliness now. I am comfortable with it. I get up, get out of my hostel, get a coffee at the bar in the Piazza at the end of the street. Coffee implies breakfast goods and I find I can live on the implication, on watching other people eat, other people love. My stomach has settled, I'm content with a cigarette, my only drive, the desire to stay away from the attentions of the restaurants lining the square, to cheat choice, to refuse to choose. Not eating robs me of energy: my gaze dampens. I can look only down at what's under my feet, but my pride in self-limiting is lively enough. Like the bag I have packed, I find I have got to need so little. The only problem with being as good as full is that it leads me to demand nothing more.

As I have spare time, and no desires to fill it with, I return to the center of Rome to repeat the bits of yesterday I liked. I have to repeat, it's part of understanding where I am. I try the same route—fountain, vicolos, Pantheon—but the bits of yesterday I liked are disappointing. My granita melts too quickly. I am anxious about the ratio of cream to ice. I am being slowed down.

The only thing that repeated itself was that no repetition was possible.
Kierkegaard, *ibid*

I decide to give myself a task: I will buy a new notebook, which will allow me the pleasure of looking and refusing, or choosing, as well as exchanges with shopkeepers, whose sense of purpose makes them so friendly and cheerful that these are almost real encounters, though they can be dismissed, on either side, with no love lost.

There are few chain stores in the center of Rome, only two or three big international brands that reproduce the same thing they do everywhere, and give a feeling of—what?—European-ness, stability, a guaranteed repeat experience? Each small shop sells a single type of object, often something so recherché as to be outdated, amusing: watches, gloves, corsetry. They open at odd times of day, some in the morning, some in the evening, and their windows contain every example and variety of this one

When the desire comes upon us to go street rambling the pencil does for a pretext, and getting up we say: "Really I must buy a pencil," as if under cover of this excuse we could indulge safely in the greatest pleasure of town life.
Virginia Woolf, *Street Haunting*

thing, but where is the rest? Where are the shops selling groceries, cleaning fluid, toilet rolls? Rome's city center is an accessory: the basics of everyday life are not here. I find a fancy stationer's that sells pens and paper, plus rubber stamps customized with elaborate figures, name, or address, and books for sorting life in different ways: a "cellar book," a book for shopping lists… It also sells address books to slice up friends along arbitrary, alphabetical lines. The books are finely made, their covers marbled, giving the illusion of stone, or the illusion of the illusion of stone like the painted-on marble of the Palazzo Spada and, oh, they are expensive! I don't think I could buy one but the problem's not the price. I no longer have a home address to write in the specially printed section on the flyleaf of one of these books. No, this is not the shop for me.

At the end of the vicolo is the Tiber. I cross the bridge and onto an island, then I cross another bridge. I'm in Trastevere, and I am amazed.

When I first visited Rome with my husband, we booked a hotel in Trastevere, because we'd heard it was the cool part of the city, but when we arrived the hotel manager explained there was a problem, and we would have to move to a room across the river, off the Piazza della Rotonda. When we returned to Rome, we rented an apartment in Trastevere but again something happened, and we were taken to "better" rooms behind the Piazza Navona. One day we decided to walk to Trastevere. From the Piazza del Popolo, we took the via del Corso, which looks like a main street on the map, because it is so straight and long. We imagined it wide and light, and found it was dark and narrow, but then we weren't familiar with Rome, and this was before

What if a person arrived in Rome, fell in love with some small part of the city that was for him an inexhaustible source of pleasure, and then left Rome again without having seen a single tourist attraction?
Kierkegaard, *Repetition*

Googlemaps: the only way to know the city was through our guidebooks, which we had forgotten to bring out with us, and the Via del Corso went on and on until it ended with the white palace built by Victor Emmanuele II, which the Romans call the Zuppa Inglese because it looks like an enormous cream dessert, and which masks the dirty broken meringues of the Forum. We weren't far from Trastevere. In fact we were heading in the right direction, but for some reason we gave up.

Instead we turned back and went into the Vatican where we looked at Michelangelo's ceiling women, who looked like men, and, through ranks of photographers as thick as the crowd by the fountain you throw coins into, we glimpsed a corner of the same artist's *Pieta*, white as the Zuppa Inglese, and it didn't look piteous, or pious: it looked like something else altogether. That night I dreamt that a white papal statue pursued me across a chessboard, which looked exactly like the cold tiled floor of our apartment.

But here is Trastevere, finally. What had seemed so difficult to achieve married is, on my own, laughably easy, as easy as crossing a bridge. Get over it: I shouldn't be so surprised. Rome is full of illusions. On the Via Piccolomini (teeny-tiny-street?) the dome of Saint Peter's appears to shrink as you get near to it and, in the church of Saint Ignatius, a hollow ceiling appears to recede into a flat roof. I am surprised I tire of Trastevere so quickly. Its non-monumental smallness has been so thoroughly enclosed for tourists. There are no vistas, there is no room for views. St Peter's might survive the hordes but you need grandeur for that.

It's lunchtime again, at least I think it is. I find a café still serving only drinks. I take out my laptop. The waitress does not know if there is WiFi. A man at the next table watches me type up some notes. He is fascinated: "It's like playing a piano."

A Roman woman walks by: a navy trouser suit, a flash of red briefcase and red shoes, the flashes, dictated by time and movement. There are bright clothes in the shops, but only the tourists are wearing them. Her briefcase swings: stride—flash—red—stride—flash—red: pattern recognition.

A Roman passes, talking in gestures into his mobile phone. At the next table, a cute guy in designer black sits alone, sipping a glass of wine. Then I see the dog collar. There are some patterns I still don't recognize.

I chase a few WiFi signals, but can't connect so instead I read your message again, then look back through our emails, and I am shocked to find them silly. Such flat words do no justice to feelings, but how would I flirt again else? Flirting's meaning deferred—that surface-y glancing urr sound, skidding on ice. I can recognize the pattern—the flash of cards dealt, trumped—a vocabulary of gestures impersonal as those I found in marriage. Flirting has its own architecture, unstoppable, built of polished aphorisms put in the gaps between the stones. How high you can build depends on received wisdom, local planning regulations. In London you can build what you like, in the shape of whatever. In Paris, you can't go beyond certain limits. I have no idea of the restrictions for building in the center of Rome. Maybe we built just because we could, because the blocks were already there, lying around, and we knew how to use them. But how do I stop the endless elaboration of my thoughts about you, the Baroque curlicues in my head?

I leave the café, find a small stationers, and buy a notebook. Oh, in Rome they make things more beautiful than anywhere else! This notebook: hand-bound, sewn, its edges tinted red as pork in a Chinese takeaway, its paper thick as fabric. For three Euros! I should have bought two, three, but in the shop it seemed one of the more ordinary, cheaper items.

•••

Back at my hostel, there's WiFi and I'm finally connected. But there have been no more of your words that arrived like flowers, so I sit down and book a flight out of Rome—where, because of the state holiday and the religious holiday, there is no room for me at this, or any other hostel—to Athens and, in Athens, another cheap hotel. I do this with no fuss, because no one knows where I am, and nothing I do now means anything to anyone.

And, because you called me a game-player, I decide to play a game with you. I reply to your email and tell you the tale of the missed ferry and the full hostel: *Will you rescue me?* I want to hook you with a story, then slip from your grasp, if only to make you want me again. I want to amaze you with an illusion as clever as the statue in the Palazzo Spada. How could you know that, having been abandoned, I have already rescued myself?

Lay waste to everything. Transform yourself into a contemptible person whose only pleasure is in tricking and deceiving. If you can do this, then you will have established equality.
Kierkegaard, *ibid*

I check out. As I wait for my bill in the performance art living room, I flick through postcards on the desk: the Rome I didn't see. The top card shows Cupid and Psyche, a statue inside the Capitoline Museum, which I have not visited this time or on any trip to Rome. It is said to be a copy of a Greek original (always in Rome, there's something older, better to refer to). Psyche kept her name, Cupid was translated from the Greek, Eros. Cupidity means greed, and Cupid (rhymes with stupid), the Roman god of love, is a jelly baby with little round belly. Eros is more difficult to say, and sounds like rose, and like something to do with sex.

The marble lovers on the postcard are two plump teens of about equal height, lit through a late-afternoon window that turns them yellow as instant custard. They are kissing, but they are walking as they kiss, heads turned to each other so they must stumble. She leans into him, and it is difficult to see how he supports himself without falling—or perhaps the sculpture has been wrongly displayed and really shows two people lying down, or perhaps it's in some way a bad sculpture. He is looking into her eyes, no, *at* her face, his finger prying her lips apart with the intrusive sensuality of a dentist or a baby. Something like a bed sheet is draped around her hips. He is naked and has no dick, or a tiny one, or else it has been knocked off.

Psyche was Cupid's human girlfriend but he would only visit her at night when she couldn't see him. Being in touch wasn't enough: Psyche wanted to look too, but as soon as she demanded more than words, he disappeared. Cast out from the temples of Juno and Ceres, the gods of home and food, she was taken in by Venus who, she thought, would help her, but who set her impossible tasks: lessons in love.

You have taught me a lesson in love. No one thinks they need to be taught how to love: it is love that teaches the lesson, and the lesson love teaches does not seem to be one that tells you how to love better, but the sort you hear in, *I'll teach you a lesson!* Not a lesson, then, a punishment. Or a warning: do not look too closely at what you love, don't ask to much of it, not if you want to keep it. On the postcard of Cupid and Psyche from the Capitoline museum, Psyche's pupil-less eyes are only for Eros, or maybe they are still closed. Has she looked yet?

"There could never be anything between us. I would ruin you," you said on that afternoon in the old city. You said it as though you were working out a problem, as though you were pretending to talk only to yourself but you meant me to hear. And that seemed such a silly idea it almost made me laugh, but also struck me with terror (as soon as words are out, there's always a chance they might correspond to something real). We were on the corner of a street and it was as if you were deciding aloud which way to go, like someone on stage, planning a quick exit, and making sure I knew it. What a performance!

I take a bus back to the rail station, which is another oculus, a gap through to somewhere else. An oculus, in art, is also known as a "station point," the point from which the artist intends the observer to view the work.

And, once I'm on the train, the view is like the view outside all the other stations in Europe, the backs of apartment buildings so subject to the railway's rattle they're few people's first choice of home. When I arrived in Rome, I'd thought *Termini* in the station's name meant an ending but, I just found out, it's named for the ancient thermal baths.

As the train leaves the station I catch a glimpse of the Terminal Hotel.

6 Rome to Athens/Vol de Nuit
28/29th April

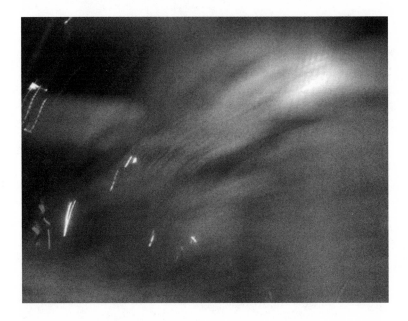

Please pay attention to the safety instructions, even if you are a frequent flier.

I can't remember what the stewardess looked like, what kind of uniform she wore, whether she was young or old, beautiful or not. I thought I would pay more attention because I am not a frequent flier. For years I tried not to fly, didn't visit places that required it. It was not Green. It was a kind of indulgence I didn't want to take. I didn't want to be the sort of person who thought some specific benefit came only with the very quickest change of scene, that I should go to other places to have particular kinds of experience, and—feeling displaced myself—I had no desire to treat other people as native. For years I stuck to it, though I found it hard not to take flights when so many of the other people I knew who worried about taking flights took them anyway. But here I am at an airport hoping, just like them, that in leaving, the most hopelessly non-specific meaning will take place.

I am about to cross a time zone, to lose another hour. *Night flight*, I am thinking, *Vol de Nuit*, which is a perfume by Guerlain that does not smell like this airport, which smells of the human props—coffee, cigarettes (for all that they're banned), cleaning fluids—that we use to keep ourselves, and our places, under control. Nor does the perfume smell of the mechanics of flight, of petrol and metal and the future of the twentieth century like Caron's *Par Avion*, which is a perfume I like. It smells of being asleep, and flying at night is like being asleep: it is easier to let go of stolen hours (*vol*, in French, also means theft), or to pretend there were more of them. Night flight is nothing happening. It is a kind of denial.

It's a small world, and easy to cross if you have the time, and the money—from airport to airport at least, if those are the places at which you want to arrive. Otherwise it can be a large world, and difficult to cross, difficult to find your way up a small track off the map once you leave the main road. But airport to airport is hardly travel. This airport looks like all the other airports I have been in. There is very little information here to tell me which country I am leaving and, when I arrive, it will be at a building very much like the one I left. The airport is a buffer zone against loss of time and place. Designed to cushion the shocks of change, every corner is rounded, each surface easy to clean: plastic, marble, polished concrete. Against a background of undemanding gray, which suggests I might be in an office, functional fittings stand out in primary colors, hinting that I might be in a nursery, or on a building site. Shops that are open day and night breathe out a scent identical to fresh passion fruit, which, I know, comes from cosmetics and not from fruit at all. Signs threaten politely in every language: *Please do not leave your baggage unattended: it will be removed and destroyed.* The airport is made to run smoothly, so smoothly that passengers slide off each other without a second glance. I go to the bar where sounds are submerged as in a swimming pool, where plastic chairs that imitate wood are decorated with cushions in fabric that imitates flowering plants. I order a drink to celebrate being nowhere, after-hours. On the floor plan of the bar at the computerized till, island tables swim in a bright blue sea.

I am waiting for your reply to my email and I have settled into a waiting state, which is an airport state of mind. Waiting is familiar and its anxiety, once recognized, is comfortable. Loving is waiting for something to happen even when I'm not: I'm always in the headlong state of being about to hear from you. The Internet, which is also so much waiting, doubles it. I could spend hours flicking from Twitter to Facebook to Email, hypnotized, waiting for someone to make contact, to tell me I'm still here. I wait and I don't do, until I find I have used up all my time, agreeably, waiting, until I almost feel I have done something. I could live in this suspended state (almost) indefinitely.

As I pay for my drink, the postcard spills out of my bag: Cupid and Psyche, their bodies rolled in puppy fat, I can hardly tell boy from girl. I bin it. Now I have started clearing myself out, I can't stop. I take everything from my bag that might weigh me down: receipts, screwed-up notes, the crumpled empty cigarette box. *Fumer nuit gravement à votre santé*, it tells me: *Smoking damages your health.* *Nuit.* Night flight. *Se nuire (vb)*: to damage—yourself or another. A transitive, and a reflexive verb, you can't do damage without damaging something, or someone, or yourself.

I take a corridor down the side of a duty-free concession, thinking it leads to my gate but it ends in an air-conditioning duct. A woman at the end of the corridor is leaning on a trolley. On it there are many things in bags, so many, and so full that I can't think how she got them through security, but they are not bags for traveling. They are ragged and made of plastic. She leans over her trolley, resting against it, as though she has been pushing it for a long time. This airport that is so bare and shiny is where she lives.

•••

All electronic devices must be switched off during take off and landing... We fly over places I have only seen named in IKEA catalogs. I never thought to have them pried off the page.

In a row of three seats, I'm paired with a couple in their twenties who are playing top trumps with cards showing the puppets from a kids' TV show. They must have learned so much about these fictional characters in order to play. They are so into each other. Like Cupid and Psyche, they look only inward, are always half turned in each other's direction, her hand always on his arm, his fingers on her thigh. When he takes off his cardigan it is her arm, not his, that reaches around his shoulder to unhook the cuff, and it looks like it is his, but unexpectedly white, short, and pointed, like a novelty dance number where one partner stands behind the other doubling his number of limbs. When he eats crisps she holds the bag and he feeds first himself, and then her. They have no independent action. Her face is pale and unformed. He pushes up the thick black scaffold of glasses to kiss her, and it is helpless as a slug.

The stewardesses offer headsets, and the passengers pay to quiet themselves. Because they have spent money, they agree that silence is necessary. The headphones link to a playlist, but there's nothing else to entertain us on this flight, which is too short for love or for action, at least the way films tell it. Instead I fall asleep and dream that I am dead. *I am still on earth with other dead people waiting to be passed on to somewhere else. By a kind of customs desk, I wait with my former brother-in-law. We discuss comic books we have read. Now we are waiting, we will have time to catch up on our reading. I ask the customs officer whether it is possible for the dead to fall in love. He looks regretful. He says, definitely, "No."* I open my eyes to find large tears burning down opposite sides of my face into the airline pillow.

A hostess nudges me awake: drink? biscuits? Although I do not want the drink, and do not like the biscuits, I eat them because they are given, and drink warm wine from a tiny plastic bottle. I cross the little boundary on the map into the shaded part of the world. Alcohol leaks in to loosen up my mind, to let stories out. Words hang in front of me as on the runway, illuminated: I cannot say them, have no one to say them to. In the seats in front of me, an old man and an old woman don't know each other. They find the stories that come out are about their grown-up children. Deal, play, trump: it's difficult for me to listen. I have planned for nothing beyond the hostel at the end of my flight, but I'm buoyed up by faith in other people's plans, as the plane is buoyed up because the passengers believe it is flying and, if we stop believing, it will fall. These particular old people talk in operatic vistas: friends, relatives marry, divorce, die, all in a sentence. Everything happens to everyone; it's no surprise. So much is concluded. Their stories have ends, and people come to them, even before the fasten seat belts sign goes off. I listen like I might learn something: they have been stocking their memories for so long, long enough, perhaps, for them to begin to see a pattern. Storytelling is a consequence of survival and each tale—told as though it could have happened only that way—irons out regret. But they don't foresee their own ends, not these people who are really not that old, in their 60s maybe. Like children they still haven't learned that things will go on beyond them.

Turbulence: people fasten their seat belts with the sound of bubble-wrap popping. Things shake and fall from the overhead lockers, as though there were a right way up, as though the plane were a house set on solid ground that could be pushed off balance. The chicken leg wheels descend from the plane's undercarriage. *Take nothing with you.* If we go down, metal stripping from the aircraft roof, if we gallop through the houses at double speed… but I've always had a problem with the might-have-been. As it is, after an interval of unsure minutes the uncrushed plane leaves a shadow of its crash across the rooftops, across desire.

7 Athens/Speaking
29th April

I'm at a café table. It doesn't matter which country. I've been traveling for a long time now. Or, not long but—how many cities in how many days? A couple of nights in each, maybe three at most. I am establishing a pattern. The first night is for flopping, exhausted, into whatever hostel, hotel, or friend-of-a-friend's apartment I have booked, borrowed or blagged. And then for getting up again, for walking the streets of the neighborhood until the moon shows above the bay/bridge/ruin/whatever, compulsively needing to find out exactly where I am on the map.

My hostel overlooks the dual carriageway in front of the station. It has no double glazing, no air conditioning, and the windows rattle with traffic, but it is clean enough, and very cheap. The hostel is hot and smells of drains and I am tired and this is where I am.

No one else is staying in my room, and the woman behind the desk smiles although neither of us understands the other. I haven't spoken since arriving in Greece, don't even know what to eat for breakfast. The coffee in the hostel tastes of hairspray. There is flabby white bread, small jewels of plastic-cased preserves, thick slices of industrial cake, oranges. I eat the oranges. I look up the phrase for coffee but forget it before I get to the corner café.

Without language I am not a traveler but a sightseer. Unable to put anything into words, I am freer: you can no longer condemn thoughts that I can't articulate. I am traveling away from meaning, can't even read the alphabet. Street signs start off OK, then the letters crunch into triangles, polygons. I can't keep their shapes in my head long enough to fasten them to what I see when I glance down at my map. In the meantime, simpering gets me a long way with waiters, with ticket clerks. Asking for directions in the street I smile and apologize, leave gaps, echo phrases, get by with words common in every language: taxi, hotel, WiFi. I could buy a little book with photos instead of sentences, and if I don't speak the language, there are machines for that: ticket dispensers, ATMs, money itself. If I prepare well enough, I won't have to talk to another human being. Brandish a banknote and point. I am freer with money because in an unknown language it does not feel like spending and because, as a tourist, it is my duty to dispense it.

Across Europe, coffee is the common currency. Sitting at the table in the café, somehow I order, flip open my computer. I show the waiter my screen. The cursor flickers in the box. He understands. He types in the code. And I am connected.

I open my inbox. There is a moment—awful, wonderful—while the page loads: microseconds spent waiting. However quick, it's never quick enough.

Is there anyone here?
  (One here!)

There is.

You are. Or I am. Or, more rarely, we are here, together. I am not at this table, not in this street, not in this café. I am not in Athens. This is where I am.

A girl, maybe eight years old, comes right up to my second tier café table, selected in order to avoid vendors and touts. She's with a couple of other children, older and younger, but she's the one who enjoys her job. Elbows on the table, she looks up into the drinkers' eyes before she offers her hand for coins. She leans over my new laptop, puts out a finger and strokes its aluminum shell, tentatively, sensually. She has never seen anything like it before.

The future's already here; it's just not evenly distributed.
William Gibson, *attrib*

When I crossed the international border last night, time flipped another hour on from England. I thought I was getting away but here you are, still. You wrote to me yesterday evening: I was already asleep. I replied this morning before you were awake. I remember when I was in Prague in the real past—post-Soviet but pre-Internet—how I stalked my building's postboxes for another love's letters. I didn't have a key—the box was my host's—but I learned to pry them out with a ruler, I couldn't wait. The drip-feed of emails is more satisfying but more addictive, like the dark syrupy coffee, like the unaccustomed sun. It is delicious to go to sleep knowing that in the morning they will be there. Is this the extinction of loneliness, or its renewal? Online we can get in touch any time we feel like it. Feel… touch. I bury my cheek in my palm, just to be in touch with someone.

Why do you fly from me?
  (Fly from me!)

When I am online, I am the place you escape to. When I am not online (when I am with you), I am in the place you wish to escape. When I imagine what I desire I still think of you, perhaps because I have never had you. For a while we were so close, if only occasionally in the flesh. When I preserve our distance, you want to be in touch, but the more I pursue you the more you recede, the more extraordinary, mysterious, you become.

That time you wrote:
  I would like to hear your voice.
  But when we Skype-called it was difficult to hear: my words echoed back to me, interfered with yours, mangled the start of your response. Did that happen at your end too?

I asked it then, that old suicidal question:
  Why do you love me?
  But all I heard was the echo:
  (Do you love me?)

Such a slender question. There is a point where voice leaves flesh, where it peels flesh right down to the bone. Voice is bone. How long could I have worked over our bare words? Not long, perhaps: one day soon after, you turned me off, your blurry avatar was gone from my contacts list. Uncharacteristically decisive of you, I thought, but then what did I know? It could have been something I said, but then, it could have been that I'd begun to say less and less. There came a point where there was little more I could say to you.

If I can make disappear what I cannot not desire, I disappear too.
Gayatri Spivak, *Can The Subaltern Speak?*

(More I could say to you!)

You had me disappeared, but I was already leaving, my voice hardly more than an echo. I have said nothing since I came to Greece. I am so quiet here, I no longer have any idea what I am aloud.

I have slipped into visible silence: some call it writing.
Spivak, *ibid*

I still don't understand how a person isn't his words.
    (A person isn't his words.)

•••

I pay, get up from the table, close my computer. If travel is passive—I am carried along, asked to choose nothing, to do nothing—then tourism is the opposite: an eternal to-do list to justify the future anterior of before the trip: *I will have done.*

Is there a radical counterfactual future anterior?
Spivak, *ibid*

How will I decide how to walk this city In Real Life, where crossing real space takes real time? An algorithm could generate my narrative, but what decisions feed it? There is an algorithm called Ariadne's Thread, which blindly exhausts the search space completely. Designed to deal with multiple means of proceeding, it permits backtracking to the last fork, the last branch in the forest. If I could type my movements into a program, would it tell me what I think I'm doing here, what I'm going to do next?

At every crossroads I turn because of a tree or the way light slants across a building or because of a telegraph pole against the unfamiliar cloudless sky. Sometimes enough similarities occur to begin to seem predictive: I'm avoiding monuments, museums, the already coded, but I make few demands. Sometimes I limit my walking to a few streets, sometimes I take it further. It depends on how much energy I have left after travel. It depends what the city's systems want of me.

This city is a dog's bark from far off. Here workmen use picks to dig up the streets: modern tarmac vs ancient tools.

If on the other hand there is nothing in particular one has to accomplish on one's trip, one can just wait for something to happen. One will sometimes see things in this way that others miss.
Kierkegaard, *ibid*

It's not a fair fight. Churches are covered with colored plastic weave, awaiting restoration. It is the same material as the large rectangular checked bags sold on the street stalls in every square here, the bags that say displaced, or homeless, or refugee. Why do I walk in cities? I think I am trying to trace the form of something. My real space map is in my pocket. It names the main streets; others are left blank. It misses off some of the smaller streets altogether. It's a tourist map I picked up in the lobby of my hostel, and it shows me the city it thinks I'd like to see. I try not to rely on it too much. I make my eyes soft, and skim its surface, hoping to find my way, to pick up a pattern in the letters of each street name, but meaning crumples.

T-shirts are some of the only things I can read.

A city-break tourist strolls hand-in-hand with his girlfriend. Across her chest: WHEREVER YOU ARE On his: LEAVE ME ALONE.

A man (a native of the city?) walks along the street from the station wearing a pink polo shirt—WOMAN LOVE ORGASM—and carrying a single rose.

"Been here before," you said, on that afternoon in the old city, and you didn't mean you'd been in Athens before, or in the city where we were when you said it, or in any place at all. You must have

Love is sequential, in other words... it's not autonomous. There are points, tests, temptations.
Badiou, *ibid*

been mapping me from another relationship. You expected certain corners, and refused to acknowledge new patterns but you can't walk one city to the map of another. "I am not," I told you, "anyone you have met before."

I keep seeing you in other people, still. I've spent the morning falling in love with men across the street who are wearing your coat, carrying your bag, whose hair is cut like yours, and Athens is full of men who look like you: dark hair, dark skin, that physique… I looked at you, and you looked at me, but I do not remember us looking at each other at the same time. I mapped you by the places I finished and you began, always from the corner of my eye. You said, "Don't look at me like that. Don't give me those eyes." And, just before you disappeared me, "We'll never see each other again." You can't know how much that hurt, not even being allowed to look. Looking evokes something else. The old Greek gods punished people who looked. They knew that witnessing was the first step to telling. Not just Psyche: Tiresias was blinded when he told Zeus he'd seen both sides of sex. Acteon was turned into a stag for looking at Artemis. Look, and you'll end up looking like something else. Looking changes you.

Could I trace how it works, that change? Probably. There's a yarn behind everything here: all you have to do is follow the clue to find out the how people change when touched by another's desire. Midas desired wealth. His touch turned his son to gold, Apollo pursued Daphne, who became a tree. In Greece, there's no such thing as an inanimate object. Women, especially, turn into things—when they are threatened, frightened—and the transformation, though occasionally punishment, is more often relief. Love objects are so difficult to hold onto as people. The very moment you think you have them they fall from your hand, as stone, or water, or leaves, or whisper into air. The men (the gods) transform in order to get sex, the women transform in order to avoid it. There are so many women under spells here. In northern Europe enchanted girls—Snow White, Peau d'Âne—can be restored, but in Greece the change is permanent: nymphs escape into reeds, stars, stones, transform into nature, not art.

May I die before I give you power over me!
  (I give you power over me.)

Under your spell, I tried to transform to keep you. You told me I must be—what? A libertine, librarian, a lesbian—and I was surprised because I was none of these things. You invented a life for me that looked nothing like my own, and I was happy to give myself up to your word. I was asking for it, like Callisto, like Daphne. I never challenged what you made of me, but, no matter how I echoed your desires, there was no metamorphosis I could use to keep you. What worked at first worked no longer. I had no shame—tried everything—but in the end it was all the same. *Why do you love me?* echoes as, *Do you love me?* Could I have tried anything else? I had no idea how to answer you, only that any answer would have the same result: No—while, before, any answer would have had the same result: Yes. There was no cause I could twin with any effect. Each route was a dead end. There is no algorithm for love.

Why do you fly from me?
  (Fly from me!)

Echo's warning-in-longing.
Spivak, ibid

In Greek myth, it's the men who do the chasing, usually. Apart from Psyche. Apart from Echo.

Echo was not chased so is not changed. Half-metamorphosed as a punishment for blabbing, she kept the same body but her voice got stuck on repeat. She pursued Narcissus, a man who loved the sound of his own voice. I could never work out why, when she gave him exactly what he wanted, he continued to fly from her.

Why was I (why am I) like this?
    I don't know.

30th April

Athens is a visitation of light on my eyes, so bright I can't recall the dark days in England. I've lost my grip on time. A week of summer, and summer will go on forever, I can imagine nothing else. I flood my eyes with strong light, with sights striking enough to defy my narrative or to supply their own. I am a tourist and maybe this is what tourists do: shock their own sad stories out of them with large buildings, old statues, juxtaposed time zones and styles, with no personal context.

The Athens metro is a large, cool bathroom: tiled, low-lit and very clean. It is a better bathroom than the one in my hostel, and this between-space is more homelike, as it reminds me of other metros in other cities. It is the center of my Athens. I take a train to Monastiriki and walk up to the Acropolis. The ruins in Athens are not like the ruins in Rome, the city built around its own hard shell. Here the city is in a park, and the park is full of monuments that are bigger and grander than the buildings in the city. The steps up to the Acropolis are crowded with people, but all they want to do is cut the buildings down to size, snapping each other, hands posed so the porticos appear to be pinched between their fingers, or offered on a flattened palm. Their cameras are digital, and it doesn't matter if they get it wrong first time. They overwrite photo after photo until they get the perspective trick just right. Each photographer turns away from the others, some toward the monuments, others toward their subject, who is standing on a vacant plinth, or between two pillars. Each tries not to notice the other photographers, wants to be the only one who looks. And what role does the companion play, who, complicit but not closed down by the circumference of a lens, sees all the photographers, but collaborates in not noticing them, and consents to be the subject—or do I mean the object—of one photograph alone?

By the Parthenon, a T-shirt (on a woman): NATURAL LOVE.

In front of the Parthenon, people are behaving badly: children kick each other, a young Japanese woman sits on a rock and plays pop loudly from her phone. No one asks her to switch it off. I can't say I blame them: dwarfed by perspectives of size and of time I'm not sure I can calibrate what's appropriate. Some of the Acropolis, says a notice, is not even original: casts have replaced the building's original "members," held in place by mechanical prosthetic limbs, their marble stained, like the rotten teeth on my crumpled cigarette packet. I photograph the scaffolding, the restoration work. My photographs look like tourist photos gone wrong: *ratés*, they say in French, which means, missed, as in *I've missed a good shot*, but it also means, ruined.

The people at the Acropolis are all in groups. No, there is one woman alone, a little younger than me. She has long unartificial red hair and is pale and freckled. She looks celtic: Irish, Scottish, or Breton, perhaps. She is dressed in a long, plain dress, like someone who wants to see things plainly, and she looks at the buildings, flatly, squarely, taking in both them and their artificial supports. I want to talk to her, about the scaffolding, and the music, and the photographers, but I don't know what to say. Loneliness again. I wonder if she is lonely. She has that quality—something I recognize in me—a quality of... what? Of being alone. I don't think she has strayed from a group. I don't think she is here on a mini-break. What could I say to her? Perhaps, *I see that you are looking too?*

I don't. I walk down the steps from the ruins. The tourists follow quickly. They've done the Acropolis, and are restless for the next monument. They don't look back. Instead they look out over Athens and photograph the view, which is transformed into an object smaller than the size of their hand.

A man with a T-shirt: LIVE FOR SOMETHING OR DIE FOR NOTHING.

I am sick of making room for couples to take photographs of each other.

On the way back down the hill is the site of an arena, or perhaps a theater, a space for performance, or maybe combat. It's lunchtime. In the shade of trees under the white rocks of Areopagus Hill, a group of Greek teen boys perform an elaborate traditional dance to hand clapped rhythms. On steps up

The arena of the two. Badiou, What is Love?, EGS Lecture 2008

to the *POINT DE VUE*, pale northern European children play games on their phones. As I climb down the iron stair drilled into the rock, a street vendor slaps down a tomato on the ground in front of me. It bursts then, miraculously, it shrugs itself back into shape. It is made of silicone: a trick, a toy, a fake. But for a moment, time goes magically backwards.

•••

I walk for a long time to find a bar that is not a tourist bar. it must be the right kind. I find a bar that is right, in a square that is not perfect, then a perfect street with no bars, then I backtrack and turn corners to find a perfect bar on a square that is also perfect. It is nothing more than a small, white house. I can only tell it is a bar because there are two sets of tables and chairs on the narrow pavement outside its door and, across the street, which is narrow and has no cars, several more tables and chairs by a patch of waste ground. I'm finally hungry, instead of that thing that feels like emptiness but not at all like the desire that is necessary to convert emptiness into hunger. So far, Athens has resisted me, offering mezze plates big enough for two. There are smaller dishes if I were only willing to choose. I could choose, I suppose, cutting off my other options, but where's the fun in that?

I sit for a while at one of the two tables on the narrow pavement. I order a beer and watch people smoke. I still have a lot to learn about smoking. Not just the language: is there a right way to do it? At a stall on the patch of waste ground, where the newspapers are weighed down with stones, a customer mumbles to the vendor, a cigarette stuck to his lower lip. The waiter passes me and I signal to him, but he does not see.

A woman at a table in the square calls the waiter for attention. He does not notice. She calls again. She is not loud enough, or tall enough, or maybe she doesn't look like she holds the purse strings. Always women have to speak louder to be heard at all. I don't mind. I don't want to be noticed. I am playing the woman who is there for a reason. I might be waiting for my husband. I might have been stood up. I must look like I have a story. Without a story, a woman can look a little purposeless, sitting in a café at least. A woman in the city is a space for something to happen: a girl alone at the table in the square looks like an opportunity, a location for an encounter, something that will change her, or the man who encounters her.

There are, said B, in Paris, plenty more fish in the sea. I didn't believe her, though there are plenty more fish on the menu. Seeing the waiter pass by carrying a tray, I'm sorry I'm still not hungry enough, not quite, so sorry I distribute my flecks of hunger between the dishes that come along. The fish are small, a starter. I could eat the fish. I call the waiter. "The fish are sold out," he says. Then I will have nothing. Having had the idea of fish, I can't imagine anything else. Another fifteen minutes—he comes back. He says, "I will go fix it. You wait here." Some time later I am eating the fish. They are extraordinary (but should I have chosen the salad?). There are so many things to eat here. You exchange money for them, and it is hard to part with the money but, once you do, it seems like nothing because—here is the food! And the food is so very unlike the money, and so very good, that one seems to have no relation to the other.

"What do they eat here?" I asked you. We were in a bar somewhere I'd never been before but somewhere you had, and I was hungry.

"What do 'they' eat? Don't be such a tourist."

"But I am a tourist here. Aren't you?"

"I know this place inside-out. I'm as much at home here as anywhere."

The café we were in looked a bit like this bar, like someone's house, but it was dark, and we did not eat, and the dark came down early to expand our drinking time… But now I'm sitting at the table in Athens, outside, and it is still light although the sky has turned deep round the edges, and I am eating the fish, which are cheap, and drinking beer, and it is very good, so good that I am no longer pretending to be a woman alone: I *am* a woman alone. My default position—hunted—I have forgotten all that. I relax. It leaves me, perhaps, vulnerable.

The waiter comes over. He says, "A man has sent you this drink."

The waiter says, "He wants to improve his English."

I look over to the man. He looks at me. He raises his glass. It seems there is nothing I can do. He comes over to the table. Greek, in his fifties, older, unless he isn't. Heavy silver bracelets, heavy gold rings. He folds his fat across a chair. He says, "I like white women. Everything around me is black." He says, "my name is Christos, like Christ."

The gods here are so close to mortals, and goddesses are always being thrown over in favor of some girl. They're not like the Roman gods, of whom things can be asked: Greek gods ask things of their worshipers. The only difference between them and humanity is that they're in charge, and we're not.

"Pigeons," he indicates the birds in the square, "they are dirty birds."

Now everything in the square is dirty.

"But the others," I say, "Doves. Ringdoves. We don't have those."

The doves are rose-dun colored, their shape longer and lower than English pigeons, with rings of white around their necks. Are they really ringdoves? I know the word. The ancient Greeks said the gods had their own language. They called things right. I put the word together with what I see. I would be happy for them to fit.

"Yes," he says, not looking at the birds. "We have those too."

He says, "I lived in Bolton, Manchester. In England the people are not so open, and after twelve o'clock, everything is closed."

I say, "Your English is already very good. Were you there for work?"

He says, "I was married to an English woman. One daughter. She is twenty. She comes to stay here, sometimes."

"Are you married now?"

He says, "No. I am traditional. Once is enough." He says, "Why did you come here to this bar?"

The ringdoves rise from the square through the tangle of telephone wires.

Fly from me!

We were in a bar, like this bar, small as someone's front room, but in another city, and the dusk had come down early to expand our drinking time. A girl came through the door, with a man—older—and they sat at the next table. You said, "She's pretty, but listen to her." You said, "Imagine waking up to that." I sat with you there—a non-fag-hag. "That girl," you said. "How old: eighteen? A student, you think?" "Twenty-five," I said. You could not spot the crenellations of experience in her. I could see them.

The door of the bar swung not only in, but outwards: forwards, back. Inside, outside. Would she cry out, during sex, in that voice? Would you mind then, or would it be only in the morning?

The girl with no door on her mouth.
Sophokles, Philoktetes (trans Anne Carson, *Gender and Sound*)

You can chase your desire and, unable to touch it, you can have it disappeared. If you're a god, you can turn flesh to wood, to grass, to gold but—watch out, Midas!—cut the reeds, and even nature accuses you. Few girls have doors on their mouths, and we are nothing if not natural, unless we're not.

Why did I stay with you in the bar that night? Why didn't I walk out? Because, doorframed by my mouth, I found a home in our conversation. Dialogue is erotic, even when it's not. I must have conversation, and the conversation must be ongoing, if I am to go on.

The ringdoves wheel and settle in another part of the square. Christos looks at me until his eyes hook mine.

"Where are you staying?"

"By the station."

"It's not safe there," he says. "You should watch yourself."

He wants me to be safe; he tells me I am not. I did not intend to drink two beers. He buys me a third. I am drinking out of politeness. I am beginning to feel not safe with him. I am beginning to feel drunk. Two men come over to our table. They speak in Greek, then he appears to send them away. They are also dressed in tracksuits and gold chains, gold as Midas. Unlike the ringdoves, I cannot put a name to the way they look—or I could, but am reluctant to make an error in translation. Christos has already asked me to look out but, being a tourist, I cannot read their look accurately enough to see.

Christos says,

"You are leaving tomorrow? You come for a drink with me later, a last drink in Athens, I will give you my number. There is a club. It is very nice, very clean drinks."

Christos takes my notebook, finds a page. His chains clank: I am blinded. The sky is black now. He writes a number. He looks at me, into my eyes.

He does not give me back my notebook. I do not say yes. I do not say no.

(Say nothing: to speak is to be punished: think of Echo, think of Tiresias).

He holds my notebook, and he looks at me.

Then he presses it hard into my hand.

"Now,' he says, 'go back to Plaka where you will be safe."

Athens
Mayday

Space × time. In each city I spend an evening arriving, a day mapping, a morning leaving, or preparing to leave. If I have an extra day inserted between the second and the fourth, the morning of departure, I begin to link up separate sites of the city, walking between them instead of taking the bus, the metro. Today, I'm leaving. I can't stray far from my hotel. I walk to the station, twitchy for departure; unable to concentrate on the city I am in, already looking for the next.

I have given up paying on the metro. The turnstiles are always open. There are no ticket checks. A white-tiled elephant built with EU money that the Greeks can hardly afford to staff. A guard patrols the platform, his uniform marked "private security." I wait for him to challenge me but he is only interested in hassling a beggar. Outside the station the touts surrounding the cafés are unconvinced, unconvincing. They know the city's civil servants are on half-salaries, that no one really expects to get paid.

It's May 1st, a day of protests. In front of the parliament in Syntagma Square I wait for something to take shape. Outside the building, the police are sitting, nervous, in armored minivans, waiting for a mayday signal. They have guns, but their road-blocks are made of plastic ribbon, polite as velvet ropes in a live museum. No streets are blocked off. I have been kettled on demonstrations in England, pressed against the glass revolving doors of multinationals, scattered by police horses. In Athens someone lets off a firecracker and I'm the only one to fling myself flat to the wall in a time-slowed moment of real fear. Later I hear rumors of the expected violence but by then the protestors in the square are all gone. By the metro, a man sells wind-up toy soldiers to no one. They creep on their bellies across the pavement. A flock of pigeons takes flight.

I go down to the demonstration and walk behind the black flag, half on the road with the protestors, half on the pavement. On the Bank of Athens' facade, the capital's name crossed out and BANK OF BERLIN scrawled above. The anarchists' chant is a low humming like plainsong, then a sudden shout. They wear black in the heat. They have appropriate hairstyles, and they look like professionals. Some of them have homemade riot gear: bike helmets, pieces of wood shaped like baseball bats. Some protestors shower leaflets. No one picks them up. Some spray stencilled slogans or paste bills. Others rip them down, minutes later. Water and bread vendors walk against the flow. No one buys.

Events recede at different velocities. I walk back to Monastiriki market. There is no sign of the protests, but the army surplus stall has a sudden terrifying purpose. I go into the antiques market where there are stalls selling fake and real turquoise eye-charms, and fake real-or-fake-wood dicks with bottle openers at the non-business end, as though their purpose might otherwise be in doubt. There are also *real olive leaves, silver plated*—garlands for heads and necks, Midas-halted by a desire to keep them, hold them.

In front of a stall of antique toys, a woman swathed in white with a white painted face, the imitation of a statue, wants to shake my hand. I make a gesture of refusal but she insists, silently. I offer it. She grabs it and kisses it, wetly, then presses a pack of tissues which—now we are linked by touch, by saliva—I must buy. I wave her away, too shocked to speak. I thought I was about to be part of a performance not designed to end in such an abrupt exchange. She expects money. She is the first person I have met here who expects money, and she has gone to such elaborate lengths to get it. She has reminded me what touch is like, reminded me that I do not like always to be in touch. Still silent, she mimes her disappointment. Her arms are spread toward me but her feet are rooted to the spot.

Why do you fly from me?

Because May Day is a holiday as well as a strike, I follow the path from the market up the Pynx, a green hill in the middle of the city. In a wildflower meadow outside the white-bellied observatory, groups of Greek twentysomethings with guitars picnic, form impromptu rebetiko orchestras. Flat-profiled men from

Greek vases, their torsos surging up from their legs with the perfect balance of centaurs, gather flowers for their girlfriends to weave into garlands. They could not do anything that is not beautiful. The grasses tremble and bob. Time stops. Or, rather, it never was.

Everyone wants to hear less from me. Already I am talking as little as possible. If only I could say less—but books are made of words. I take out my notebook and write with a blunt pencil. I'd prefer to type, but to open my laptop here seems wrong. From here I have a bird's eye view of Athens, like Procne, like Philomel, a star's-eye-view like Calisto. If I could arrange words in patterns, like a landscape, if I could do without sentences, if the linear could be laid out flat, if the algorithms worked…

Echo shrank and died, but I will not die if you do not answer me. I will harden. Voice peeled back from flesh; *her bones were turned to stone… It is sound that lives in her.* An echo is part of the landscape, or is produced by the landscape. She is, and is not, nature.

Meantime, an echo changes the meaning of what it repeats, cheats time, stops it, throws the story back, makes possible another solution in repetition.

Echo in Ovid is staged as the instrument of the possibility of a truth not dependent on intention.
Spivak, *ibid*

There is a kind of "suspended" time, writes Anne Carson in *Eros, The Bittersweet*. It is the time you get at festivals, when things are speeded up or slowed down, sectioned into moments of significance, and each significant moment—however small—an echo of last year's ceremony in words, or objects: a ritual: the same plastic-limbed fir-trees umbrella'd up (ornaments attached), the same spectacles-testacles-wallet-and-watch, the same *Nam-Myoho-Renge-Kyo*. This echoed time

Some Greek philosophers have already maintained that eternity is the moment.
Badiou, *In Praise of Love*

opens up possibilities outside the everyday. As does the sort of time that you get on holiday, and the kind you find at protests. And in love.

I lie back on stone. Above is a blank of light. I am not like the Greek lovers with their garlands. I am not from here.

I'm at home here, as much as anywhere.

Are you? How must it be never to find yourself a stranger?

Here as much as anywhere…

My eyes go white. In the very material afternoon I'm suspended between two nothings. It is delicious.

8 Sofia/Boring
May 2/3rd

I thought getting to Sofia would be easy. The distances looked manageable. But I got to the station in Athens to find the direct sleeper train had been canceled three months ago. I could see the stops clearly on the map, and the line that seemed to link them, but joining the dots proved more difficult. I'd assumed connecting would have been easy, or at least possible.

Yesterday in Athens, the Larissa Station was rammed with people sitting on bags, on suitcases, on the floor. I left my hostel at 11 p.m. but the expected train did not arrive at 11:30, nor at 11:45, nor at midnight. The people on the platform grumbled to each other, and queued at the ticket desk to ask questions they knew had no answer, but it was still May Day, still a holiday, and none of them seemed truly distressed or in too much of a hurry to leave. The ticket clerk, overwhelmed by requests, sat his pretty un-uniformed girlfriend on the counter in front of him and gave her a spare mic. She giggled, and began to read out a list of delays, cancellations, and suddenly we were in the brightness of black and white, no longer everyday people waiting for a train in a station in Athens, but actors in a movie about everyday people waiting for a train in a station in Athens.

I wasn't bored. Even if I'd had to wait there all night, I could have waited, watching the beautiful screen, for ten more minutes, and for ten minutes more. I'd checked out of my hostel, which locked its doors at midnight: there was no going back. Besides, it was a holiday, and though the trains did not run, suspended time (ritual time, revolutionary time, party time) was still in operation. This time is the opposite of boredom, a time when everything goes as fast or as slow as you like, or when you like how fast or slow time goes—or when liking and time seem, for a moment, to be the same thing. Maybe this also happens when things go wrong: as order crumbles, something opens up, and there are moments people cut themselves some slack. At around a quarter to three my train arrived, not the sleeper, but a train with regular carriages that took me only as far as Thessaloniki near the Greek/Bulgarian border. I lay in a corner seat and wrapped a scarf over my eyes to block the already rising sun.

How do things stand concerning this horizon of time? How does time come to have a horizon? Does it run up against it, as against a shell that has been placed over it, or does the horizon belong to time itself? Yet what is this thing for, then, that delimits time itself? How and for what does time give itself and form such a limit for itself? And if the horizon is not fixed, to what is it held in its changing?
Martin Heidegger, *The Fundamental Concepts of Metaphysics*

From Thessaloniki I meant to continue by train but found the railway system collapsing: price rises, staff laid off. With more miming, more scribbles, more silent offering Euros and pointing to maps, I crossed the city by bus to the coach station only just in time to catch that day's one connection. All morning the Sofia coach followed the railway. Ghost carriages, orange with rust and graffiti, clogged the track. By the roadside, hastily built petrol points with lean-to cafés: TRAVEL SHOP NON STOP. On the Greek border, solar panels on every house, solar panels and steel gates with barbed wire: the edgelands of self-reliance. Once over into Bulgaria my coach stopped almost immediately at a roadside bar, where the Euro stopped too. Having no Lev I could buy... nothing. While the other passengers ate, I smoked a cigarette next to a rancid swimming pool teeming with tadpoles and discarded beer crates, all the while watching the horse that has been put out to graze on the central reservation.

In a field across the highway, a man tilled the soil with a horse-drawn hand plough. There it was again, the past turning over the present. He could only wait and hope for the future to take root. To choose to move on is privilege... probably. Other passengers joined me, breaking down their wait into hand-rolled cigarettes, another kind of ritual time—the preparation, the anticipation, as much the ritual as the act itself. There's an extra pleasure in pleasures that are rule-bound, sanctioned only at certain times, in certain places.

The diners and smokers finished. As we climbed back onto the coach the air was full of sinister floating seeds. And suddenly there was a sign for Sofia. I'd been asleep. The railway was gone and we raced tram lines into the city, the coach shaking, I didn't know why. Wait. Yes: we were on cobbles, the present rattling over the past.

•••

When does counting the days out become counting the days back? I've turned a corner, am beginning to feel the need to leave more quickly. Though I seem to have been traveling for some time, I'm not sure how far I've got. I'm bored with doing things. I no longer want new places. A friend emails, tells me to *enjoy myself*. This makes me angry. His vocabulary for what I'm doing seems a bit limited.

In the breakfast room of my hostel loud pop and news play simultaneously from screens in opposite corners. I can hear a third strand of music from reception. I'm getting bored with hostels. I'm beginning to feel a revulsion at the going down for breakfast in the morning, never sure what, or who, I'm going to get. I am bored by my room, which is actually a gloomy apartment smelling of unfiltered Sopianaes, decorated in sinister moss-colored apparatchik luxe, in the bathroom a snot-colored circular bath with a jacuzzi, which I use to wash my clothes. I am bored by the corridors with carpeted walls and dusty dried flowers—those little obeisances to decoration, nervous attempts at friendship in a foreign language. In the breakfast room there are just two other people, a mother and daughter perhaps, the younger dressed plainly in jeans, the older smoking, dressed flashy and cheap and, at the same time, slovenly. There is something about the way she hangs around that makes her look itinerant. She is waiting for something but also ready to leave. It is this and not just her dress that makes her look like a prostitute.

No, that's too much like something you would have said, and I am nothing to do with you any more.

I have nothing to do with you any more.

What would I do with you anyway? I can't think of anything I could do with you. The thought of you is boring. I never thought you could have bored me.

To be bored with someone is the start of rejection. Before he dumped her, André Breton wrote that Nadja began to occupy his company, *without... the slightest concession to my own boredom.* They were in a café, which is a place people wait for one another and also a place people wait with each other: a place made for waiting. We met in cafés, sometimes. And how I must have bored you! The more you talked, the less I spoke, but not Nadja. She bored Breton by a repetitious performance of her own abjection: stories of the men she slept with (he assumed, for money), of her moments of breakdown, exhibitions of pettiness, small vulgarities. Nadja bored Breton because she resembled too closely the places of her life: the dreary streets, the enclosed train carriages of her Paris. She bored him because she could not, her mind could not, choose to leave those streets. And

Breton was, he writes, *grateful* because boredom evoked disgust, broke his attachment. Boredom is close to disgust and, like it, is so physical as to prompt a prompt withdrawal, an eye-watering yawn. As for us, your words became an object that sat between us, pushed us apart: a pair of dirty gloves peeled seamy-side out on the café table, a reason for leaving. As you got bored with me, whatever bored you about me stuck to you and as we separated it peeled from us both until there it lay. And you took it for my life. Perhaps even I mistook it, for a while, for something alive

I don't know what there can have been, at that moment, so terribly, so marvelously decisive for me in the thought of that glove leaving that hand forever.
Breton, Nadja

because of the attention you paid it—but it was the dead shell of boredom.

Whatever it was, that rejected spare part, like Breton you thought the woman across the table would not survive without it, or without the contact that created it. *Nadja*, says Breton, *seemed to live only by my presence without paying the slightest attention to my words*. What Breton didn't notice is that Nadja was also clearly bored, that they both sustained only the illusion of connection. And, as for me, I was ashamed to find that you bored me, didn't want to let it show. When boredom occurs between companions it hovers like shame, never settling, reflecting now on the boring, now on the bored. Where to lay the blame? Boring is bored's flipside, *bored with* is the twinned reverse of *bored by* (that parental cry—how I believed it—*Only the boring are bored!*).

Characteristics such as "boring" therefore belong to the object and yet are taken from the subject.
Heidegger, *ibid*

The two women have gone and the breakfast room's empty now. What shall I do? I don't know... I ignore the spongey white bread at the buffet and finish my coffee, then I walk out of the hostel, down the broken boulevard, over the lion bridge and into Sofia.

•••

The road that runs from the river ends at the central market, housed in a large hall. In the outdoor market the stalls that sell cheese do not sell yogurt, but the stalls that sell yogurt sell some cheese, and also margarine or cheese spread: the coffee stalls sell some chocolate: the chocolate stalls do not sell coffee but do sell powdered soup and sometimes tinned food. The system is the same in the indoor market, which does not offer anything more, or anything else, just repeated goods sold over a clean tiled floor instead of broken tarmac.

I've reached the last page of my Italian notebook which, in Sofia, looks more and more of an outlandish luxury. I see no stationery shops, and the bookshops outside the market—of which there are many—do not sell stationery. In the outdoor book market I linger over the stalls although I cannot read the books. I cannot find my pen. I can neither read nor write. I am at my most helpless.

If I could ask someone, *where...?* but my free map of Sofia suggests inflexible phrases that would elicit answers too complex for a novice speaker to understand: *How do I get to the airport, What time is the next train to..., Where am I?* There is no *please*, no *thank you*, no *beer/wine/coffee*; no *big/small*, no *one-two-three*, no *how much?*

I'm no longer thinking about you. I've given myself another task: I'm in pursuit of a new notebook, ordinary task which is the opposite of desire. I want to resist. I want to live extraordinarily. The more I pursue you the more you draw back and the more extraordinary you become, but if I stop pursuing, leave too much of a gap—of time, of place—you become first ordinary, and then boring. I do not like to be bored, finding boredom a fault in me. How can I restore your extraordinariness, my desire? Perhaps by forcing myself to be less bored, to pay more attention. To what? I don't know. I can start only with everything.

She was sucked back into the whirlwind of ordinary life continuing around her and eager to force her, among other concessions, to eat, to sleep.
Breton, *ibid*

OK:

Everywhere in Sofia, there are few traffic lights but always the drivers are courteous to pedestrians. The pace of everything is measured. Streets that seem narrow take an age to cross, as everything happens in strict order. Everywhere here the WiFi is very good and usually free, but there's so little online about Sofia that I cannot find anything to interest me about the city. That's the boredom gap: if a place doesn't meet with its written description, either the city or the Internet becomes a restless tedium, and I might as well be elsewhere. Every city has an elsewhere, a place it aspires to. Sofia—finding itself uninteresting—looks for an elsewhere in Italy, its upmarket shops named, hopefully, *Italia*, and *Vinoteca*.

If naming marks desire: the bigger the gap between the name and its object, the greater the leap of desire that marks their coupling. And, when the name meets its unlikely object, there's a moment of delight, a bit like ritual time. Perhaps this is why I want to know little about my destinations—too much knowledge can blunt these chemical reactions—but, knowing nothing of Sofia I'm already bored here. How can I be bored when I have never seen this place before? Is it because the city is bored with itself? The McDonald's on the main shopping street is empty. Homeless rifle dumpsters but so slowly, so leisurely, that poverty might be a pastime. Sofia is flat, built in a shallow basin surrounded by mountains lying at enough distance to be picturesque, but not beautiful. Unlike Nice, Athens, Rome, Paris there is no high ground, no point of view. The city's streets issue no challenges. I can't imagine where to go next.

I search for a toilet and find one in the only luxury department store, in reality a badly lit barn with ill-stocked concessions, no sales clerks standing by the tills. A sign on the door indicates, in pictures, *no dogs, no ice cream*. But there are none to be seen. As I exit, three military helicopters fly slowly over, one suspending a large Bulgarian flag. Above them, a lazy tourist plane crosses the city to the airport.

What makes Sofia boring is time's abandon. A city bored by its own history, Sofia's waiting for something that hasn't happened yet, so that here and now are telescoped into nowhere. By the traffic lights workers are sorting cobbles to mend the road; a little further along, a man replaces bricks in a wall, choosing carefully from a pile to be reused. It's the opposite of Rome, an anti-ruin, both an ex and a potential city. Builders are everywhere, not building but restoring: outside my hotel, outside the public buildings. The streets are wide, the facades monumental, but empty. The population barely fills the city. In the park fitness stations await workout freaks, but are used only by children. Sofia is waiting for a larger population, more up-to-date, more suited to its scale. It is waiting to be populated by giants. In the meantime the city is overstaffed with menders and cleaners making ready, picking up litter, maintaining the highways, polishing the floors in the metro, preparing for the day the new Bulgarians will arrive.

•••

I wait (or I am bored, or at any rate I sit) in a park full of lilacs and irises. There is a playground with bronze statues, fancifully conceived according to the myths that boys will play with girls, and that all ages of children will play together. I have never been so happy or so lonely. I am happy because I no longer miss you, and I am lonely because I miss no one. What I miss is desire. If I'm bored I can't feel desire, as desire is never boring, it unfolds one fascinating petal after another. When desire stops, boredom flows in and creates a gap, with hardly a gap between.

What would the lover ask of time?.
Anne Carson, *Eros The Bittersweet*

If boredom is a nudge to pay attention, I must work at new ways to wait, to skip the gap. The bored are always waiting, waiting for boredom to end, unable to make the leap because—language-less as I am in Sofia—they are unable to say why they are bored, to name a cause which could

Boredom is a function of attention.
Susan Sontag, *As Consciousness is Harnessed to Flesh*

lay the ground for a solution. Boredom recedes an object's capacity to mean anything, or the object recedes from its name— there is a peeling off anyway—until boredom yawns in the gap between, and nothing has anything to do with anything else.

But a lover, waiting, is always charmed: desire fills the gap, self-inflates until it's as outsize and as pregnant as Sofia's department store, creating the opening of ritual time via love. I remember the moments before each time I saw you—the countdown in train carriages, in empty bars, in bookshops—in hallucinogenic detail: each coat-stand, picture, drinking glass, each page of each book, each phrase half-caught from the next table—more clearly than I remember our meetings which plunged experience into something like drunkenness. Often you made me wait, and the wait was as much a hallucinogen as any drug I could have taken to give boredom the slip. *Euros/pounds/dollars in my hand*: any trip's framed by the time spent waiting for the drug to kick in. The wait, the wait, the wait *is* the kick.

Independent of what happens, and what does not happen, the wait itself is magnificent.
Breton, *Mad Love*

Where should I wait for you now? Not by the telephone, as Breton did, not any longer. My phone travels and waits with me. Should I go to a bar, a café, for the WiFi? Perhaps, but if I'm waiting online, any scene may substitute, the setting just as abstract as a message from a lover who never appears in the flesh. There is no ritual, never any kick. In hell—perhaps also in heaven—no one waits: everything has happened already, and everyone is bored, there is no time, so there is no gap and, to fill it. There no desire, and there is no hope.

In the park in Sofia it is school lunchtime but the children aren't playing games. Pairs of teenagers snog on the benches. One girl is draped over her boy's knee. She looks boneless, helpless, physically, or mentally, ill, while he hangs over her, administering mouth-to-mouth. His posture says pity—*pieta*—until, suddenly, she shifts, stiffens and by turn he looks vulnerable, flopped over her, stringless.

In between the lovers there are other figures: statues, but not the old Communist statues—they've been moved to a park outside town. The new statues look like they might be Communist statues, although they are not, because they are often in groups, rising in waves for or against something or other, because they are vaguely female, draped in abstraction and long flowing garments, because they gesture dramatically. They are named for huge emotions but their features are smudged and all the same. Some of them are cement, but they say nothing concrete. Their huge gestures tell me only that they're big, and their names—JOY, HOPE, FRIEND-SHIP—are never made flesh. Named hopefully—the children of an anti-revolution, of a country trying to detach from its own history—the statues' handles come off in your hand. Perhaps they were once named otherwise, their original names erased like the faces in Stalin's photo album. Boredom is what doesn't happen between a thing and its name.

Our names are not our own. Our names are social.
Denise Riley, *Impersonal Passion: Language as Affect*

Giving a child its first name is a small violence.
Riley, *ibid*

The Bulgarians could have destroyed the Soviet statues. Some states did. Boredom, the opposite of revolution, of ritual time, is not the opposite of violence (more parental voice: *Vandals! Hooligans! They did it because they were bored!*).

I don't know why I was so angry with you—you, in an email, after a tedious evening of quarrelling, waiting, together (for what?). (*I don't know why I was so bored with you.*)

This being detained alongside particular beings that refuse themselves.
Heidegger, *ibid*

Yes, boredom is a dom: a king-dom, a domain, an area of power—of power within a state, or power between two people. It is visited on the powerless, in politics, and in love. The bored and the boring are the waiter and the waited-for. The bored can do nothing until the beloved arrives, and the power relation they create is so physical it's almost a space where the waiting lover is trapped. To make someone wait—to bore someone—is to claim power over them, but to be bored, to find someone boring, is also a power relation.

When we make it into an object in this way then we refuse it precisely the role it is supposed to have in keeping with the most proper intention of our questioning. We refuse it the possibility of unfolding its essence as such, as the boredom in which we are bored, so that we may thereby experience its essence.
Martin Heidegger, *ibid*

One sees the aging Don Juan blame the state of things, never himself, for his own satiety… it is ultimately a choice between two evils—between still and bustling boredom. This is the sole choice left to him. Finally, he realizes the fatal truth and admits it to himself, after which the only pleasure he has left is imposing his will on others, of doing evil for the sake of evil.
Stendhal, *On Love*

I wanted to deny that you bored me, priggishly believing the grown-ups: that to find someone boring would be a failure of my own imagination. But those evenings drinking when you repeated your piggish *truisms* to the point of hysteria, I, refusing to take the bait, did my best to bore you back. Did you bore me on purpose, to pass the buck of rejection? Did I choose boredom as an expression of my own violence? Or were we both just killing time, as we had time to kill, and no one else to kill in it?

You're fragmented, you said. The bored pick apart their objects, searching for a little meaning, until they appear only broken and rotten: that's where disgust leaks in. Disgusted by you myself, I let you become bored by me, until I looked no use to either of us.

I have been your Echo, your mirror. A mirror never says it's bored, not with the dreariest corner, reflecting on cobwebs and faded wallpaper. Perhaps no mirror is. But a smashed mirror reflects only fragments. Break me and you break yourself, and anyone might be angry to see himself look back in pieces. "Who," you said, poking around my remnants, "do you think you are anyway?" It was hardly a question (*can these bones live?*), and at the moment you said it I could think of nothing. So you gave me the lie: "You're nothing. I bet you'd sleep with anyone." I examined myself and found neither of these things was true, and, for a moment, I was free. Still, there's no getting away from you. If I refuse to be what you say, I still have to be what you don't. Even now your boredom with me creates a negative image of its own negative self. And every time I'm bored by your circling memory, I think about what you were to me and—another double negative—I am interested again. You interest me because I allowed myself more freedom with you than with anyone else. However much we bored each other, when I was with you I never bored myself.

But the wider the gap between us, the more difficult it becomes to hold you together, and the more painstaking the process of curating your strung-out words into some sort of coherence that could still be loved. As you write less often, the gaps between your words have become so wide that you've begun to fall apart and, as you do, I'm frightened that I might too.

In becoming bored by something we are precisely still held fast by that which is boring, we do not yet let it go, or we are compelled by it, bound to it for whatever reason, even though we have previously freely given ourselves over to it.
Heidegger, *ibid*

I'm still pasting over your cracks with the residue of what I still seem to be able to call love. I could paper all over you—your eyes, your mouth. I could mummify you into an acceptable entity I wouldn't still want to hold onto (if we met again, your reality might really make me angry) but that would be like keeping the Soviet statues standing, or like making new statues and naming them grandly, but vaguely, for no history. It would get me nowhere, and I can't keep on going nowhere in a world where everything is so obviously going somewhere, even here in Sofia where around the statues in the park there are banks of flowers growing so quickly and, circling these, small roads, where the sparse traffic flows round roundabouts. And I am beginning to reattach reasons to events, like car-jacking leads, like wires on a life-support machine, to different nodes of meaning none of which are anything to do with you. I am beginning to make stories about myself that bypass you alto-gether. Am I moving on?

You said, "I don't know why I was so angry with you."
     It might have been because I told you you were boring.
     Face-to-face, that might have been the last thing I ever said to you.

You only kill time when you are bored, and I must have bored you half to death. The opposite of killing time is spending it. Sofia would like me to spend more time—in its parks, its restaurants, its department stores—but the capital just hasn't got the hang of capitalized time yet: it can't fix desire to duration with the glue of brochured words, and make me pay for it, though it's trying. Beside the statuewomen, I have passed other huge women on signs for casinos and for strip clubs, and they are not named HOPE or FRIENDSHIP, but SEX, or MONEY. The women on the front of the RENT-A-GIRL MODEL AGENCY look just like the women on the poster for *Business Girl* magazine that covers the newsstand, and I'm getting confused. In the meantime, the city tries its best to bore its visitors, as well as its population, who have no doubt seen too much of boredom's alternative form: violence.

I wander into the park's gated summer-house, iron curlicued, with stained glass stained over with urine-colored drips of graffiti, and I find it—blink and you'd miss it—that moment I can keep boredom ajar, pry it open with jaws of life, and rescue myself through its iron teeth.

The moment of vision is nothing other than the look of resolute disclosedness [Blick der Entschlossenheit] in which the full situation of an action opens itself and keeps itself open.
Heidegger, *ibid*

4th May

Next morning I'm waiting again, this time for the coach which will take me on to Budapest. My fellow travelers—a scowling fat girl in an off-the-shoulder sequinned T-shirt and gleaming leggings; two thin women eating cold McDonald's from brown paper bags, a number of blocky, shaven-headed men smoking and drinking coca-cola—are hulks of solitude. We are all heaving around what's inside us with no common language, no hope of an exchange. The coach is late and we are all bored and the waiting is not at all like waiting at the Larissa station, although I was waiting there too, and for longer, and with less certainty of arrival.

The station cannot properly be what it is supposed to be for us as long as the moment of the train's arrival is not there. The dragging of time as it were refuses the station the possibility of offering us anything. It forces it to leave us empty. The station refuses itself, because time refuses it something... How much time is capable of here! It has power over railway stations and can bring it about that stations bore us.
Heidegger, *ibid*

Then three Hungarians arrive, who look out of place. The two girls are round, but on the hips not the belly, and they are not dressed in anything tight, or black, or shiny. The boy is wearing hiking shorts, and the shoes of all three are lumpy brown pastries. Their drinks are unflavored, unsweetened. One of them has a bag with the threearrowed symbol for RECYCLE, and the word, NATURA. That's it! They're North-western Europeans. I haven't seen anything like them for a while.

The coach arrives and we drive over cobbles then concrete, through the rings of stained gray apartment blocks that circle Sofia's perfecting center. We cross the point at which the monumental pulls away from the everyday. The roads are broken up, something's pushing through, the outer city invades the inner. We stick in traffic by a ragged street market: each stall selling one kind of veg, and not much of that, its shopkeepers balancing goods on hand scales, stalls set out on scarves, on bits of carpet, on the bare pavement, stalls selling odd objects someone gathered together with I don't know how much hope of a sale. Old women leak in amongst the posters of business girls and casino girls— SEX! FUN! LUCK! MONEY!—trickles of black coming up through cracks in the pavement.

Small puffs of clouds: the first I have seen since Paris.

I take some of my sky photos but I'm getting sick of my point of view. Telegraph poles, new-builds, dereliction, train lines, tramlines: avoiding one cliché, I'm stuck in another, if it's possible to be stuck in an aesthetic of change, of movement.

The photos have become a task, and the task has given me something to do—like buying the notebook, which I never managed to track down—but it has also numbed me. Putting something down can do that. I could take more video clips, like the ones I took rattling over the cobbles, like the one I took from the Italian train or, in Athens, through the window of a taxi at night, street-lamp after streetlamp rising up to meet me, but I've forgotten where it's all going... I check myself in case I've become too happy with my unhappiness, which has, after all, proved to me that I can still feel, breathe, think, that has proved to me that I am still here.

Budapest is thirteen hours away. I doze, a defense against simultaneous Hollywood blockbusters and anglo-pop broadcast through two screens, one at the front of the bus and one halfway down, both soundtracked by the louder radio. I am the only English-speaker. Because I can't hear anything distinctly, I watch for patterns. In the movies women appear only at moments of high emotion—to cry at the hero's funeral, or marriage, or graduation—the rest of the time they go unnoticed. We appear to be either boring or hysterical: no wonder men despise us.

How do people who don't look like film stars have love affairs? It never happens in the movies. The film is trying to make its stars look boring as everyone else by dressing them in shades of brown, mussing up their hair. The stars used to be silver, platinum. Now they are sepia. Everyone on the coach wants to look like a movie star, but as they look at the awards ceremony, not on the screen—the men in black leatherette the women in rhinestones and lycra, the special flipped with the everyday—except for the Hungarians who are matte, absorbing instead of reflecting light. There's so much of them, and everything about them is quality! Their fabrics are thick; their watches are chunky, their mobile phones and music devices are slim. They take possession of their seats, expanding, until they overflow the inadequate fold-out table with gourmet crisps, bottled water and glossy magazines. At a pit stop they get out for more. They are so prolific. They amaze the whole coach with their ability to order coffees and cakes and juice and sandwiches. Don't they know that they could have waited and saved twenty, thirty euros (goodness knows how many Lev)? Don't they know they could have bought better, tastier bread from the bakers' at the corner of any street in Sofia for less than half a euro? But they order in at the pit stop bar and everything comes to them immediately, and readymade. They expect no less. They expect no more.

Back on the coach, we cross the border into Serbia where there are so many new cemeteries, so much dumped trash. The white and black of the rubbish sacks gleams in the sun with the same shine as the new gravestones, marble, granite, obsidian. From a distance it is difficult to tell one from the other. The screens blink, and the movies switch and I try to catch a new thread but there are too many words, too many stories. I can't hear, can't think. I fall into utter passivity.

What do the bored do? They section out time, like Albert Speer, Hitler's architect, who, postwar, walked all the way to America, never once leaving his prison cell, multiplying the space of his enclosure by long division, writing his diary on a thousand sheets of toilet paper, each day a weightless perforated square. The bored divide and sub-divide until each moment becomes a grid within another, each pavement split into cobbles, but however much they break down time, they never cover any more ground. Boredom is freefall: even if you break into a run between any two fixed points, you never really get any further.

This project is… a battle against the endless boredom; but it is also an expression of the last remnants of my urge toward status and activity.
Albert Speer, *Spandau: The Secret Diaries*

If boredom fragments, it also builds, as anything fragmented gains borders, more of them, and longer. Whether you were bored by me or by your own

The enduring of the "during" swallows up, as it were, the flowing sequence of nows and becomes a single stretched "now" which itself does not flow, but stands.
Heidegger, *ibid*

capacity to be bored, whether boredom is visited on the bored by external power—of a state, or a person—whether it's a failing of the boring, or a sin unaddressed, it insists on a border, an outside and an inside, a bored to be bored by, a you that is not part of me. To be bored is to lay claim to some personal territory, at least.

Tiny unavowable interdictions to infinity.
Barthes, *A Lover's Discourse*

At the Hungarian border the coach stops. An exercise of official power: we are asked to descend, and to wait for a long time, a long enough time to be broken down into many units of canned drinks, candy bars, cigarettes. The people I have traveled are beginning to look familiar, friendly, almost family. The trashily-dressed fat girl, too tired to scowl, turns and softens, tendrils of hair escaping from her scrape-back. The harsh, skinny women who smoked continuously at every stop, josh each other. A shaven-headed man with DIY tattoos grabs my bag from me, unasked, and carries it down the coach's steps.

Outside the customs point we wait again on the motorway's verge. Dusty grass: a used condom. I am constantly on the verge of… something. We're called into the checkpoint and lined up by the wall. How do the border-guards verify me? At the Bulgarian/Serb border they searched my bag. At the Serb/Hungarian border a guard takes my passport, looks deep into my eyes and says my Christian name.

9 Budapest/Timing
4th May

Travel happens either too quickly or too slowly to describe. Time passes and—traveling again by rail-replacing bus—I am in Budapest for the first time in years, perhaps to the day from the last weekend I was here. How do I know time has passed?

Well, here and now, as opposed to then, there are doormen, and entry halls, and multiple locks, and buzzer-intercom systems, and notices promising security and dogs. City of Janus, double-headed Budapest looks both ways: Buda, to the west, and Pest, to the east. Leaning to the west, even the public toilets have door codes.

Awareness of change is the condition on which our perception of time's flow depends.
William James, *Principles of Psychology*

A friend of a friend has left the key to her apartment in a tourist shop with a bell and a double entry.

"Are you here for a holiday?" The owner asks. She doesn't wait for an answer. She goes on. "I cannot understand people who photograph Budapest when they could go to Switzerland. The Alps are beautiful!"

"Have you been?"

"No, but I will go one day. I would take photographs there."

In a building next to the shop, through curlicued metal grilles, then a porch and an entrance hall, I climb a flight of wide marble steps that curls around the iron cage of a lift. Behind three backwards-turning locks the apartment—amazingly—overlooks the Danube, has white walls, a parquet floor, avant-garde mid-twentieth-century paintings, and avant-garde mid-twentieth-century furniture. Now it's behind the times, but once it must have been ahead of them. Untouched by anything contemporary, it's out of time, seems to never quite have been of it: something about it never happened.

It's late. It's getting dark. I have no idea what time it is. I sit in my dazzling apartment, dazzled by Budapest, by the white walls, and the moon and the moon-globes strung along the city's banks and bridges reflected upward in the river.

5th May

The next day, I walk the streets. Budapest is a relief. I can read the signs again, even if I can't translate. It's Saturday and every man here is let loose from a stag party. An agitated group tries to find a brunch place, already booked. Along the riverfront the men pass Italian, Greek, Japanese restaurants, but not Hungarian: those are hidden down back-alleys.

Brunch? I haven't had breakfast, can't get my head around the money. The currency runs into thousands: just under three thousand Forint to the Euro. I can't bring myself to spend notes with so many zeroes. I withdraw too little cash but, with the tiny thousands I have, I find I can still buy thousands of calories. So much on sale is fried or smothered in cream, or icing. Maybe that's where the thousands come in.

But Budapest means café culture, no? So that's where I should go. On the main square (of Buda or Pest? I'm not sure?), is Café Gerbeaud, its facade layered in chocolate and cream. Everything on the menu's so expensive—those rows of zeros after each digit: surely there's nothing I can afford. In the currency of coffee, an espresso is the smallest unit. I look down into my tiny cup, shrinking into it as an old Englishman and an old Englishwoman dressed in icing-sugar pastels sit down at the next table. The man looks up brightly from the menu:

"Oh, nice coffee!"
  "Iced coffee?"
  "*Nice* coffee!"
  "Iced..?"
  It goes on. And on. They might have played this many times before. It is a game—but only just.

I'm not very hungry anyway. Let the tourists eat cake: Sachertorte or whatever... No! In Budapest, in the Café Gerbeaud in Vörösmarty Square not Sachertorte, which is Austro-not-Hungarian, but Dobos cake, or Esterházy.

I leave and queue for a cake at a cheap stand-up café round the corner.

What do they eat here?

Don't be such a tourist.
But I am a tourist. What else should I be?

OK, I'll show you! So that's cheesecake, right, and those are strudels? And that thing there is Esterházy cake, which is layered with, on top, a design of cobwebs in icing. And the Dobos, which is the same tight drum but the layers are slimmer and, like the zeros on a Forint, there are more of them, the top layer a hard lid of caramel. And, oh, they are people's cakes! The first jogs the memory of its sponsor, Prince Paul the Third of something, the second, its creator who popularized the cake by traveling across Europe distributing samples. There are seven layers in an Esterházy cake—like the Dobos, an odd number—if you don't count the icing on top which, being so slim, and of a different material, I don't. In the Dobos there are five layers, clasping four of buttercream, though at the Café Gerbeaud, there are an extravagant eleven: five of cream and half a dozen of the other (in each cake, the extra slab, always, of sandwiching sponge at the base). These stacked cakes stand out from the others, slow the gaze, bring it to a halt, break it down into layers where it would glaze over smooth cream. They give the eye a handle so it can afford some grip: the more edges, the more grip, that's how gestalt works, and that's why these show-stopper layer cakes draw *Oooh!*s and *Ahhh!*s each time they're put on a table. There's some competition: all the cakes in the shop are layered, rolled or stacked and all of them contain a hidden surprise of something inside something else. The unexpectedness of the inner thing makes these cakes memorable, gives the memory extra purchase—unless you've had one of them before, in which case the delight must be in discovering the expected surprise as though, for the first time, again.

When a scene has little or no apparent structure, we are likely to be confused and frustrated: the eye will roam fruitlessly seeking interest & points of connection, from one fixation to the next, without much success. Simon Bell, Landscape: Pattern, Perception and Process

"That!" I point to a thick slab of white cream, or to its neighbor, black with poppyseeds—I don't mind which. The till works east European old-style, in three layers. You ask for your cake then, sandwiched in a middle queue, wait for it to be wrapped, then finally you queue again to pay.

As I leave I'm surprised by a poster in English: YOU CAN'T SAY YOU'VE BEEN TO BUDAPEST UNLESS YOU'VE TRIED KUSTOKOLAKS HUNGARIAN SPECIALITY! I don't think what I've got is a Kustokolak, and it's not something I remember from the first time I was here. Am I going about Budapest the wrong way?

I sit in the central square to eat my cake, and do the math: I work out that all those thousands spent in the shop and the café were equal to less than one Euro. In Budapest many prices are displayed in Euros, and these prices are written larger and more clearly than anywhere else I have been. Only the beggars' notes are still handwritten in Magyar. While the rest of the city clears its memory banks for a reboot, they're living the past, their data already out of date. Good luck to them, waiting for a repeat of the expected surprise though, now with these anglophone tourists, panhadling's hardly a piece of cake.

Repetition and recollection are the same movement, just in opposite directions, because what is recollected has already been and is thus repeated backwards, whereas genuine repetition is recollected forwards. Repetition, if it is possible, thus makes a person happy, while recollection makes him unhappy.
Kirkegaard, *Repetition*

The beggars and junkies congregate in a panic corner at a particular entrance to Ferenciek Ter metro, which is my stop. At different times of day I see: a man bellowing in the voice of a town cryer, another shaking and singing, a woman offering tiny bouquets. Then something unseen scatters them like a gust of air. In other parts of the city the beggars sit placidly and wait for loose change. Here something animates them, keeps them moving but doesn't move them on. It's... disturbing.

I get up and walk down the main shopping street, which I was told to visit by the woman who wanted to go to Switzerland. It's a disappointment of tourist tat. There is active selling going on here, though. It's not like Sofia, or even Athens: people have money, and street vendors approach hopefully. I pass a sign: BUDDHA BAR HOTEL OPENING SOON (hotel, like taxi, like WiFi, the same word in every language). Another: MAX-MARA OPENING SOON, then NOBU OPENING SOON—more machines for holiday making, all located somewhere in the future. In the fashion streets, the local boutiques are all 30 percent, 50 percent, 70 percent SALE. There is something unfamiliar, still particularly Hungarian, about the way goods are displayed. In the flat, narrow vitrines women's clothes are stretched across boards, or on dressmakers' dummies, pinned between the panes like butterflies, refracted as though through deep water that only appears shallow, making long distances seem shorter. If the past is everything known and the future's everything unknown, the present, trapped mid-way, hardly knows where to look. Even in Janus Budapest it's difficult to turn both ways at the same time. There's one remaining local supermarket, NON-STOP DELICATES, but I have returned too late: the city has already been sold.

It's getting on for lunchtime, and I could eat lunch for once, so I have all the bother of finding somewhere. I head for what, from a distance, looked like a Hungarian café with outdoor seating. Closer, it's an "Irish pub," the prices (in Euros) high, and the menus in English.

I wander through the iron-ribbed market hall where displays of plaster mushrooms show species and variety, and there's something northern European, something I don't quite like about this casual intent to inform, to catch you, fill your head while you wait in line to fill your belly. The market is closing when I see what I want. I queue to eat lángos for the first time in—how many?—years and the long queue moves so slowly through the piles of shining fruit and veg that I am about to cry with impatience. I'm almost out of time.

Time flies like an arrow.
    But then:
    Fruit flies like bananas.

Bananas are curvy so maybe time flies less like an arrow, more like a boomerang, or maybe time flies are the flies that zizgag below the square old-fashioned-modern lamp in my apartment, turning back on themselves as they bounce off invisible borders.

The last time I ate lángos it was because it was cheap and I was hungry, and I had no expectations, never before having eaten anything like the deep-fried salty dough pillow glitched with oil and garlic. And now I'm repeating that stop in time to grasp at who I was that time in Budapest before—so many years ago I might have been a different person in a different city—but it's something like trying to hold onto a smell, or a color, or the feel of a string of beads passing through my hand. There are no adjectives to describe time's passage. It can pass slower or faster, like a volume dial can turn louder or quieter, but no more than that: it has no texture, no timbre. Sound can be loud *and* cheerful, or loud *and* sad, or loud *and* aggressive, but time can't be aggressive, or cheerful, or sad, not really, only the things that happen in time, which means these events must be made from different material to time, though they are woven with it. It's the quality of these events that turns time's dial, speeds it up, or makes it hang heavy.

This is the reason there is a world. The world consists of repetition.
Kierkegaard, *Repetition*

Time is not just what I pay attention to, but how I pay attention to it. Looking back I notice there must have been gaps in my attention. This gray water to be bridged between the banks of now, and then, shows that memory too has edges. But it's these blind spots, and the sensation of grasping, that make it memory. The unmeasurable widths of these gray areas are time's increment. It would not be the past without this gap.

I've moved up the line by the lángos stall, almost without noticing. Well, time flies when you're having fun. If that's so, when time stops you must be having the less fun. I'd say it's more fun—the most—when something's memorable enough to halt time, but I suspect it's more likely I've got it wrong about fun: time can be so painful that the definition of fun might be anything that makes it pass quicker.

I get to the head of the queue a minute before the mechanical bell sounds to signal the punters to leave the market, and I eat the lángos impatiently, searching to repeat the first surprise.

Is this repetition? I became immediately out of sorts, or if one wishes, in precisely the sort of mood the day demanded. Kierkegaard, *ibid*

•••

Crossing behind the market's car parks, I step from Buda, (or is it Pest? I can never remember) onto a bridge over the Danube. It looks like it's supported by white classical columns, but up-close, the columns are cables and they shake slightly as I walk. Many of the people already on the bridge are taking photos of one another. A man photographs his girlfriend repeatedly at ten meter intervals. Any bridge is a photo-op: it's something to do with scale, and it's something to do with the joke of being on neither one side, nor the other. A good-looking girl is photographed by her less good-looking friend, who makes up for this difference by being in charge of any amount of complicated camera equipment. An older man photographs an older woman. She holds a cable, poses as though poised to swing like the Blumenfeld fashion shot of a model halfway up the Eiffel Tower, but she stays still. She is performing, for the camera, an imitation of a photograph of someone moving, and she's still posing the way they did in the nineteenth century, as though exposure took minutes. If she goes on like that, she'll never get anywhere.

From the center of the bridge I can see both ways: Buda (or is it Pest) behind me, and Pest (or is it Buda?) ahead. We understand things by their edges: that's where the eye grabs them, sorts one body from another. We know cities by their borders: the unmarked (you can tell as soon as you're in a suburb) or the inalienable, the steep drop off a cliff, or into water. A city is where it crosses. Budapest's first bridge was built in 1849. What did the Budas and Pestians do before that? I don't know. Was it that technology couldn't span so broad a gap, or was it that nobody from one side of the city wanted to get to the other?

In the eighteenth-century German city of Königsberg there were seven bridges and the citizens, wanting to free their lives from the tedium of repeat experience, searched for a route that would let them traverse the city crossing no bridge more than once. In Budapest there are eight bridges, running from bank to bank, or to and from four islands—and these two even numbers up your odds of being able to cross without coming across a passed version of yourself.

Each bridge in Budapest is built in a different style, visual proof of the passage of time. From North to South they're the Megyeri (2008); the Árpád, once the Stalin, built for the workers (1950); the Margit (1876); the oldest—the Chain—(1849); the Erzsébet (1903) rebuilt in 1964; the Liberty (1896, reconstructed 2009);

the Petőfi, once the Horthy (1937—a website tells me it is, *possibly the least inspiring of all the Budapest bridges*); and finally the Rákóczi (1995), once the Lágymányosi, that is lit by lamps reflected in downward-facing mirrors. There is also a northern rail bridge (1913, rebuilt 2008) and a southern rail bridge (1877, rebuilt 1953) which, if included, would bring the bridges again to an even number, and which, because they cannot be crossed on foot, we shall not count.

(*We* shall not count? How easy it is to do the math, so easy to slip into the impersonal, the first non-person plural: multiplied, diffused, expanded into authority. And when demonstrating, how painful to cross from the first person to the second: "His times were so different from hers. Sometimes he demanded an answer right away, at other times he did not answer for weeks.")

But, back to crossing the bridges in the order described above: yes, it is easy to cross all the bridges in Budapest without recrossing once. Even easier as, in Budapest, the bridges from and to the two islands count as one. But what if I've come to see the bridges, not the city? What if the city is incidental? What if the bridges are the ghost nodes in this algorithm, and the tourist streets with their castles parks monuments shops cafés, are the arcs, mere vehicles to the next crossing point? What if I've come to visit not a place, but a time?

If I want to make sense of time passing chronologically, as historical time continues to pass me by at its own monumental pace, however time loops my own life, then, by the date of original construction the order of bridges would run: Chain (1849), Margit (1876), Liberty (1896), Erzsébet (1903), Horthy (1937), Stalin (1950), Rákóczi (1995), Megyeri (2008)—that is, if a bridge is still the same bridge when it's rebuilt or renamed, even when it crosses from and to the exact same spots on the bank.

In cities space doesn't run parallel with time. A city can overwrite me while I stay still. All I have to do is wait. If I don't think the Árpád is the same as the Stalin, because it no longer has the same name, or if I don't think the Erzsébet of 1903 is the same as the entirely different bridge of 1964, joining the same points, also called Erzsébet, I might prefer to rank each bridge by its latest incarnation, and the order would be: Chain (1849: though the bridge gained extra lions in 1852, it is still the oldest), Petőfi (1937), Árpád (1950), Erzsébet (1964), Rákóczi (1995), Megyeri (2008), Liberty (2009), Margit (2011). Then, instead of going from Erzsébet to Liberty my path would lead first past Petőfi to Rákóczi, though Petőfi would have moved north to sit under Chain. Either way, making my way from north to south, it would be no more than a matter of time before I recrossed at least one.

Time can be reckoned by the distance between the beginnings and ends of events, and the gray water that flows between them. Like cities, events are defined by their edges, and it's easiest to square events by their borders in space: *that Summer in Paris*, or *that Winter in Bratislava*. I can measure time as the difference between these edges, but I'm never sure if I'm measuring the difference in the place, or the difference in me. There is no unit for personal small change (should it be counted in tens, like Euros, or thousands, like Forints?), and there is no standard exchange rate for personal with historical time.

Well, I'll cross that bridge when I come to it. For now I am very comfortable on a bridge, balancing over the gap between one sure thing and the next.

In 1735 mathematician Euler found that, in Königsberg, where every bank was linked by an odd number of bridges, there was no solution to the Königsberg problem. Because the number of banks with an odd number of bridges was not two (or zero), it was impossible to make your way to all points in the city without crossing at least one of them twice. Nowadays Königsberg has only five bridges. Time has passed, and it is possible to cross them all without recrossing, but only if you don't mind ending up on an island. Besides, the city is no longer called Königsberg but Kaliningrad. It is now in Russia, and Prussia—where it once was—is no longer even a country, which means more time has passed, and that it has passed through different units of the currencies of politics, and nationality. In 1945 the Soviets cleared the Germans out, both military and civilians. Only Russians live there now, and Poles resettled after the Second World War, so that the city, also almost entirely physically destroyed, is near unrecognizable. Although you'll still find German on the tombs in the graveyards, one of them belonging to Immanuel Kant, in Königsberg you can no longer cross the same bridge twice. It has become a city with no memory.

•••

Once over the river, in Pest (or is it Buda?) I'm back in city break territory. Silver wedding couples walk by hand in hand. I regret nothing. They don't look happy.

The districts of Budapest spiral clockwise in ever-increasing circles. Buda is 1 and Pest is 5, or perhaps it's the other way around. Whatever their numbers, the two halves of the city center are binary: one high, the other flat, one *stary*, one *mlady*—but that's Slovak, not Hungarian. I lived in Slovakia for a short while, in Bratislava, a slim border's width from Budapest. That's how I first came here. It's a couple of hours away by the train, following the river that severs both cities.

I'm following the map to the Rudas Baths but, as in Nice, I find I'm helplessly ascending, this time through a scrubby park to

Budapest castle. I don't mean to climb but the roads curve upwards and clockwise, like Budapest's districts, like water going down a sink—or not, as I've read that water goes down either way wherever you are in the world, according to factors as local as the slope of the plughole.

It is no longer so hot and I realize how much effort, in the south, I'd put into comfort. In Sofia any touch was unwelcome. Here I'm relieved to put on a sweater, a jacket, to put layers between myself and other people. The corkscrew streets are scattered with massage parlors, places where you pay for touch, but the pavements are almost empty, although the statues of undressed women on the art nouveau buildings detach themselves from their iron-framed facades. No longer supportive caryatids, they cross from the fascias into the streets. They are almost amongst us.

Then, just like in Nice, there's no more up, not unless I want to pay for the castle, and the only way to visit and not to pay is to pay, instead, to eat at the restaurant on the ramparts, newly terraced with tables and moated by modern defenses where perspex, not water, preserves the signposted "view" but allows no entry, not unless you're both hungry and rich enough. Standing at the summit is a pair of sixty-something female twins with matching haircuts. They are dressed in identical pink leisure outfits, just as they might have been aged five.

At the bottom of the hill are the Rudas Turkish baths, which I have chosen because they are the oldest in Budapest and were really Turkish when the city was not-EU-not-Soviet-not-Austro-but-Ottoman-Hungarian. The bathhouse is under renovation, hidden beneath plastic sheeting, and the flyover leading to the rebuilt Erzsébet bridge. Entry is not expensive but, last time I was in the city, I had neither the time nor the money nor even the sense of direction to visit, though I did have an inkling that soaking myself in thermal and, as its website tells me, *slightly radioactive* water was something I would like, though I had not done it before, and though I have done it many times since in various cities across the world.

The stone interior of the baths is flaky as ancient skin, and the main pool's ceiling is vaulted like a church with, instead of a font, a tap set over a stone basin at one end with a sign promising something to do with health, or youth. Though I can't read what it says, I fill my plastic bottle up to the top because whatever it is, I want it.

Health? Youth? Age is the elephant in the room: wrinkly and Dorian-gray, it's spent too much time in the baths, which are graded by middle-aged temperatures: 38, 40, 42, ages most of the bath's patrons have long passed. Cold-blooded and slow-moving, with wrinkled rubber-capped heads—clown's wigs covering already-bald spots—their increments are showing. But, as I creep nearer to them, the distance between me and them has telescoped so much I can see the connections, can imagine how time will bridge the gap between us. I'll be there one day. But not yet.

An old man with long gray hair, bent double, his swimming trunks almost transparent with wear, sits under a pipe, the thermal water cascading onto his back. He directs the hose around his shoulders, letting the water caress him. He's taking care of himself. No one else will.

The last time I saw you I remember holding your arm because you slipped as we walked up the some steps—a legitimate touch—and, just after that, a girl with tight cut-off shorts passed, going up the steps in front of us, her buttocks a slim continuation of her legs. You made lewd fingers. You always let me know that youth belonged to you, even if you were no longer young.

You took off your glasses, said, "Of course I look twenty-eight." Though you might have been, you didn't say, "I'm only playing."

To stop time dead with love is for teenagers. It's not meant to happen at my age, or at yours, or if it does it's comic. How could we ever have bridged the lifetime we have between us of believing love is any particular thing?

But wait, what's this? A chronicle of the Middle Ages?
Ere half my days, in this dark world and wide?
Midway upon the journey of our life, I found myself?
Chronic! (That's what they used to say at school for *rubbish*, or the boys said it, while the girls minded their language). Chronic! Don't make me laugh.
I'll laugh like a Medusa, though they don't have them in these waters.

The "waters of youth" are warm in my bottle. I take a gulp, determined to stomach them, but they're too sulfurous to drink. I'd rather get old than swallow that, hook line and sinker. Is that the catch—you can never drink enough for it to work?

•••

Along the river from the baths I find an outdoor café by the Danube. I eat (again!). I order fried carp because I ate it once in Slovakia, years ago, fished straight from the same river when the water was still brown, and probably slightly radioactive. I am disappointed. Whatever I've ordered, it's not the same. I am leaving tomorrow: I had only one chance to get it right. To make things worse, at the table behind me a grating Hungarian voice speaking in English makes a hateful comment about gypsies and I turn, ready for scorn and am amazed to see that she is young and, what's more, beautiful, with the kind of beauty particular to youth: a tall, slim, dirty-blonde with straight white teeth, cut-off shorts skimming the tops of her honey legs and T-shirt that says MIAMI (will she ever go?). And she is the girl on the bridge, still facing her less beautiful friend whose complicated camera equipment is heaped up beside her plate. The beautiful girl has the face of a fashion model: like a girl's but at the same time like a woman's because she has no young-girl fat on her cheeks. And, because she is so beautiful, and so young, I am shocked and condemn her more harshly than I would have done had she been older or less beautiful.

The last time I was here, I was her age, and in another how-many-years I may come back to Budapest, and I will know more but I will look less: that's the trade-off. I'm only material and that's how time works on it, in both directions. The only way round is fiction: those too-wise girls in books—or is it just we expect so very little from girls? The last time I was here I must have known things. I had a degree, my head stuffed up with things that must sometimes have leaked from my mouth, and a few of them at least must have made sense, but I can't remember. So much time was passed in speaking, and I can remember the feeling of it, but nothing that I said. It's the gap, again, that makes it a memory.

Now I talk less and the fewer words tumble out, the more each means. It is terrible to age until each phrase is more than the sentence that contains it, and finally every word—so loaded with meaning by memory, reading, experience—conjures so many others, like nodes with a hundred arcs. Now each word has more edges, and they are sharp: your words are more defined now because, though you still write to me, there are fewer of them, and they come less often. All those words we used to have, and now we're monosyllabic! Each stands out, sparser therefore more distinct, changing the focus, making it difficult to judge how far away you are from me.

No more words, please, as I get older. Words are for the young.

•••

Primitive creatures like us steer by light. Walking back late a supermoon reflects the globular street lamps. In front of the expensive riverside hotels vendors sit impassively draped with HANDMADE LACE TABLECLOTHS centimeters from the tourists eating on the hotel terraces. The tourists look back at them, trapped.

And then the noise, and the parties. Budapest is full, fuller than it could be with only the people who live here. I've lost track of time. It's late. It must be—it is!—Saturday night. Time may not happen to everyone at the same rate, but at least we all agree it's the same day. Here in the spacious present the hen and stag parties have come to another city to mark time. Hurtling toward settling down they're in a rush to get old, to set a date, and to fix the setting with some kind of wildness, a fixed, ritual wildness within which, nonetheless, much can happen that is uncertain.

The specious present.
James, *ibid*

How can it be too late for me, for us, even now? There is still so much that is happening to me for the first time, still so many bridges crossed which I have no recollection of crossing before.

A limo streaks by. Out of the sunroof the upper body of a girl in a white satin bustier, her lower half hidden like a blonde doll's torso sunk into a cake. Is she a bride on her wedding night, or on her hen night? Or was she picked up by one of the stag parties? As she passes she lets out a long scream. Of joy? Of terror?

6th May

And the morning after, the streets are empty, and the bins in every street are full of empty champagne bottles, with more bottles beside them queuing outside every club entrance.

I have to get to the station to catch a train. I've been unable to buy a ticket for the sleeper from Munich. The German network requires a reservation made a week ahead with tickets sent to a terrestrial address. Terrestrial? What century do they think we're living in?

On my platform a sandwich-boarded girl walks up and down looking grim. After Athens I imagine she is protesting. Then I recognize a word on her chest, the same as in the cake shop. Oh it's an advert! Apart from Sofia's ads for casinos and strip clubs, I haven't seen one of those for a while. On the wall, another poster with the translation: YOU CAN'T SAY YOU'VE BEEN TO BUDAPEST BEFORE YOU'VE TRIED KÜRTŐSKALÁCS (not *KUSTOKO-LAKS* then. How did I misread it the first time, or did I only misremember?) HUNGARIAN SPECIALITY! Well, perhaps I can't say I've been to Budapest, but I can't say I care. Sitting in the station I've already left the city. I am waiting, in the waiting zone again, happy to be relieved of the responsibility of where to go, what to do, which was beginning to make me anxious. Chasing edges is a tough job. I am happy to leave decisions on where the borders are to others. We're not so similar then, you and I: you never took the train, liked to be in the driver's seat of your old car, although you might not have looked it. "I bet you thought I couldn't drive?" you asked me. Well, it wasn't really a question.

And you liked to tell me stories about myself, and your stories surrounded you like the shell of your old, brown car, with you in the driver's seat. *How now brown car?*

How now? I've no idea how we could be now. Could we be apart, could we be something that happened in the past, and still be something? Could we be like Heloïse n' Abelard? Could we be like Eva Figes n' Herman Hesse, Muriel Spark n' Derek Stanford? Could we be like Socrates n' Diotima (love is pain, art is pain; love is over, art is what's left)?

I get onto the train and am immediately handed a schedule of the stops in German and English. I know where I'll be and when. A passenger speaks to me in German. I understand and, to my surprise, am even able to reply. I show her my timetable, and we are both reassured. There is no longer any possibility of breakdown.

How long have I been traveling? Only a few weeks. Feels like thousands. That's exchange rates for you. Have I got anywhere yet?

That depends where I think I'm heading.

I am heading back to Paris.

The journey is not worth the trouble, because one need not move from the spot in order to be convinced that repetition is impossible... then one travels more briskly than if one traveled by train, despite the fact that one is sitting still.
Kierkegaard, *ibid*

The Travelling Salesman problem asks how I can get anywhere via the shortest route, alighting at each necessary station. If I traveled from London to Paris, Paris to Nice by train, then on to Rome via Milan, then took a plane to Athens, a bus to Sofia, another to Budapest, it looks for the best route to take me back to Paris, and whether my journey would take longer if I didn't cross the same bridge twice, and if, when I got there, I would have got any further than if I crossed back on myself, even if it took exactly the same amount of time.

In most cases the distance between two nodes in any Travelling Salesman Problem network is the same in both directions but there are cases where the distance from *A* to *B* is not equal to the distance from *B* to *A*, and these problems are called *asymmetric*. Asymmetry is more likely to occur in real cities, thrown off balance by one-way streets, traffic systems, dead ends, and cities where you arrive by plane, but can only leave by bus, or where you land at a certain airport, or station, and must leave by another.

That's not even taking into account accidents, delays, changes to the timetable, or changes of heart. More often than not my nodes have been dictated by their links, their arcs, rather than the other way around: in Rome I took a plane and, in Thessaloniki, a bus, other links having entirely broken down. As well as the main points on my journey there have been sub-stations, at some of which I could have taken a quicker route, or changed direction altogether, as the parameters of my problem are not fixed. I have bypassed other points, which could have been nodes, like the most beautiful stretch of coast in Italy I didn't see on the fast train from Ventimiglia. Maybe my journey's more like The Chinese Postman problem in which all streets must, in time, be visited with some, usually a minimal number, by force of necessity, twice.

But these are nice, nice stories, these problems of time and space. What makes them memorable is that they are about towns in Germany, and bridges in now-Russia-then-Prussia-and-in-between-the-Soviet-Union when they could just as easily have been points A and B, Alpha and Omega. Math is dirtied with metaphor and metonym: who was the salesman, and why did he cross Germany? Was he selling vacuum cleaners, or Universal Vegetable Slicers, or was he distributing samples of Dobos cake? Could one of his stops been Königsberg, and if he visited that town, did he cross all of its seven bridges, and which bridges did he find he had to cross twice... or did he miss his connection, or run out of samples, or were the things he carried in his case simply too heavy?

Time cannot be perceived by itself.
Kant, *Analytic of Principles*

The point in each of these algorithms is to travel as little as possible, and to reach the destination quickly, but I have nowhere to stay in Paris until I have made two days pass, and one night in between, so I must go indirectly, via enough nodes to ruffle up my time. If I break time down into memorable activities, more crossings, more halts along the way, it might be easier to go the distance. If I layer time up with events it may seem to pass more slowly or more quickly—the jury's out on that—at least all the time will be filled and, by stacking up more routes, the time I spend between cities will grow bigger until the journey has the significance of a city itself, with its many streets and tall buildings, its downtowns and uptowns squared by their different atmospheres, its islands and bridges. I will put this city of time between us. Making this time longer (or do I mean quicker?), am I getting any distance on you?

Travel makes time pass more keenly, even if it's just a trip across a bridge. As the train pulls out of the station it crosses the motor-way and I see two tents pitched on the central reservation, and a couple who look like tourists, not vagrants, doing something that will make their visit something to remember: picnicking, pointing, and watching the traffic.

10 Budapest—Munich—Paris Train 6/7th May

At the first stop out of Budapest a young couple, with a child aged about five or six, get on the train and colonize the table where I'm sitting. The parents bring out food, a handheld games console, magazines, toys, until all surfaces are covered. The father, who wears a gold teddy bear on a thick gold chain round his neck, is attentive. He gives the games console to the child, who plays it loudly on repeat. The father does not turn it down or give the child headphones. The train runs parallel to a disused railway line. May bushes flower between its tracks. The father brings out a commercially pre-drawn teddy bear for the child to color. Opposite them (next to me) the mother, who wears a hair-band with a pink plastic bow, sleeps. She wakes occasionally to eat: prepackaged pastries, salty snacks. The child ignores the coloring sheet. He is not bored yet. The father draws a grotesque bunny of his own, like nothing in nature: the animal of a television watcher, an easter-egg eater. He brings out an array of small, new plastic toys. The child selects one filled with sweets, price label still attached, excavates and eats the candy, then loses interest. Something about him is kidnapped: a prisoner, jollied along by his captors, whom he humors, and something about this is distressing. I want to leave but there are no other seats. The father plays with the new toy, now empty. The boy ignores him. The mother wakes. I eat a square of chocolate. She looks at me resentfully and pops another biscuit into her mouth. She sees the father's rabbit and, taking the paper, begins to draw her own. The child wails for the paper. The father snatches it and gives it to him. The child pretends to throw something at the mother and she starts back, shielding her face.

I am heading for Paris, where I know people, know the language. The tough part of my journey—the traveling towards unknown words, cities, currencies, the journey away from meaning—is almost done. I have put myself in distress but I have rescued myself. I don't need you but I can't help wondering where you are. No contact today, yesterday, the day before, but I have no connectivity. I can't read the messages you might have sent me. Still, at Munich station I hope there might be WiFi. I hope for connection, and my hope runs to the rhythm of the train: I hope. I hope…

I have only a fistful of Euros but the beer on the dining car menu is cheap. I think I'll sit and drink all the way to Munich.

•••

Travel is suspense—don't strangers always meet on a train? It offers glimpses, lends itself to stories, but I so rarely see their ends. The beginning of a story is an acknowledgement of distance, of the distance between us, measured in an ignorance that prompts curiosity. Each story yearns toward completion in such a way that distance, ignorance, is no longer passive waiting, but becomes something active, as the noise of the train carriages pulled helplessly along develops itself into a rhythm, though the pattern may be only in the eye of the beer-holder.

Absence persists, I must endure it—hence I will manipulate it: transform the distortion of time into oscillation, produce rhythm.
Barthes, *A Lover's Discourse*

In the dining car a group of jolly fifty-something German men buy a beer for a woman perhaps half their age, her skin twice as dark. Having cornered her with the gift of a drink, they play at guessing where she comes from, speaking English, their common language. "Yes there's the war on terror," she says, "but it's not as bad as it sounds." "No burqa then?" the men laugh, quarrying her with questions, pressing her into personal confessions: "How much are you allowed to drink in Pakistan?" "Well," she admits, "I drink more in Europe." "What do you do there?" they challenge her. "I work for a UN organization," she says, "I want to go back and work against poverty." They don't like this, chase her into details, trying to trip her. Does she know what poverty is like? "I spend one week of the month with my father in the fields." She is not what they thought. What can they do about it? How can they get rid of the thought of her—young and pretty— also decided, intelligent, engaged. They dismiss her: "But you can't be typical: how many girls in Pakistan are like you?"

The men do not look as though they work against poverty. "I have a little factory," says the ringleader, the one with red trousers who karate-kicked his way into the dining car (his apology to her, their introduction). "I make wooded floors. And laminate. That look like wood." He pats the formica surface of the dining car table. "But that's oak?" she says, hesitating only slightly in her assertion. "No!" he exclaims triumphantly, "plastic!"

The girl leaves. The men discuss her in German. I can't tell what they are saying, but I know it is about her. Still I am envious even of their harrying attention. Was she their type? Why did they choose her, to press with their questions, to laminate with their stories? The Pakistani girl is younger than me but is acne-ridden and a ring of fat surfs the gap between her blouse and her jeans. Why didn't they choose me? (Am I no better than them?)

Quite frequently it is by language that the other is altered.
Barthes, *ibid*

The sky covers itself with clouds. We are entering northern Europe.

A young woman in a miniskirt passes through the dining car. The men's gaze turns to a new prey. They watch, enjoying her struggle to wrangle her heavy suitcase through the narrow exit by the bar. She's gone before they can stop her. There are two other women alone in the dining car. Will they pick one of them next? Or me? Or should, or could I begin a conversation with one of those women. No. The space of travel is erotic. There is no encounter that is not sexual.

"Don't take it personally," you said, "but you're just not my type."
Atypical then, maybe.
"I don't seem to have a type," I said.
(Of course you meant me to take it personally.)

Atopos... Not my type.
Barthes, *ibid*

Two women enter. They approach the three men remaining at the bar (their ringleader has gone after the miniskirt). The women are around fifty and are dressed girlishly in holiday tops and cropped trousers, one entirely in yellow, the other in white.

The tables are turned.

The women order beers and comic plates of slippery-dicked hot dogs. I watch them flirting in a foreign language, like a silent film, as they put on a performance for the men about whether they should have cream on their torte (they give in, miming a feigned reluctant acceptance—appropriate to their femininity— of pleasure). Typical. Their show's a dead circuit, will never strike sparks. But they don't really mean for it to go anywhere.

But, however little I like the look of them, I wanted the men to choose me! Is my need to be desired all I desire, and does it matter who meets it? No I also desire my desire's annihilation in meeting its object, which, if it's you, is something quite particular, atypical.

It's my desire I desire, and the loved being is no more than its tool.
Barthes, *ibid*

The atypical is what can't be pinned down to one topos, which means category, but also place. The ancient Greeks used *loci* (place) to think things through: each place a *topos*—a meeting of space and idea—a topic. Every topos was a mnenomical journey in which a location prompted a memory, an emotion, a stage in an argument, creating a junction of thought that became typical of ground covered, or fought over. But this process was pre-Socratic and, it being difficult to write while walking, most of their thoughts were lost. All we're left with is the word. *Loci* is plural, the opposite of locus—place—which is an end point, static, so what they learned must have been discovered between places, along the arcs between nodes, though we don't know what sort of places the Greeks moved from, and to: if they stopped for the man-made, or natural; if they halted at every town, every house, every tree; whether the features that made up their minds were near each other, or meters, miles, countries apart.

I have stopped in passing places, in elevators, on escalators, in corridors, streets, and in the narrow carriages of trains, and thought of you, and, while moving through these moving places I have thought particularly about our walking together, and talking, which is a memory prompted by a similar movement, until this memory seems never to have existed in real space but only as revived by my journey in the present, reattached to a new topos, becoming a new topic, so that I am only almost sure this walking together was something we once did.

As a pattern of argument, a *topos* tends to travel backwards, from the concluding principle back to the qualifying example to be proved, e.g.: if you and I agree love is X, then there must—or mustn't—have been love between us. Though it seems odd to travel in this backwards direction, I have, in these passing places, stopped and wondered whether I could backtrack to ask you to meet to walk, and talk, with me again—nothing more—but these thinking paths have led me nowhere but circled back to the point at which I find asking you impossible.

Like the men in the bar, it was always you that asked the questions. To participate, I must acknowledge the place from which I argue, but you claimed the topography. I'm never still, always abroad whereas wherever you travel (or so you claimed), you're on home ground. Typical.

The atypical is always out of place, like the Pakistani girl. The more she's pursued, the further away she gets. If he can't get her, her pursuer fills the gap with a placeholder story, which replaces, but pushes what she really is further away.

My refusal to stop you moving, to typify you, is my defense against you, though it's a suicidal one. I refuse to fail to admit there are aspects of you I still love, I refuse to reduce you to a type I can embrace or dismiss. The atypical remains unspoken, never set down in words, and love, especially, is so not like love, not like love at all, because the experience of love is always atypical, based on the particular in the beloved. It is outside anything normal, including its own name. All I

can speak about is what it is not. What I didn't say to you must have been evident. I said next to nothing, which was statement enough.

The passivity in which I waited for your story to stop for me, is my strength—after all it is my desire's annihilation I desire. Instead of breaking you down, I let you break me apart so my words and my actions differed. Tears may have poured from my eyes but I always refused to speak less than calmly, which must have looked entirely out of place.

Maybe I let myself get carried away.

At the table next to me, an older and a younger German woman sit down. The older opens an elaborate cardboard box, gilt-etched. I cannot see what is in it but the gold interior of its flaps catch and toss the evening sun back and forth until there is a gold fire burning between them, as though the box were full of it.

I sit and drink. I don't work. I don't write. I don't read.

Now that I am moving, I still want to disturb you in your familiar places. I still want to move you but any time I set you in motion, instead of walking with me, you leave. Thinking of me, I want you to be distracted, displaced. If I could email you now, would online be place enough for time and place to coincide? Love seems not to take place in normal time, so why should it take place in normal space? Perhaps cyberspace is its most appropriate venue. Or, for second choice, a train.

The older and younger German women are now sitting in front of plates of giant cream cakes. The fire in the empty box is still blazing.

All I have is this story, which travels forwards, not knowing how it will end, and any story is in the waiting. It's a matter of knowing how to receive ideas. Better not to miss the train I came to catch, better to be in place, on time (by which I mean, as usual, slightly early). Then, when the train, or the story, arrives, I will be ready.

A story must also know when to leave itself alone.

The hiding must be seen.
Barthes, *ibid*

I take out my book.

You never saw me reading. We never traveled in companionable silence together.

11   Paris/Replaying
7/8 May

I am lonelier because I am in Paris. I arrive to find friends are out of town. Not finding them in familiar places, I know where they aren't. And I know Paris, don't have to walk it, look at it. I spend my time online, working.

I am staying in L's apartment. She's away in another city. On the overnight train from Munich, which was so very different from the sleeper trains in the movies, I didn't sleep on my bed, one of six stacked like morgue slots in my compartment, fully clothed as a corpse under a gesture towards a sheet, textured like a wet-wipe. All day I sit in L's apartment. I empty out my bag. I will take my clothes to the *laverie* on the corner to wash, but not now. Tomorrow…

All I can see of Paris is the mansard window opposite the window of L's apartment, a fifth-floor walk-up with a tiny iron balcony and a tiny iron table and chair. It is so Paris that I don't have to see any more of the city than this view. I know exactly where I am. It's May now and it's hot here, and I burn my palm cooking pasta in L's tiny kitchen. Used to gas, I put my hand down on her electric hotplate and, though I switched it off a while ago, it's still hot. The kitchen overlooks the back of her block, which looks— the dingy stairwell windows running stains down concrete walls—Paris Paris too, but in a different way. In the evening I go out to a bookshop to hear D read. This is what I came to Paris for. The bookshop is full. I arrive late and stand outside on the street listening to her disembodied voice crawl through the speakers. Afterwards she invites me for dinner with several others. We eat couscous, drink a lot, then smoke outside a café until 2 a.m. The next day I'm hungover. D and my friends have returned to London. I stay all day in L's apartment with my pile of washing, I don't need to go out.

So what happened in Munich?

I missed my connection. Or rather, I was not allowed to catch it. I arrived at the station about 9 p.m. and all over the concourse were food outlets of every kind: pizza, pasta, sushi, donuts, pancakes, everyfood, all closing and—closed up with hunger, having eaten nothing all day save a few squares of chocolate—I sat down at the first one, or rather the last to still have lights on, and lucked out: it was cheap and good, but maybe any of them would have been.

And afterwards, loitering outside a closed coffee shop, there was connection: WiFi. You wrote, a single line:
    I'm in Prague. Why not come?

And why not?

What does your name do to me? A sick lurch of pain, or hope (can I tell the difference?). When you get in touch, I feel it like a clamor. Still. Blood rings in my ears like an airplane taking off, numbing all other sensation. It is overwhelming but I do not want it not to replay, and I don't know why. You told me once I'd never hear from you again, and I believed you. There was something wonderful about that. I really thought you had that strength. By giving in you made yourself human, made me wonder if this imperfect breaking off was just something you do with everyone. I'm always surprised that I am surprised when you get in touch; it should hardly be surprising because something in me is always waiting for that coincidence.

Come to Prague, you wrote.
You can stay at my place.

On the one hand, it's the only generous offer you've ever made me.

On the other hand, it's the *only* generous offer you've ever made me.

L emails, to make sure I got in. I tell her about your message: should I reply? *Sure*, she writes, *Want to get burnt again?*

> The complex of melancholia behaves like an open wound.
> Freud, *Mourning and Melancholia*

Well, I don't know.
But, still, I don't answer. And even if I do… I have to remind myself it's just talking. Remember, nothing's happened. It's only a string of words, it's only online. Remember to keep everything at the level of fiction.

That's what L said the first time I told her about you. "You didn't sleep with him? You only fooled around?" Then you were just "talking," or whatever sorority phrase. Your tongue in my mouth: did we speak truer when we spoke online, without bodies, sounding tinkling with the tongues of angels?

Yes yes. I write *I'll come to Prague.*

That's all I write. No *to*, no *from*, no *love*.

No.

I press delete.

Then:

Will you be there next week?

I don't press send.

We always sent emails without an X at the end, without salutations. I can only send Xs to people I'm not in love with, and to call you by your name… you were too exceptional, too particularly yourself to have a name I had already heard wrapped around so many other people. Writing about you to the few who knew, I used your initials, frightened, perhaps, of invoking you fully.

Next year, one friend wrote, intending consolation, *you won't even remember his name.*

You complained once that I did not use your name, but you seldom used mine either. When I hear my name spoken aloud it shocks me, like something falling onto me from a high shelf, like being hit by something not heavy but unexpected. I know who I am but a name that has served so many others… I'm still surprised to find myself attached to it.

You forgot my name once too. You were introducing me to someone, a chance meeting in the street, and you floundered. And all the time we wrote to each other you supplemented mine with the names of people from books. You called me Macabea, (insignificant, ignorant, dirty) from Clarice Lispector's *Hour of the Star*, you called me Gudrun (bluestocking) from *Women in Love*, you called me (epicene) Shakespeare's Viola. I was named and un-named. I loved it when you did that, felt I belonged to you, but I could never make you belong to me. To call anyone as though he belonged to me seemed wrong, though I loved to be possessed by language.

Come to Prague, Joanna, you said (you wrote).

Are you mine because you called me back? I don't know whether I want anyone to be mine the way I wanted to be yours, because I'm unsure I can be yours and my own at the same time, and that's not something I'd ask of anybody. But surrender to another is also a kind of possession: *How dare I claim to love you*, you said, *knowing so little of you?* You don't know how easy it is to know someone when you love what you see, each time you see it repeated. You didn't know how much desire is observation, naming. But there was always more to notice, to catalog. It was as though I spotted you across a crowded station, I tried to keep track, but when I caught up you kept on being a different person, not the one I recalled. You were a moving target. Whenever we met in the flesh, I felt

Thus the shadow of the object fell upon the ego.
Freud, *Ibid*

foolish to have garnered a different image of you in the online space between, and given it your name. *You are what you have loved:* I'm wise to Freud's idea that, whenever I talk of you, I'm also talking of myself. Each small thing I knew of you is what I still can't leave. If I lose you I lose a world—behind your eyes, beneath your tongue—not only you: I lose myself.

Nothing requires me to remake myself like love. Except perhaps the Internet, and online I can call myself anything I like. A *nom de plume*, a *nom de guerre*—in writing or fighting there's the same requirement for disguise. I add "writer" to my profile, and here I am, a writer. It's nice to say it in public because I've been writing all along. And aren't I writing to you now? I check and recheck emails I sent you, and it's like checking a manuscript, except that

I can't edit what has already been published, still searching for some evidence that could have turned the story in the wrong direction. Pre-Internet lovers only ever possessed one end of the conversation, could never reread their own love-letters; once sent, those private feelings became private from them.

But it's difficult to know if what's made public was ever truly private, as all we know of anything private is what's been shared. Love letters: what a performance!—even when made public to no more than a parliament of two. Any performance requires an understanding of privacy, of an inside to turn out until it's performative as a soliloquy, a torch song. I wasn't only your lover: I was your audience.

AMOUR FOU IS NOT a social democracy, it is not a parliament of two. The minutes of its secret meetings deal with meanings too enormous but too precise for prose. Not this, not that—its Book of Emblems trembles in your hand.
Hakim Bey, *Temporary Autonomous Zone*

And, when I do something online in public, I'm aware I'm doing something private too, as I'm usually alone, and there were times when I felt, seeing you were also online, I was performing only for you, a public performance with a private intent that paralleled my public purpose, an intent that remained private, even from you, and sometimes—until later—from myself.

The Internet demands from me not a response, but that I am responded to. The last time I was in Paris, I remember, B said, *proliferation*. First email, then Gchat, Skype, texts: our profligate communication proliferated, became uncontrollable. I should have known, this is when it begins to get serious. Shifting from one online identity to another, there became several angles from which I must not be the first to write back.

Lightness is the ecstasy of communication without the irony, it's the lie of disembodied cyberspace.
Kraus, *I Love Dick*

So you're in Prague now? There's a girl in Prague you have talked about, and I know her too, though she does not know we know each other. I know she is single. And, because she and I do not know each other well, these are more or less the only things I know about her, though I can find more about her on the public net. I wonder whether you have spent time in Prague with her. I try to reconstruct your weekend via other people's public profiles, which are not entirely reliable. Posts disappear: tweets are deleted, or fall off the timeline. Could there be anything private between you? I still don't know. Tracing her Internet foot-print, she seems to have spent the weekend with friends, no mention of you. I try another site, another angle. If knowledge is power, I want to know everything about her.

I am jealous (not envious) of your public conversations. Online envy is normal—the caddisfly-shell public profiles conjure glamorous lives—but jealousy is something else, the desire to possess. The jolt was physical when I discovered you had Inter-net personas I didn't know about. I wanted a stake in all of them: Instagram, Twitter, Facebook, Tumblr, I desired to be linked into you through every one. I wanted our connection acknowledged, "official," but, superstitious of connecting too publicly too soon, we never followed one another.

I scroll down the list of connections from your profile, which links to hers. I hyperlink, displace myself. If I keep going I might come across everyone you've ever known, their friends, their relations, their relations' friends. Then I try to trace the degrees of separation from my profile to yours, and after a while, the names come up of

If the object does not possess this great significance for the ego—a significance reinforced by a thousand links—then too its loss will not be of a kind to cause mourning or melancholia.
Freud, ibid

friends of friends, of acquaintances, of people you might have met, and the suggestions go on and on until the names become unrecognizable. But I never come across you. Careful not to perform our private lives in public, we are not linked. Our Internet remains private, one-to-one. How astonishing!

Online you can cut off, unfollow, but you can always declare a return of contact. Or, press a button and there's always somebody else: each contact weighs the same, if all you're counting is numbers. A message of congratulation: you've gone up a level!—there's never any end to it. But whatever button I press now, you will not be there, nothing beyond your shiny public shell. That you go on, visibly, publicly, after "we" ended is still hard.

What is strangest is inseparable from love... mens and women's sexual organs are attracted to each other like a magnet only through the introduction between them of a web of uncertainty ceaselessly renewed.
Breton, *Mad Love*

Every day I have to renew the decision not to search, not to write, not to look. Each day is a not-end.

I used to search for your photos as though looking could conjure you, and then I stopped, as though not looking could make you disappear. I don't want to look you up much anymore, haven't looked for you for some time. I know that if I see you, I might be tempted to get in touch. But today I'll try it, or I'll try myself, and see if you have changed, or I have. Memory is necessarily incomplete, it looks for a revelation in something outside itself. Your message prompts a need to find you still exist, so I spend the morning, not walking through the city, but stalking you through the Internet. How will I find you? By typing your name, though it is such a regular name that I have already found both its parts attached to several other people, who have all become tangential to my idea of you, until I've forgotten who it is I desire. I try a game: how many letters do I have to type

The existence of the lost object is psychically prolonged. Each single one of the memories and expectations in which the libido is bound to the object is called up and hyper-cathected, and detachment of the libido is accomplished in respect of it.
Freud, *Ibid*

before Google turns up your name. I hardly dare to enter your final letters, don't want to leave the trace of you on my new laptop. Slot machines. Banana, lemon, cherry: all instances of your name become you, and I can accommodate them all in my desire for you. Online, love is not narcissism, but its inverse.

I'll search a different way then, looking for a tell, a giveaway. Because I think they'll tell me something of you beyond words—something barely voluntary—I'll look for photos. This segue from *read* to *look* takes me scrolling through Google images to find the pictures to which you've outsourced your identity. If I type in your name, all those other people who share it stare back too, and I have to search for you in the crowd. Your name triggers several sets of faces, one via your first name in full, another if I abbreviate. Scrolling I confuse your avatar with someone else's which, from a distance, looks like yours, but it is a face in shadow, the negative made positive (the shape behind you in your photo is a window).

Between the snaps of others, I see your public face again and again in all its states, each sharing the same stamp of manufacture. I have no private photographs of you. You did ask me to take a photo once, of you in front of an art gallery (we met in art galleries, sometimes, spaces as impersonal as a coffee chain, or a bus station). I took my phone out. No, you said, use mine. Superstitious, you didn't want me to have a piece of you recorded. A photograph steals the soul, traps the ghost in the machine, if the ghost and the machine can be called separate things. I returned your phone and you looked at what I'd shot, deleted it, said it made you look old. I didn't think so. Some people exist only at certain ages. Some old men have boyish wrinkles: some small girls have the faces of middle-aged women waiting to happen. Well, we put what we can into our faces and scrub them each day—they are our mirrors, better keep them shiny—but they wear down as though they were the rags we used. You never looked, how you "looked" in any case. I had to describe you once. I was waiting in a bar, that might not have been the right bar. Had you been and gone? "What does he look like?" the bartender asked, and I used words that fitted no more than your outsides. To delineate your quantifiable ordinary shell seemed a betrayal.

The wrinkles and creases on our faces are the registration of the great passions, vices, insights that called on us; but we, the masters, were not home.
Walter Benjamin, *The Image of Proust*

As I type, the burn on my hand from L's hotplate inflames. Maybe it's my wrist's angle; maybe the ibuprofen wore off.

I do not click on any of your photos. If I did, my computer would remember, and bring you back to haunt me. And even if I had, a photo is not reality. I'm ok. I didn't get in touch. I've stuck to fiction. I still needed to be able to conjure your image on the coach across Serbia, on the train from Budapest; most especially during moments of difficulty, or boredom. In Paris, where I have friends (although they are not here) I need it less.

A page further down, and there are no new photos of you. There is a mirror above L's desk. I glance up to see what I look like when I look at you. I look hurt, but maybe it's a trick of the light.

Why this compromise by which the command of reality is carried out piecemeal should be so extraordinarily painful is not at all easy to explain in terms of economics. It is remarkable that this painful unpleasure is taken as a matter of course by us.
Freud, *ibid*

Why do I want to burn myself this way?

9/10th May

I empty out the ends of change I have from other countries, looking for spare Euros to feed the washing machines in the *laverie* across the road. I don't have enough. Unsure how soon I would return to the Eurozone, I'd spent coins or given them away. There is a change jar on L's dressing table. She's not in the country, and you only store change when you know you're coming back. You may never use it, just as you may live in Paris and never go to Versailles, or Fontainebleau, but it's nice to know it's there.

I'm bored and alone so I take a long walk, crossing, not by chance, the streets in Paris that bear your three names. The approach to the café I'm looking for is oblique, triangulating by the Gare du Nord, that Monop… Inside the café there are already Macbook Airs x3 flipped out (I remember the Greek girl who stroked my laptop), though no WiFi. Disconnected, the world is different; it's like being underwater, or behind a screen.

There's music in the café, and I notice it because I'm not connected. In this café the songs' words fill the gap where online words might have been, so that the people here don't have to talk to each other, or write, or even read and—if they're waiting for someone, alone—the music masks their disconnectedness.

International songs play in all the cafés in Europe: the same tunes for all of us. Adele's "Someone Like You" has been playing in all the gin joints in all the towns in all the continent. They're playing it again now, and I notice. I've learned to pay attention to songs that make a mark, and I know that the songs I notice—the songs that come to my lips or circle in my head—tell me something. If I notice I'm noticing a song, I slow it, pull the words from the music and strip them down them for clues.

When I am in love, songs mean more to me than almost anything else, or perhaps they mean more to me than almost any*one* else—except to all the other people in the café, each of them with their own internal musical hooks.

Everyone knows that what is written "Especially for You" is subject to copyright.
Theodor Adorno, *On Popular Music*

Songs are like names, impersonally personal, vehicles for emotions I never knew I had. And they never change, however often they're played. Or do they? Sterile bandages—not so sterile though: dirty with their singers' love or loss—they can be applied to anyone's hurt. And every time they play it again, it pulls off the plaster, exposes the wound, and adds to it the pain of revelation. *You must remember this...* Musical clichés are just waiting for us to happen to them. They snag me with the universal, hooking my specifics, never changing yet altered by each instance they are played, so that even songs that seemed banal when released sound amazing today. The time between adds something, if only the weight of time, *as time goes by*, or maybe this time erodes context, leaving the song washed up out of time, an instant curio. But a current hit—always on your mind, always on the jukebox—doesn't refresh like that. Repeated too often, in all contexts, it can't attach itself to anything specific, can't mean anything new.

Once it was difficult to track down old songs but, online I can telescope the gap. I'd been willing to let those feelings go, no wish to revisit them. Once a feeling is set down, sung out, it's dealt with, but when a song can be replayed just the same over and over, the feeling's never finished. The songs I replay are the same every time and each replay satisfies the same thing in me,

The moment of recognition is that of effortless sensation. The sudden attention attached to this moment burns itself out instanter and relegates the listener to a realm of inattention and distraction.
Adorno, *ibid*

though it never satisfies me so much that I do not need to hear them again. My problem, now that I can listen to a song whenever I want to, is that I can't *not* want to, and when I listen I know it distracts me from doing and feeling other things I might need to feel, or do to move on.

Adele is still wailing about memories. The best love songs are all about remembering-about-forgetting, without which the ghost of emotion remains dormant, unplayed, unrepeated, and all songs are sad, because all songs know that, no matter how many times they replay, they're going to stop, even those that fade out in denial of their own ends. What little of you not lost is caught in the past. What we had is not ongoing, so I crave ways of replaying, and I will do this any way I can, because *someone like you* might walk in at any moment.

When the audience at a sentimental film or sentimental music become aware of the overwhelming possibility of happiness, they dare to confess to themselves what the whole order of contemporary life ordinarily forbids them to admit, namely, that they actually have no part in happiness... at last one need not deny oneself the happiness of knowing that one is unhappy.
Adorno, *ibid*

Adele's finished, and another song—*She may not be you... but she looks just like you...*—whines from the corner box, before the sound stutters, starts to splinter. The waiter crosses the bar to change the CD—back to Adele again. A CD? More out of date than the Bossa Nova hit it's playing, which must have been recorded as analog before being remastered on digital.

On vinyl, analog waves manipulate the air in just the same way as the singer's voice—a sound so physical it's called "warm," still warm from voice, which is still warm from love, or hate, or whatever. Digital converts sound into code, makes a translation of feeling, while analog's analogous, a recreation of the real thing that stands beside it, as love songs are analogous to love.

When analog goes wrong—a scratch, a piece of dust—the sound warps but is still recognizable as human, though a love song on vinyl loses fidelity through repeated contact with the machine that repeats it. Some people love analog all the more for its human imperfections, its slow decline of memory—but digital shatters like a mirror, each shard reflecting a single element of voice: a pattern, not human at all. For back-up, CDs contain not one recording of the song, but many, layered. If one fails, parts of another come in, then another, and more again. But if there are too many false paths, their memory corrupts completely. The errors may have been there all along, as every digital disc is full of errors, but they're not ones we can hear. Some people say digital has no soul.

Slow decay or violent shatter. How do you like to lose it? Is there anything you can do to smooth the gaps, make the letdown less

There is no gradation between the vague recollection and full awareness but, rather, a sort of psychological "jump."
Adorno, *ibid*

devastating? Depends what technology you prefer: digital's dither and jitter, or analog's wow and flutter. Jitter correctly spaces samples or blocks of sound, and dither smooths the digital jags, the jumps from sample to sample, step to step. Wow and flutter balance analog sound through the machine it's played on. Digital or analog? The consensus is, one's no better than the other, and fidelity depends largely on your equipment.

Beyond CDs, which we're all but beyond now, we hit a "memory wall." Random Access Memory means computers process faster than they can store, that memories can be replayed more easily than it can be laid down. Our storage can't keep up with the playback, with the songs, and the experiences they revisit. Analog memory is linear: reads only from front to back in the direction of its vinyl spiral. CDs read and write data in a non-linear, but predetermined order. The digital model—RAM—is necessarily non-narrative. It reads in bursts, is "volatile." RAM can cut straight to the emotion, hard as you like. Whatever is accessed at random each time RAM replays is, perhaps, something other than memory, is bent to the intention of the music as much as that of the listener.

This inexorable device guarantees that regardless of what aberrations occur, the hit will lead back to the same familiar experience, and nothing fundamentally novel will be introduced.
Adorno, *ibid*

How can I continue to know you from what I remember of you? I mean both drawing from memory, but separating you from its qualities. A song replayed warps memory even as it's triggered, like the background hiss on vinyl, like background noise in the café, adding another layer of memory to musical memories that are not even mine, derailing them with fresh replays of songs that recollect for me.

Mechanical substitution by stereotyped patterns. The composition hears for the listener.
Adorno, *ibid*

I like to think I am my own pain and happiness, but perhaps I am only the parts I remember, and perhaps I remember only what is replayed for me. To be replayed, something has to be over. If I remember things that never happened to me, or misremember things that did, it's not a fault of the recording but of the playback. Like RAM, songs point at information but don't store it themselves: the memories are stored elsewhere, in the listener. But, even in the heart, the brain, memory is not a single thing: emotion related to an event is stored separately (in the amygdala) from the recollection of the event itself (in the hippocampus) and, each time a strong emotion is remembered, the adrenaline it releases strengthens the reaction to that memory. Perhaps some of the things I remember about us never happened at all or, at least, not the way I recall them.

The complicated in popular music never functions as "itself" but only as a disguise or embellishment behind which the scheme can always be perceived.
Adorno, *ibid*

Passivity alone is not enough. The listener must force himself to accept.
Adorno, *ibid*

Our memory—yours and mine—never having being joint, relied on the crutches of external things. We didn't exchange love tokens but we did swap music, and the songs we sent stuck to each other making meanings analogous to themselves—like that time you sang a song to me, and it wasn't a love song, but it had the name of the place we were in, and you sang it as a joke, which seemed loving and, oddly enough it was a song another man had sung to me once, also as a joke, though we were not in the place it referred to at the time, proving no more, I guess, than that songs are transferable. When you sang it to me, I thought it meant something. I was wrong. Or I was right, but only for 3 minutes 55. Problem is, you're part-constructed of the songs you sent me, and I don't know if revisiting them now in new places gives you an altered reality, or casts your shadow over the here and now. I was *always looking* for you to come and inhabit them.

Always Looking, that's the name of a song I first heard just before I met you, when I was looking for someone who, coincidentally, became you, and you snagged onto that song like a pocket on a door handle. When we were together-not-together, I listened to that song a lot, and now, you've gone, I'm still looking, still listening, and if I hear that song in the street, in a café, by chance, I take it as a sign, though of what, I don't know... The problem with the songs we exchanged is that now I keep thinking you wrote them all, or that I did, and I'm never sure whether all the men in the songs are the same man, and if all of them are you, or if all the women in the songs are me. When you sent me songs I thought you were sending me everything in the song, from the words and the sentiment, to the notes, to the breaks of emotion in the singer's voice, and the crackle of vinyl or glitch of bytes. What you sent me, I welded so strongly onto your being I almost thought you'd made every part of it yourself. I won't make that mistake again. Some of the songs—the ones where I only knew a phrase, a chorus—when I go back and listen to the whole thing, I realize weren't about what I'd thought they were at all. Some of them weren't even love songs.

I don't know why the words don't fix themselves without the music, or why only both together make any feeling worth replaying. And I don't know why they play songs in cafés. Is it out of fear that in our meetings there, we could never feel anything so big, so concisely? 3 minutes 55 seconds: an ongoing moment barely longer than the exposure of a camera when vinyl was invented in 1888, though a photograph is taken to prove an experience was real, but a song played proves the reality of experience on the listener: I meet any memory only when I am ready for it. Like a photo, a song incites a desire to hear the experience through to the end, however sad, makes being sad a kind of fun. That's why I am scared of new songs like I'm scared

The people clamor for what they are going to get anyhow.
Adorno, *ibid*

of new books, or at least I think I am, then I'm surprised to find them easy, that they fit just right, or I fit right into them. I've been avoiding new music, especially by women: all those maenad albums: riot grrrls shrieking, letting loose in pain, in ecstasy, and the singer-songwriters, always breaking up, breaking down. I never wanted to be in either girl ghetto. But here I am, now, and nothing else makes any sense. So don't play me new songs, songs that will show me anything new in me. I can't take another story. How can there be more good tunes? I want the old songs, my parents' songs, emotions I've heard played out a thousand times before. I'm tired… I don't want to listen any more, but how can I stop?

I'm in a bar. I could get drunk so as not to remember again and again, like a maenad: music maddened them like wine. They were seduced by music in punishment for refusing to follow Dionysus, who was a music god, but not like Apollo. Dionysus is the god of raves, a pub singer at home in all the gin joints where music comes together with anything that blots out the memories it prompts, in the service of servicing something in us. Maenad groupies ripped the rock god Orpheus to shreds and couldn't remember afterwards what they'd done. Full up with drink and song, they killed what they loved, because they found, in their madness, a kind of clarity: they knew attraction harmed them.

The waiter changes the splintered Bossa Nova for another CD, and a song comes on, and I clasp my mouth in shock. It's that song I heard when… I turn away from something, towards the window, and catch in my smudged reflection, as in L's mirror, that look that must be there. Hearing that song out of place, where I didn't expect it, I don't move away. I want to test myself. I want to know what I looked like the week that song kept me sane with its three-chord pattern, a dying fall. That whole album, but that particular track. I know what's coming, that cough at the beginning of the song by the dead man.

We were between the bars in another city, where it patterned through my head, the only thing I could hold onto, that gave any shape to what happened, as it happened.

Say yes.

My mind loops on replay.

I turntable away from the music. But, when I look into the glass, I don't see my own face. On the other side of the window a man, seated at one of the outside tables, talks into his phone. He leans against the glass, his elbow to mine, our bodies less than an inch away from each other's. He can't hear what I hear—and maybe no one in the bar can. The thickness of a pane of glass, the space of a song: 3 minutes 55—such processes!

I get up. I've spent too long alone with you—or with your shell: your messages, your photographs, your music.

•••

I meet R for lunch. On the café speakers, another woman singing. Always women singing that they're *tired, so tired,* of someone, of something. Outside the café R lights two cigarettes, one for her, one for me. She tells me, "You're acting like a teenager." She tells me that once she went out with a man for ten years, and at the end of that time they had nothing left to say to one another. There was no reason for them to get in touch again. But, after they broke up, he moved close to her, only a few streets away. She hid from him. Once, she saw him in a supermarket, and she knew that he knew that she knew he was there, but neither said anything. They follow each other online, but she didn't want to see him again, not in the flesh.

I show her your photo. She sees the shell, says, "At his age, only hipsters have beards. Pretend May '68 Greek intellectual. Does he need those glasses or are they just fakes?" I say that you do need glasses and that you are not older than me. R says, "I know several women who have been very happy with much younger men."

Come to Prague, you wrote, but here I am in Paris, with only your pictures. I could have changed at any number of stops on the Munich train. I could have changed at Munich. It would have been an easier journey than coming here.
    Come to Prague.
    Well, why didn't I?

At Munich station the ticket offices were all already closed. Better wait for the train, and buy a ticket from the guard who, holding a clipboard, told me there were no berths available on the sleeper to Paris, no not even seats as there were in Athens, but that I could take a separate train to Stuttgart and try to reconnect with my original train there at 1 a.m., when extra coaches might be added. If I wanted to get to Paris by tomorrow, she said, I would have to take a chance.
    So that is what I did.

12 Amsterdam/Objecting
Paris–Bruxelles 11th May

"Welkom op de Nederland": how many welcome messages have I received on my phone? BIENVENUE EN BELGIQUE, WELCOME TO FRANCE, WILLKOMMEN IN DEUTSCHLAND, AUSTRIA, HUNGARY (I'm working backwards), WELCOME TO BULGARIA, WELCOME TO SERBIA, WELCOME TO GREECE, ITALY, FRANCE again. No WELCOME TO ENGLAND, which I left. I am welcome, it seems (almost) everywhere.

This time I didn't want to leave Paris, didn't want to move, but L was due back and would need her apartment, and I was promised a place to stay in Amsterdam, plus I have to be in Berlin in a week. Back on the train, having broken the connection, I relax, realize that, yes, this is home.

And being at home, I'd thought I could work, but now I'm here I can't think. The slow train rocks me. The only thought that hooks my mind is sex. I have not been connected that way with anyone for a while. I close my eyes and let the thought take me. I imagine you fucking me against a hard smooth surface (the train window?). I imagine you kissing me on the mouth; gently on the clitoris, your teeth grazing my nipples. I have imagined these things many times during my journey. Future anterior: I imagine saying, *Again. Please.* to something that has not happened yet.

Reader, am I embarrassing you?

At Brussels, I change trains, and the station is full of lovers leaving. They hang from each other's bodies, and everything they do is slow motion. A boy pushes his girlfriend's hair carefully back from her face. It takes eons. I huddle under an electronic notice board, looking for the warmth of connectivity beneath the glow of a WiFi sign, but it's another pay spot—the same all the way though Belgium, including on the train.

Come to Prague. Do I regret not saying yes?

On the Belgian train, I admire the tweed seats until the guard tells me I am in first class. I move to second which is identical, except the seats are covered in leatherette. The windows of both carriages are scrawled with graffiti.

In Brussels the ticket hall was beneath the ground-level platforms, but somehow I have tunneled under, pulling into Antwerp three levels down, ascending on escalators to the surface, which is a grand 19th-century palace sitting atop a void. I ask the guard behind a high mahogany counter for my connecting train in French. He smirks, switches sadistically to Flemish.

Pulling through Rotterdam station, graffiti: LOVE IS A BATTLE-FIELD and SOME GIRLS ROMANCE SOME GIRLS SLOW DANCE.

(both, obligingly, in English).

then, by the side of the line, a large new housing block supported by scaffolding, its interior entirely void.

•••

I arrive and it's so much later than I thought. Unlike other cities, Amsterdam draws up to its points of departure, rather than encircling them: the port and the station are at the harsh cold summit on the city where it meets the sea. In front of the station, a car park, tram stops, a long cold open space for the city's trapped wind. I cross it and do the usual: enter the lobby of the first smart hotel, pick up a city map, walk to where I'm staying. It's already dark.

My hosts are friends of a friend: a gay couple, nervous. They are going on holiday tomorrow—and planning is stressful, yes, but there is something else: something that makes me glad I am no longer a couple. One is German, the other Italian. We must go out to dinner. We must not eat Dutch. We must eat Korean. I am tired but they must provide me with a guide to their city where they have lived for years. They say they love Amsterdam but that I should not go to the red light district, which is trashy, nor to the inauthentic central, touristy areas. I should not go to the outer districts, which are not interesting. I should not go to the modern area by the docks, which is ugly. Where, then? They point out a hidden garden, a furniture designer's shop by the Anne Frank house (into which I should not go, not unless I want to queue for hours). They both work for a Green charity: one in research, the other, pr. What do I do? I can hardly say. They are suspicious of my project, they are suspicious of my work—both, I think, for political reasons.

Back at their flat, they pour me a small glass of cheap white wine, recork the bottle. The researcher goes off somewhere to do something, the pr shows me his sketchbook: canals, flower vases, café tables, ruined cottages, all the old standards. He apologizes to me for his strong interest in something that, like writing, and romance, may not be directly relevant to Green politics. But he loves the things he draws. And he is sorry that he loves them perhaps more, or as much as he loves environmentalism or pr. I need to sleep but I cannot shut him up.

Before breakfast they're gone. I cling to my sheets as they pass and repass my couch-bed, pretend to sleep. As soon as they're out I get up, try to work, but I have been traveling for too long. A walk to a café will wake me. Perhaps.

I'm back in Northern Europe and it's cold. The sky is white. I am exhausted. My fingers are pale and waxy. There's a swelling over my right eye. I find the café my hosts recommended. I don't want to eat. I want only insubstantial things, things that are bad for me. I order: chocolate with cream—*mit sahne*—no, that's German but Dutch is almost... well a move away from the latinate at least—yes—*slagroom*. No need to chew it, it dissolves. I'm too tired to bite, and I could eat *warme chocolademelk met slagroom* endlessly without getting full up, seeming to care neither for my outsides, nor my insides. I could even pull off the magic trick of eating sugar but remaining thin, if I eat nothing but. But appearance is a side-issue: most of the time right now, I don't need, or want, anything else.

In the café window reflected colors vibrate and separate, orange and blue, like primitive film. There is a WiFi code but the Internet does not work. I am blank. I notice nothing, write nothing, feel nothing. I go back to the flat and back to to bed. It is midday.

I wake in the evening and it's dark again. I go out. Ten foot windows of light hang framed on the sooty walls. Are they shops or interiors? They look like they must be selling what's on show: the cushions, the books, the life. I have just left an apartment like this. I didn't belong there, was on the wrong side of the glass. I walk through the red light district, where my hosts told me not to walk, not for safety but from a sense of aesthetic disgust. The head shops are full, but the sex shops are empty. It's Saturday night, and the streets are full of stag parties. They wander, but they do not enter. The groups of men stick to the main drag. It's in the side streets that I find the window girls—mostly Dutch-Asian, flesh crammed into tight dresses and shallow vitrines like shop dummies. As I pass they activate like movement-sensitive clockworks. Although it is dark I put on shades, still in my pocket from the Paris sun. I feel shame, but not for them, for me. I want to tell them I am not part of this looking. A man passes. One of the girls taps on her window, beckons, and suddenly she is on the outside and he is on the inside. He doesn't go in. Transparent about sex, opaque about contact, Amsterdam is a city not for touching but for peeping.

No, you never fucked me. Though we went to bed once or twice, you never replayed the physical jolt of what we did online. There was something sensual about the call and response of our emails, texts, Skype all at once, like breasts, cunt, clit, neck, mouth—so hot, so responsive, rhythmic, inventive, like sex. *Well*, almost... But there's something about saying these words with my mouth that's like sex again, that's physical. I'm like that with words, have to let new ones live in me for a bit, use them, say them, feel them. It takes me time to understand them else.

We will never have done with sensation. All rational systems will prove one day to be indefensible.
Breton, *Mad Love*

Why must our dialogue be erotic? I imagined there was a connection somewhere, that sex is what words lead to, but words are where the fuck stops, and visa versa, I mean sentences at least, I mean full ones stop. Some people say things during sex, verbs I think mainly, though I have fucked people who came out with full sentences like an instruction manual. Using dirty words too often tames them, like the Amsterdam storefronts. Pass them everyday and they're no longer shocking, even the live girls in the windows. Sex lives at the edge of language. Like art, like religion, it dwells more comfortably in images, and in objects. As soon as words make sex comfortable it's fucked. But, if we don't have sex, there remains no end to what we can not say to one another.

Is this a blow-job of a book, then, a book around a dick, around its absence? I want to fuck you through words, or fuck you up, fuck you over. The first is the only way you let me, the last two, all I'll allow myself now. Words conjure fucking perhaps better than the bodies that, so often, can't or won't match them. How else will you let me *resentir* (that's French again: re-feel) re-evoke the physical? I took your hand, once.

"Does that help?" you asked.

"It helps me."

You said nothing.

Did I embarrass you? Am I embarrassing you now? Well, the men who fuck me are never the men who talk to me. I can't stop talking about fucking, and nor can this city. Maybe from time to time it even does it.

I never had sex with you—that's why you're so good at it. But I have imagined you when fucking other people, and this has

What doesn't stop not being written.
Jacques Lacan, *Encore*

Of course I really have Dick to thank for this, because he gave me someone to write to.
Kraus, *interview, Artnet*

made the sex I've had better than it might have been, for them as well as for me. Sex is its very own simultaneous pornography. And pornography—sex that remains potential—can never be finished with. Everyone watches porn now, it's all over the net, and who could avoid its confusing promises? I got my early porn from words, looking up the dirty bits in books, where all I knew was that they were words about sex, so each felt sexual, each feeling prompted directly by the word's unfolding because I had no images, no objects via which to connect to them to my body. But sex on the net—porn, I mean—do I like it? Well, depends what it's like. That's the problem with porn. Sex never feels like anything else. It doesn't even feel the same as watching it.

Porn looks like sex, and at the same time, not. The people on-screen are "actors"—professionals whose job is to make us believe, though sometimes they're called "amateurs" which is a word that means they don't get paid (though sometimes they do too), and which is also a word that (in French) means they "love it," though they may only look like they love it, and, though, sometimes you know they're also acting like they hate it to make you love it more. And sometimes, yes, they do act too, even the amateurs, dressed up as plumbers, secretaries, students (though some of them might also actually be these things too; how can anyone tell?). But what is always real is the fucking. When we see them doing it there's no doubt: there they are, really fucking. The problem is they might be acting fucking all the time they are fucking too.

The porn clips I've seen are the opposite of the sex I've read in books, which is built from words. In porn, the fucking happens like a silent film though, sometimes, a soundtrack covers the embarrassment of silence, as in a restaurant or a hairdresser's. There is no soundtrack to the Amsterdam girls sitting in their soundproof tanks. There's another one of them now, above her a sign: REAR ENTRANCE NOW OPEN. Hoho. Well, we are in the

Nether Lands, and it may be the early hours of *pun*day by now, but *fucking* is not a pun. Though everything around it is: the blow-ups the push-ups, the teasers, the ticklers that mean the same as bodies, but are not the same, because, like puns, their extra meaning can be strapped on, stripped off. Fucking never means anything but itself, does not translate into its limp accessories. No, fucking is never a "thing," not even here in the never-Netherlands.

Here sex is not sex but nostalgia because it's sold. At the point of sale, it's rendered out of the spontaneous and into the past tense, its duty to simultaneously remind the buyers of what sex is like, even as it plays itself out in broderie anglaise, or transparent plastic, or edible "silk" until sex is something to have and to hold (though they won't be able to have it and eat it). No wonder its shell is pure kitsch, from the plastic frills lifting off the plastic bodies of shop dummies—a gap between the hard synthetics and their harder flesh—to the names we have made for all these things that fill the gap between a woman and what she is in fantasy: *garter-belt, brassiere, thong.* So alien, those intimate things that have to be specially applied: what a carry-on! They make me alien to my own skin, which, they inform me, should be smooth-surfaced as latex, or lycra. Looking into shop windows I don't look like the dummies, so know I'm not a woman. And if that's what men look for, what hope is there for them? Both sexes have failed, substituted for sex, sex objects, which, though lacking a pulse, look more like sex than the real thing, and up the ante with leather, or with lace, until what you buy is better than what you can get for free. Intercourse—that word that means talking and fucking—comes from the Medieval French "entrecourse" or business—which means both sex n' shopping. When goods leave the shop,

Das sind die wahren Wunder der Technik, daß sie das, wofür sie entschädigt, auch ehrlich kaputt macht/This is the true miracle of technology, that it breaks that for which it compensates.
Karl Kraus, *Nachts*

they lose half their value at least. The only difference is, if objects survive long enough to become antiques, they accrue it again, or more, which can't be said of us.

Though I'm walking in the red light streets after midnight, I'm left alone. Women on the street here are not hassled. Like me, they are not cut from the same cloth as what's on show in the shallow vitrines. Only one incident. On my way home past the design porn of the hanging windows, a man (a boy?) grabs my arm, shouts, HELLO GIRL!—a T-shirt slogan that shows he does not speak English, has no idea what he just said. I am shocked, not because of the sudden contact, but because he stops me as we're crossing a busy street in opposite directions. "Sure," I snap, "but not in the middle of the road!" He's already gone. What he wanted was so non-specific, so unable to admit a reaction, that he has dismissed it already.

Give me a word, you have taken the world I have! Well, we never had the same object in mind. I was only a virtual-girlfriend, a blow-up, a strap-on. If you wouldn't fulfill your promise in the flesh, at least I knew you would write to me later. When you got home late, perhaps a little drunk, a last reflex before sleep: private talk, intercourse...

Give me a world, you have taken the world I was.
Anne Carson, *Tag*

12 May

Even in May, Amsterdam is dark, and cold, and sometimes it rains. I stay inside, but I don't feel at home. I work from café to café, transcribing my notes, trying to find one where I'm comfortable. I sit in a café alongside an image of myself working in a café. I am working hard. Perhaps this is not the right café, but how quickly I become loyal to the latest place: the café with the hot chocolate this morning, the one I'm in now (finding the first one full) where I am drinking a beer. I sit at a table inside, and I decide I like it. From the speakers: something about cold and the month of May. It is May here. But not that kind of May. Denial. My temperature is still wrong: my blood has been heated by the sun. I look odd: I am wearing all my clean clothes at once.

I wander. Or rather I walk because I need to keep warm, to have something to do. The cafés are small enough to look like domestic dining rooms and, through long windows, all the canal house dining rooms look like fashionable restaurants. Amsterdam is full of shops whose vitrines, between the long, shining uncurtained windows of the houses, showcase second-hand books and only-just-antique small domestic objects. "Perfect taste, not too ostentatious: that's Amsterdam," my hosts told me. As I walk I realize I am looking for the hotel in which I spent my honeymoon weekend—so anxious that the little time and money we could spend be modestly tasteful—so many years ago. The hotel was chic enough: a black-faced canal-side building—I remember the approximate location—but we slept in a small bare room at the top floor back which we could afford, and which did not live up to the ground floor windows' promise. I don't find it—but then I'm not looking very hard.

I find the flea market and the sun breaks through the low flat cloud. Leafing through a stall of second-hand books I find Daumier's nineteenth-century cartoons, *Scenes From Marriage*: an art book, heavy and thick. I can't afford it, couldn't, in any case, drag its weight around with me.

"Are you married?" the vendor asks. (Muscular, fifties, mustache).

I hesitate, before I say, "No."

"Ah the husband wife thing!" he laughs. "I've been there."

Everything on sale here once belonged to somebody else, and their ghosts are still hanging around in the way the heel of a shoe is worn down, the creases made in an old pair of jeans, the inscription worn wordless inside a second-hand ring. Disembodied bodies are everywhere. If none new are found to inhabit them, these things will return, unshaped, to their boxes for weeks, months, maybe years. Why buy second-hand? The charm of other people's things gives us—what?—romance—what?—gravitas?

These abandoned objects are part-human through association. Eyeglasses, hairclips, belts and braces so intimately complete us. They also supply emotions. In all objects there is a promise, wordlessly spoken. Like the bodies in last night's sex-shop windows that filled the latex bras and plastic lace, they are suggestive, hinting at the promises of flesh. I have memories of you but no remembrances: we exchanged no presents.

My lord, I have remembrances of yours. That I have longed long to redeliver. I pray you now receive them.
William Shakespeare, *Hamlet*

We all need somewhere for our desire to sit. If we are lucky it will be in gewgaws, and our desires will be easily satisfied, drip by material drip. If we are less lucky it will be in people or ideas and, finally, in their absence, but every thing here is so promising that I'm glad, when things were promising with us (those plastic bodies are so light), we didn't lean on them.

The flea-market sells mostly everyday objects, but not for their original purpose. They now exist to be looked at, but they carry a *sillage* of use, though we have forgotten what some of them were for. That's normal: very little can be looked at without being judged for use—or maybe only art, which is why art causes such a kerfuffle. Use stops at the border of its frame—or velvet rope, if it's unframable—and that's why art makes people angry. The flea-market objects suggest derelict uses without end-users. They've moved away from us in time more quickly than things that are so useful they break or wear out before they arrive on these tables: that's the generation gap. No longer understanding what they're for, we are invited to knot them, group them as they appear here thrown together—the whatnot by the lavaliere, the lorgnette by the pre-electric sewing machine—to invent scenarios for the chipped, the non-functioning, the incomplete. But, how to group what's at hand into anything not unfinished, imperfect, wrong, how to make meanings from this broken-alphabet? After all these are the cast-offs of somebody's life, the things someone wanted to get rid of.

I'm sentimental, oh yes, but not about things to which my memories do not attach. Sentimentality, from *sentir*: to feel—that word again for physical, and emotional memory—is a feeling that objectifies. It crystallizes feeling into a souvenir, a thing that holds—but cannot feel—emotion. It can't carry on an exchange but, when you don't have anyone else to care for, or when there's something wrong with the feeling you offer (it's re-sented), or because those you love won't always care, or listen, or speak through anything else, yes, we use them.

"Don't you own an empathy box?" After a pause the girl said carefully, "I didn't bring mine with me. I assumed I'd find one here." "But an empathy box," he said, stammering in his excitement, "is the most personal possession you have! It's an extension of your body; it's the way you touch other humans."
Philip K Dick, *Do Androids Dream of Electric Sheep?*

Bon à penser.
Claude Levi-Strauss, *La Pensée Sauvage*

Oh yes, goods are good to think with.

But, smash the memorial object—throw away the ring, break the birthday vase—and you have to reformulate, maybe even have a conversation with someone, if that's still a possibility. But people don't smash things, not on purpose, not often. This market is full of the sort of objects people couldn't get rid of. I know all about the things that stick around: that if you buy cheap, the wrong style, a commemoration of the

When objects are lost subjects are found.
Sherry Turkle, *Evocative Objects*

wrong relationship, a compromise of any sort, you can be stuck with them for life. If you never bought into the right version then, buffered by firewalls of the imperfect expressions you own, and reluctant to send good money after bad, you can turn away from the whole subject, refuse to think things through. These half-used things that block emotions are most likely to hang around even after you die, when someone else gets lumped with them. It is good to have the younger generations: if not for them then who could go on living? After a certain age everything we have accumulated for ourselves loses meaning, but meaning can be re-given by passing these things on, or by promising to. Belonging neither to us, nor to our inheritors, heirlooms acquire value without meaning. Even in the virtual wold, the objects we inherit give us a kind of inheritance.

Provided we can escape from the museums we carry around inside us, provided we can stop selling ourselves tickets to the galleries in our own skulls, we can begin to contemplate an art which recreates the goal of the sorcerer: changing the structure of reality by the manipulation of living symbols.
Hakim Bey, *Temporary Autonomous Zone*

In Object Oriented Programming, "inheritance" means a set of behaviors that can be used across different "objects." An object in programming is not 3D of course, but a set of data, plus a method. A programmed object is its characteristics plus how it is used: its data is encapsulated in its functions. Why call it an object at all, why fit it to a figure of speech? Well, programming is semantic. Names are grasping tools, bridging the gap between concept and code, and what they grasp with's physical, or so it appears. The language of programming is one of metaphor: its "objects" correspond to things found in the real world. When we think of data + method as a "library," or a "checkout," it's easier to understand, to maintain, and to evolve the virtual, but this also means our behaviors are carried over from meatspace. A virtual object's a real white elephant in the room, a whatnot, a bibelot, a conversation piece: useless in itself, until it prompts our response.

As in the real world, "inheritance" gives rise to a "hierarchy"—behaviors carried across from one object to all its relations. Via concrete metaphors, we repeat our Real Life mistakes online. It shouldn't have been like this. The net should have been perfect in its abstraction. It should have given us another chance.

We make objects without entirely knowing why. Maybe it's for the joy of making. We say we make objects to meet our needs, which we so barely understand. It would be wrong to know all the uses of an object, to create an object entirely for use, as we can never see the ends of things: how a milk bottle will become a vase, or a urinal, a sculpture by Duchamp. And we can't say when or how things will leave us, whether they will break, or wear out, at what moment any particular pair of tights will run, or whether a glass will meet its end thrown across the room in anger, shattered (you might have hit someone with it!), or if it will survive us. So we discard them to show them who's boss, give them away, throw them out. We have to disassociate ourselves from objects in order to use them. For us to function, things must be different from us. We must make sure we are the non-objects.

When categories do not ideally exhaust their objects, then the contingent is in all respects preferable because it gets the imagination going.
Kierkegaard, *ibid*

"You're just not my thing," you said, once.

You meant that I was nothing, or virtually. In any case, you said, my eyes were never your favorite color. Well, if you looked around Amsterdam's flea market, you could probably have found some glass ones that would have suited one of us better. You broke me down for spare parts, or I did, willingly dismantling myself, for what it's worth, or for what each part might be worth to you. I knew my market, am used to being taken apart by different men. Break it down: there is no better way to come together again—or perhaps to come to terms with my brokenness. There's something in me that wants to break things, even myself.

I sit down at a café that elbows me in the ribs with chunky pottery from the 1960s and 70s—mismatched coffee cups, worn chintzy textiles—asks me to notice the conversation these things are having with the customers—who are both handsome and entirely contemporary—and with each other. The objects in the café are all from different eras, but all "retro," echoing the marriages of objects on the market stalls—a brass lobster peeking out of a wine cooler, cooking pots full of plastic bananas—that look like Surrealist art. What makes the objects surreal is their conversation, their "intercourse": the way these objects are coupled. New sex partners are always exciting, and no red-light district live sex show could be so novel. The things on the market, and in the café were not designed to belong together. The sentences they make are screwy. With no conjunctions, grammar becomes impossible: a teapot without a lid, a pencil case full of rusty keys-without-locks, the single arm of a shop dummy, gesturing, at what?

Bricolage… this universe of instruments is closed and the rules of the game are always to make do with "whatever is at hand," that is to say with a set of tools and materials that is always finite.
Lévi-Strauss, The Savage Mind

If one calls bricolage the necessity of borrowing one's concept from the text of a heritage which is more or less coherent or ruined, it must be said that every discourse is bricoleur.
Jacques Derrida, Structure, Sign and Play

Why do we need to hang onto this old stuff? Is it because the new stuff's scary? Things don't need us any more. We remake them anxiously, like the furniture designer my hosts sent me to see, whose tables and chairs were made from reclaimed sleepers, whose clothes were complicated stiff arrangements in denial of her flesh, and who wore a necklace made from the cogs of an old watch, like the sign made from interlaced cutlery that hangs above me in the café. We don't need things to function any more. We pass them around as novelties, sell them for prices high as Dutch tulip bulbs, just for the way they look, for what they evoke. No wonder they have abandoned us. In supermarkets the last barcoded apples nudge each other to signal the forklifts to restock. Though I've never seen it done, I've heard your fridge can do your shopping for you, that your car can book itself in for a service. Now objects speak to each other virtually, they no longer fulfill our fantasies: we may fulfill theirs.

The tyranny of an object, he thought. It doesn't know I exist.
P K Dick, *ibid*

It's always happening in Korea, in Japan. It's always happening somewhere else. But even here the web can net me just about anything I like. I can ask for knowledge, sex, love, and it will appear In Real Life a little later, through the post, as a printout from a 3D printer, on a high stool in a singles bar. There's still a wait, a microvoid, so small sometimes as to be unnoticed, that means the net has an uneasy relationship with the real, as uneasy as a word with its object.

All objects are now surreal. It's not only the vase that's out of date. It's any vase. Any use of an object is ironic, every *thing* is kitsch. This café speaks the language of kitsch, which is necessarily international, and full of queasy humor. Like an off-color joke, kitsch is more comfortable with objects that are once removed by class or nationality. And, now any thing's a sign—more than the thing itself—it's easier to make a joke than a promise.

But not everything in the café's old. There are the other things here that look old, but aren't: skeuomorphs (that big clock on the wall, crackle-glazed, yellowed, purposely—perversely—dented: rust spots spray-painted on) are promises we know will never be fulfilled because a promise is conditional on the future, and here there has been no time-lapse between cause and effect. I was in a place like this with my dad once, on the wall a distressed tin sign listing drinks. He couldn't tell the difference between the "aged" and the really old. Antique himself, he's too old, not for retro, but for its imitation. Maybe one day I'll hardly know the difference either. There'll come a time objects will outdate me—they're tricky that way, that's how things are. Is that what it means to be objectified?

I said we had no love tokens. Not quite true. Sometimes you sent me things—no, they were images of things: ASCII art, Instagram "Polaroids," photos of retro chocolate bars obsolete before the web: reality twice removed: first by time, then by technology, the sort of pics that are passed round the net like cigarette cards, photos of things that never made it into the future, their heads stuck in time's railings subject to taunts and kicks. Think and you'll recognize them, like any classroom bully. Sci-fi writer, Bruce Sterling, calls this marriage of retro and high technology "atemporal" (how much of the Net is defined not by technologists, but storytellers!). I understood, played the game, sent you a clip of Buckminster Fuller's proto-car, a smooth-parking manatee of a machine: a possible future that never went into production. I re-shot the grainy 1930s black and white film stock on my crystal-clear smartphone in a Paris museum. Atemporal enough? An exchange of gifts is traditional in courtship. Each image, as it crosses the microvoid between us, a virtual bunch of flowers.

But online is a place where objects don't matter as much as the connections they can make: the grammar, not the nouns:

I still live in a castle of meanings, not things.
Italo Calvino, *Numbers in the Dark*

any noun, any object will do. Perhaps that's how the clip of the car worked: what mattered wasn't what it was but that, as it never became, it was available as a word for use in a private vocabulary, its meaning always unfixed, potential, personal.

"Why don't we buy a farmers' house all together?" Five smart urban Dutch drinking coffee at the rustic table behind me discuss possible retro-utopias in English. They want to live in the country, like the old days, but with friends and technology, like in the city. They're young, don't have kids yet, so everything is easy. "We wouldn't need much, could live more simply, share everything." One man shrugs: "It's always going to be a balance," (he cups his hands, weighs them).

"I know it's gonna work really nice," a woman tells him, "You should move there too."

"It's tough work," says another woman who, she tells them, used to run a b&b.

I sit, and type. "Ah," says the owner of the junk stall opposite, "you're one of those people." (How many women, I wonder, has he seen, riffling through his broken goods for something that might complete them.)

Amsterdam 13th May

I get up and, disobeying my hosts again, walk to the docks.

The windows in the modern developments are smaller here, but I still pass coy arrangements: on stage between curtains, lacy as crotchless knickers, a topiary bush, a designer pendant lampshade placed centrally, for show. Both say, here I am, framed. Look at me. Mirror, window? Still as my host's still lifes. *Nature morte*: is it living or dead, and, if dead, what can live on in it?

Amsterdam is made entirely from material things. Maybe it's because they had to make the land, pulling it back from the sea, brick by brick. Already, by rights, I should be more than half below the waterline. The new buildings here, where they do not look like shipping containers, look like ships. This area used to be rough, I was told. Now rough-sided warehouses, their raw edges carefully preserved, are bars and flats, a gallery, a museum. Gentrification is a northern European thing: it's shabby chic—to take something old and remake it not so it looks new, but so it still looks old, and then to say that it is better than new things. I don't mean old like an antique—echt, kosher—I mean old like an old, old thing— down at heel, worn by use—and to say it's a better thing than something new, or shiny or functional, to say it is more authentic because of what has been done with it. That's puritanism. And though I'm a puritan, the kind that could worship the absence of an oculus, I'm a little too absent-minded for this kind of material.

I find a café, write up my notebooks. Thirty thousand words. That's a lot, I guess. That's when you email to ask when I'll be back in London: *Can you see me?* I answer that one, right away. You write back. You *might* be there then, *which train will I come in on?* I tell you. Nothing more. Those are the rules. Object oriented programming: love points at a space and some kind of data arrives to fill it. Data + behavior: an object is created. I answered you again. This is inherited behavior, and there is nothing I can do to make it die in me.

Amsterdam–Berlin, 14 May

Time is so very useful when you want to catch your train but, maybe not for other things.

I leave Amsterdam, later than I'd hoped. I am increasingly slowed down.

I speak some German, though I don't speak German, not really. *Wan geht das nexte trein nach Berlin? Nach: (preposition) up to, and including*—but not including Bad Benthof, where we are delayed for three further hours due to something that happened some time ago, somewhere else down the line. On the platform there's a small store selling chocolate and an obscene lone dildo of a frankfurter displayed in a glass steamer like the window of an

Amsterdam sex shop. I can stray from the station, but not far. And I don't get far. The roads are wide and lined with green trees, but there are no pedestrians and many cars. Across the triple-laned highway there is a cheap clothes shop, and because there is nothing else to look at, I jaywalk the highway to see, but there are no more shops by it, and there is nowhere to buy a coffee, nowhere to sit, to meet, and nowhere in the distance down the long road in either direction that will answer any of these thoughts: nothing but white low modern houses from which nobody comes and goes, but beside which cars pass at frightening speed, having other places to go. I seem to be getting nowhere fast, whatever speed I walk. I'm not used to this. It takes such a long time to get back across the highway to the station. Bad Ben-thof is the opposite of the city: a suburb. I had assumed the opposite of the city might be the country.

Back on the platform, I smoke a cigarette and wait, peering in both directions towards potential distant trains and, watching for the same trains, there is a dancer who is traveling to Weimar. He is beautiful, young and nervous. He lights my cigarette, asks me what I am writing. I tell him.

He says, "I don't like to talk on the Internet. I always have to explain myself twice. I am not good with words."

"But you speak four languages." He has already told me: French, Dutch, Spanish and English. He understands a little German too, yes, he says. But not to write, no.

"I'm the opposite," I say. "Also, sometimes a good writer will write something that means two different things, even at once, and in the same language."

"Ah," he says, "now that is very confusing."

13 Berlin/Dreaming
14/15 May

Berlin is my last city, a city I do not know, am too tired to meet. At the station—a glass jigsaw with eight levels, and many shops, which has no link to the U-bahn—no one meets me, and I can't leave. I am too tired to leave, almost. I find a map, but the city is so big: bigger than Rome, Paris, bigger than Amsterdam, Athens, Sofia. I give in, for once, take a taxi.

I want, here, to know nothing. I have, here, nothing to say. I'm dropped in the main street in the center of Kreuzberg outside a friend of a friend's flat in a hof. Each hof is a castle courtyard with towers, four-cornered, near identical, each blue square above each hof the same with birds flying over. Each tower I try is the wrong tower. I call my friend but her words could meet any tower, any hof. My phone is running out of charge when I find it. The flat in the hof is one room front, one room back, no central heating, a shared toilet on the stairs. In the entrance between the two rooms, a vast and rusted machine that could be a stove, could be a boiler. It does not work. No one has lived here for some time. It's so cold. I switch on the tiny portable heater, lie awake under a thin slice of synthetic duvet, get up again, call the friend, who has another friend who lives around the corner, who has a spare room. I walk to his apartment, which is in another Berlin, also so Berlin, in his hall an androgynous mannequin, 30s movie posters. Does he wear a bowler hat? Does he have a small gray moustache, does he want to talk? Does he give me red wine and does he ask for the same thing all my hosts demand in payment: my story? Because of the red wine, does my story slip out smoothly along its grooves, though I am surprised it does because I am so tired. Do I regret, resist this smoothness, which is not what I sought, but is what I have? Yes, but there's nothing I can do. I am a storyteller now.

I go into the small spare bedroom with red walls, only slightly bigger than its sagging single bed, and sleep. All night the room rattles. The mattress, a network of springs. Outside my window a metal shutter beyond the glass excludes all light. Builders wake me at 6 a.m. I sleep and sleep. I do not see Berlin.

I dream that there is a party at my house. My parents are there (I never give parties, though they do). They have invited their friends and parts of my house have expanded to fit them. It is three, four in the morning and some children (who invited them to the party?) are still awake. In my dream I am still married. My husband is in bed upstairs. Things are getting out of hand. I am supposed to put the children to bed to placate my husband, who thinks they should not be awake, but my parents' friends keep arriving. I answer the door and it is you. You are on crutches, dressed for winter in your coat and hat. You look terrible. We kiss. You didn't know I was still married. I have to find you somewhere to sleep without disturbing the children, my husband, my parents. I put blankets over you on the sofa and lie down with you. There are various incidents, but by now it is nearly morning. Your parents arrive with your fiancée, whom you had not mentioned, and who I find both ugly, and utterly unlike me, though I am determined to like her. She has on a red coat with square shoulders and gold buttons, a military coat. Her hair is short, blonde, businesslike. I am shocked you want to marry someone like that. But it explains everything. You leave with your family. I know it's over, but I have the satisfaction of knowing that neither you nor my family have discovered each other's presence.

Is this the end of mourning? I have conjured the dead in dreams before, called them up to puppet goodbyes, forgiveness, to touch, to hear a voice again. Or perhaps I allowed their visits.

16 May

How long does it take to know a city? I don't know, don't care anymore, don't walk in Berlin, only down the main street in Kreuzberg, to the park, along the canal, and back, and round that grid bounded at all sides by main roads. I walk with a friend who points out copper circles in the pavement: the names of Jews deported from each block. I no longer notice, no longer want, no longer need to know such things. I have no more capacity for new things. I am exhausted.

Well that's what I traveled for, to fill myself up with new things until I was entirely empty, to travel so fast I disappeared, to see what was left. That's why I took so long a route. And, finally, here I am.

By the side of the canal the year rewinds. It was like this when I left England: the rain, the cold only just giving way to spring. On the banks of the canal, blossom begins again, easy as reversing a film.

The last month may not have existed, or I might have fast-forwarded through the next eleven months, compacted, telescoped. What do I have to show for it? My pockets are full of crumbs and pieces of paper: receipts, addresses, door codes: notes for oblivion. My phone is clogged with the names of WiFi networks from bars, hostels, cafés, libraries, stations. In my purse, still a couple of coins from that time I met you in another country. I throw them into the canal. They were never yours anyway: they were mine. In fairy tales things thrown into rivers come back as something else entirely. But that's in running water. What about still?

I have friends here in Berlin: J, who pointed out the copper disks, on our way to get Turkish pancakes, T, who runs a café, V who tells me she will read my Tarot. I meet her in a café in the basement of the university where she works. It is empty. She spills her cards onto the formica table, asks for my birthday, asks if I know yours. I tell her.

I used to consult my cards, interrogating them far beyond the rules of the game.
Breton, *Mad Love*

I choose six cards, blind, from the pack. She makes an H formation: three for you, and three for me, linked by one central card. She turns them over. On your side: Art, Power, The Prince of Cups ("A muse, or an artist." "You, or me?" I ask. V says, "I don't know."). On my side: the Three of Wands (virtue), The Ace of Swords (reason), The Ace of Disks ("a beginning," V says, "from the physical, the material").

In the middle, linking us, The Lovers.

"About love then?" "Yes," says V, "but also other things: fantasy, projection, a union of opposites."

I am strictly rational: I believe in signs, symbols, magical portents.

But why do you get all the good cards?

I walk back through Prenzlaurberg. Prenzlauerberg was in East Berlin, right by the wall, the other side from Kreuzberg. It's one of those places you can still see the Cold War bullet marks pocked on the stones like pollution. To the north is a park called the Mauerpark, which means just, Wall Park, where the wall was. It is not a smart park. In it is some kind of stadium, I don't know what for. Here it is still winter. The grass shows bare in patches and the ground is uneven. Paths wind, although there are no bushes for them to wind around. Some of the paths look unofficial, beaten by feet, though they are not short cuts and are as twisty as the official paths. There is some statuary, all graffitied: a smaller-than-life polar bear, vulnerable because white, is covered with words, its eyes drawn over with blank bronze squares. I am frightened of the people in the park because something about the park is frightening, despite the fact they are often families with young children, despite the fact one woman casually exhibits an expensive camera. It is cold, not snowing, though it could, for all that it's May. The sky is blank. The people here are trying to have fun.

At the very end of the park are outdoor cafés serving gluhwein and food, but it's too cold, and I'm looking for somewhere inside. Then, on the steps beyond the park, where it meets a market, the usual people with towels spread out: old men and women with hopelessly curated small broken objects, a white rasta with a box of creased paperbacks, an art student selling earrings made from the legs of tiny plastic dolls, around fifteen people with a large green banner and petitions: SAVE THE ENGLISH THEATRE IN BERLIN...

Go to Berlin, since you were there once before, and you could in this way learn whether repetition was possible and what it meant. I had come to a standstill in my attempts to resolve this problem at home.
Kierkegaard, *Repetition*

I daydream in May, in a café called November. Why name a café after such a month? Lovely lovely Berlin spring: a long low dusk that starts at four.

I want you to walk in now unexpected, like in a movie or a stage play at the English Theatre. No, like in a romcom. You said I wanted to live in one, and, yes, no one else I know is capable of fulfilling so unlikely, so ridiculous a role as its hero. But have you been to Berlin? "No." Why wouldn't you? "It might have been interesting in the 90s. It's not the same now." But how would you know?

How long does it take me to know a city? In any city there are streets I will never go down. That's normal. I am tired of this. I don't want to know cities any more. I am carrying something that drags. It is a not thing. It is you-not-being-there, and its heaviness has only begun to weigh on me again since you got back in touch. I will never see this city with you, cannot even trace your footsteps as you have never come here. There has never been a time we could have walked it together. I am impatient with Berlin. Whatever direction I walk, I will not find you, no, not even your memory.

I remember you showed me your city once. You took me to look at plinths with famous men on horses. If they had only two hooves on the ground, you said, they had died in battle, if one hoof was raised, then they had died of wounds after. I said this was an urban myth, that there was no system. You seemed insulted, assured me there was. You gave me the facts, or things that sounded like facts—

Two people walking near each other constitute a single influencing body primed.
Breton, *Mad Love*

information, at any rate. I was surprised you thought they mattered. These were things I did not need to know. You asked if there was more you could tell me, more you could show, but I'd never wanted to see any of it. I'd come to see you and, when I was with you, I was not anywhere else, including there.

You hurried me round historic streets, my arm in yours, but we went into malls, not museums, into chain cafés, not cathedrals. We stopped to sit on benches in new shopping precincts. You would take me to other places, you said: the art galleries where you'd seen good shows, the concert halls where they knew you, and would give you tickets for free, but somehow we never went. We walked close, touching, side to side. We leaned into windows together, our faces almost meeting. *Are we nearly there yet?* Your talk about women redoubled. Any girl was beautiful: the waitress, the policewoman, the woman across the street. You were eager to show them to me: a girl you had seen working at a newspaper kiosk earlier that week. You insisted we make a detour: would she be there again? When we found the shop, she wasn't, so we sat on the steps beside it, where I reached across and curled a strand of you hair round my finger. We sat there in silence for probably a minute after. It seemed like longer of course, but I can estimate these things quite ruthlessly.

I always came to see you, never the other way round. You dismissed my city as nowhere anyone would want to see, but when I arrived in yours, you told me, "Don't hold my hand, someone might see us." See what? "See that I'm with someone." I don't think you expected that, the possibility of being seen.

What a dickhead, feeding you that load of bollocks. How could you? Yes how could I, even as I knew you were, and at the same time also weren't, because you were so much else besides. Well, we're all human; we have only each other and, aggression having been a marker of men's attention to me, sometimes it happens like that. I'm too tired to give a fuck. In the café, in Berlin, I am running out of power.

I go back to the apartment and power down for real.

So we finally went to bed (in my dreams) and in this dream I own a sweet shop. The counters are old-fashioned, worn oak with barley sugar supports between the niches. I look for sweets but there are none, in the corners of the recesses only dust.

Behind the sweet shop is a bedroom, a damp lean-to with fiberboard walls, a worn pink chenille bedspread, a double bed, things strewn on nightstands, again wood, also dusty and ringed with the ghosts of glasses: a syringe I forgot, a used condom I forgot. Dust motes in the sunlight through the ugly long low modern window, the kind of window I know well enough to look for the damp, the moss at its corners. We go to bed. You look nothing like you. Someone from the shop keeps interrupting. You come too soon. And then you go.

After I giggle and blush with the shop girls. They know what happened. They are happy for me. They are proud.

Should I take this as a sign? Dreams are predictive, and those that do not come true within a short space, said Artemidorus, the second-century Greek who wrote the earliest extant book on the interpretation of dreams, may be considered allegorical, symbolic. Only the very virtuous dream the long-term future, and I already know I am not one of them. But I am not one to worry about the state of my soul. Sex dreams, Artemidorus said, are always about some-

The gods spoke directly to souls that are pure.
Michel Foucault, *History of Sexuality Vol. 3*

thing else, though Freud said that dreams about almost anything else are usually about sex. Like a mirror, a dream is all opposite, yes like a reflection, not a photograph. My dreams show you the wrong way round until I've become so used to seeing you like that, that when I see you in London, I may no longer recognize you any other way.

I don't know what I do all day. Maybe nothing. It's evening already. German prepositions of time and space confuse me. As well as *nach*, which means both "up to" and "after," there is *nur* ("only just" but also "excluding"), and *jetzt* ("not yet" but also "already" and "from now on").

A city is the way you cross it, but I'm too tired to engage. On the U-bahn, the seats are upholstered in pretty, kitsch red, white and blue. The cushions are shiny but the backrests are gray. Are they dirty? Are they more worn or less polished than the seats? I can't be bothered to decipher. I am going to meet T at the café she runs in a cool street where cold Berlin saplings are just beginning to leaf. T says Berlin becomes Berlin at different times of day. As in London, she says, the city runs on different time zones. She used to go out with the other black girls in London to the hairdressers at midnight, exit at 2 a.m., get to the clubs when the white kids were leaving. East Berlin used to be cool, she says, but now this area of Berlin is cool because it's multicultural. Now the non-Germans in the city, *"by which I mean the English, the Americans,"* she says, prefer to live nowhere else.

After dinner with T, I walk back to the U-bahn, and, at this time of day, the street is so very Berlin, so very different from the afternoon city, which was so very Berlin too. Some of these people making this type of Berlin on the street right now surely couldn't be the same people who appear here at other times of day or, if they are, they look different. Some people only exist at certain moments. Like me. I'm on two time tracks, living in the future at the same time as the past. I hardly exist at all.

You said, *You're such a tourist.*
　　You said, *The English abroad...*
　　You said, *I didn't think you'd be like them.*
　　I have no answer for that, none worth telling.
　　Been here before, you said.
　　I said, *I am not anyone you have known before.*

Time spent with you was so hard and so bright that I asked myself afterwards, why I didn't do anything—anything!—to prolong it. But how do you extend a moment, and how can I compress the time here so I can cross it quicker to arrive at our meeting point? I am trying to get to the end of this time. If I sleep, my mind will take up the time for me. If I dream, I won't stop being impatient, but I will feel it at one remove.

It takes such a long time to cross the Berlin night back to where I'm staying, so I can sleep away this city, which is only one of the terrible places people have made for themselves to live in, as cold and strange as the twenty-four hour neon signs on the street outside, promising all night on auto.

I wake up to the rattling metal blind. I open it. Behind, it is not morning. I sit up, check my email, (a reflex), write to you, *Happy birthday. (It is your birthday?)* V's tarot made me replay the date. (If I write to you about everyday things, retexture the gap with invisible mending, something might be strengthened.) When we talked in the past, I'd wake up before you messaged me. Knowing you were online in another time zone, I'd become insomniac mirroring you. I wake again, several hours later. You've written back. I'm wrong. You tell me your birthday's date. I could have sworn… Superstitious, I'm disappointed with myself. I have invalidated V's reading? Worse, will I have altered our outcome by finding out I was wrong?

What are you doing at the other end? I don't even know whether you're in day or night. What do you do when you get insomnia?

17 May

V rereads my tarot on a cramped table in a coffee shop. *That last reading was wrong then?* "No," says V, "no reading is wrong." But she will not reread the same formation. Instead she will read my immediate future, the next week. I pick seven cards, which she deals in an inverted V: Art, The Lovers (again!), The Star, The Hierophant, The Prince of Daggers, The Devil, The Tower.

The situation: The Lovers. Art, a collaboration, a joint project.

The Hierophant—the obstacle—an advisor, a received idea or direction, way of going.

The present: The Prince of Daggers, practically planting seeds for the future.

The Devil—the card in the position of the future—"Secrecy," says, V, "concealment, consequent social opprobrium."

The Tower (the center card, a hinge): chaos, destruction, an end and a beginning.

Outcome: The Star, moving between heaven and earth, dream and waking.

This time the trumps are all mine.

I go back to my room, put on perfume, lipstick. I want to look like a woman, to find a situation a woman might find herself in. I want to go out and drink and flirt—I don't care who with. I want to fool around. I think of you but not for long or seriously. Though the thought keeps coming back, the game's not worth the candle.

I meet a friend, an artist. He's big, a continent. Canadian, but he's been in Berlin since the 90s and before, starting in squats that are now chic apartment buildings. He's 100 percent Berliner, 100 percent authentic. He asks, and I tell him my story because it is now so easy to tell, so easy it sounds like someone else's. He laughs, and I'm not sure I like it. He opens wine. I balance on the kitchen sink to photograph the Berlin night through a tiny high window. We go to a supermarket and he buys two fish. He invites me to cook them and I wonder if he has noticed the perfume, the lipstick, but that he requires a further performance, some kind of test of femininity, or just that he is old, old-fashioned, that I owe him as he paid for the wine, the flesh. I cook the fish on the gas ring in his studio, and I cook them badly. They are both burnt and undercooked. I have not cooked for so long. He does not like the fish and, though he says they are ok, he can't say it with conviction. When we are about halfway through eating them he lunges with no warning to kiss me on the lips and, seeing him come at me so slowly and also without conviction, I have time to move to one side though he keeps on coming in the same direction until he has passed right by me like in a cartoon.

He says, "I thought you wanted to experiment." This is not something I have said. I say, "I'm sort of committed to someone back in London." "Oh," he says, disgusted, "A 'romance' thing."

We finish the fish, and I leave politely. I walk back angry. He feels cheated. I feel cheated. I had thought he was too old. He had not thought I had thought so. Perhaps he does not know I think so. Perhaps I am wrong to think so, but he is, at least for me. It would be boring to be cross, naive, but I am allowed to have a preference. Am I cross? Who knows. I'm tired. I don't care. I'm enervated, slightly ecstatic. Something has woken up in me. Something has happened in my blood. At any rate. I feel sorry for him.

It was my story that got him. I loved it when you told me stories. I didn't care if they were all the same, stuck on repeat. Tell me again. Story is a disease. One of its symptoms is desire, love even, though I find it impossible to describe love in a story, not without dissimilitude, for as soon as I show one side of love, another side's face down, a playing card, a six-sided dice, a twenty-sided dice. Everything I do is about telling my story but no one will ever know the whole thing all at once: on paper I can never be 3D all the way around. For my convenience you have become a story, have coalesced temporarily at least, and I have used you to provoke lodging, friendship, lust. I am ashamed at my proficiency, and it is the first time I have been ashamed of anything on this journey so far, with a shame that comes from something I have done, not something that has been done to me. That's progress, perhaps! All the same I won't do it again. I will not explain you to myself. I will not explain you to other people. I do not like any longer not to find stories difficult. Let me put things back into the wrong order. Let me not get them straight. Let everything be fresh and terrible again. Let my thoughts of you not be worn down by the thinking, let me be too tired to think at all. Elegance comes with experience, but one can be too elegant. I need all those *lets* to put the brakes on words that slip out too easily, as I let my story out hand over hand. I need the *nots* to tie it down—without them, it's so easy to slip up.

And in the morning I am back at Berlin central station as though I never left. It's early and I'm hungover after last night. A man comes up to me in shades, at 6 a.m., black leather jacket. He looks like Lou Reed in *Berlin* (I mean the album), he looks like the ghost of Berlin (I mean the city, or the dream of it anyway, as I have seen so little of the reality). He walks up to me and says, in German-accented English, "Gimme ten Euros." "I'm sorry…" an automatic reply. He turns sharply. "You're sorry? I'm sorry. Don't cry, baby, boo hoo." I want to call him back, to explain that I'm not sorry for anything really: that it's just something the English say.

On the train, I sleep. I am getting closer to the moment that might take place between us, if it's possible to use that word, us, again. I hope I will dream about you. If I dream about you I hope there will be no reason not to dream. Love like hope… I hope, however hopeless, that you dream about me too.

I think it is unlikely.

I dream you are driving to the airport in your old brown car. I am in the passenger seat though I will not board the plane. We are on a fly-over which is, I think, in London. The car's steering wheel is on the left, like the cars on the continent, but it is still your car and when I look across at you, you are sitting on the right, as you would in England, but I think you are driving on the right, as you would on the continent, and that the traffic flows as it would there too. I know that you are leaving. You have written a stack of self-help books, or perhaps they are travel guides. They are on the seat beside you. I am also on the seat beside you. But they are there too and, at the same time I am not, and when I am there, they are not, and yet there they are.

Why did anyone ever think dreams told the future? Only the simple dreamer dreams directly, said Artemidorus. Ok then I am simple, conjuring only what I know I desire, but my dreams pull no punches, they bring something to an end, which I do not desire, which is something my waking mind will not do. *He will come back*, my dreams say or, more often, *he has gone*.

The first time I dreamt of you was the week after you ditched me. *We were in a foreign city, you'd been going to get married all along. My job was to help your girlfriend choose a dress.* Who would give me such a job? I don't know. Perhaps I gave it to myself.

And why do I deal you all the best cards?

The dreams I have are images, mostly. I dream in color but I don't remember sound. Words happen in my dreams, but they are rarely written and never heard, like in a porn clip. My dreams, post-Freudian retrospectors, show porn films from the might-have-been. Only in daydreams do I hear you speak—those romcom fantasies, those meetings cute, whole conversations I have had the leisure to invent. The different outcomes play helplessly on loop across my mind, but only when awake. I am, perhaps, more helpless awake than asleep.

A dream can be a repetition of desire, or a repetition of absence, as a successful diet is a repetition of absence. My dreams are a regime of some kind, but I did not ask for my life to be mended. Awake, I don't want to forgive, or condemn you, to find excuses for your behavior, or reasons. And I do not want love softened to liking, friendship, to pity, or to dismissal. What is my brain playing at?

19th May

I stay in Paris overnight: a friend's floor. So now just the wait… four hours… not even that.

Sitting opposite two women on the Eurostar I hear the money talk, and family talk. I've only seen the social ribs since I no longer fit, and now they stick out: the children, the holidays, the boyfriends, the plans…

One says, "I love Paris, but I wouldn't want to go on my own."

They other says, "Well, you've got your life now, haven't you?"

What *is* that?

Whatever it is, it makes me furious.

I've never not wanted to go anywhere alone. I like to be on my own, but my "own" isn't something I've *got*: it's as slippery as *my life*. What I own of my life is often in relation to someone else, but I don't need them always to travel with me. Yes, other people own parts of my life, and, if they tear their part of it out, well, that's torn it, but it's no more than a rip. How old are these women? One is 50ish, one looks younger than me. And they've both "got" their life, already, mortgage paid, rent-free. How repulsive to have caught hold of that slippery thing that will soon die for being held, a fish out of water. "Forget about him, get a life," that's what some friends have told me, as though love were outside of life. Or do they mean that grieving for love, missing someone, is the opposite of life, that a full life should be stuffed full, with no room for this necessary nothing happening?

The time we'll meet is moving towards me. I can feel the elevator movement, the rush of falling. It's like when you know you're about to spill a glass of water before you do, and you carry the movement through almost on purpose. It's like when you're going down a steep hill in a car, and your stomach anticipates the lurch. I could do something about it—but only in the negative. I can't speed up my arrival, but I could postpone, could cancel it altogether. No messages for the last 24 hours. 36 hours ago, you were "probably" (leaving for London) "today or tomorrow morning." I'm cowed by your terseness, can't pare things down further in reply. The only way I can go is into silence. We used to email twenty times a day, more. You're not one to lie, at least I think, but, are you being economical with the truth? At least you're traveling toward me this time. You've never done that before. You told me what time your train gets in. Regulated by timetables, so long as you're on board, you lack the opportunity to be late.

I sleep. I will make myself nothing until you wake me.

I don't write to you.
        You don't write to me.
        I don't dream about you.

14 London/Ending
19 May

So, in the future perfect, which is now the past, my train will have pulled into the station. We will have met. We will have drunk a couple of strong afternoon cocktails at a nearby bar for dutch courage, then I will have put my hand in yours and you will have leaned toward me and kissed me and then you (we) will have stopped and, you will have said, *Welcome to England.*

And that will have been a great moment.

But it wasn't of course you weren't when I got to at was, when you that will met way over, no not yet that wasn't which, whenever where we? Were we couldn't not, not, only glass, the things between glass light mid-afternoon was tick off people not, not no, no all of them not, no. Not, glass breaking, light broken no wasn't, and still there isn't, will, will be is light, lighted, lit.

Lit: past tense, yes, that's all for the present. Something separated, orange and blue as through glass, leaving me on the side I wasn't before, with that fuzz in the head—adrenaline is it, or vertigo?—that tells me I have put myself at the mercy. Of what? Of something, someone: you? Me? You weren't there. Of course. I knew it already.

I had always known it.

What else did I expect? You were often late, but absence has a different quality. It wasn't that you weren't there, your not-being-there had gone somewhere else too. Something about it had already passed. The moment spun into the past as trees turn from a speeding train. It had seemed that they were moving, but it was me, and you can't stop a train like you can stop a car. A passenger, passive, there was nothing I could do to go back. The moment became an object. Already I had wrapped it up and put it away, put some time and space between me and it, such a little time and space, no more than from the train to the platform but, as I looked back, it narrowed, so quickly, to almost nothing, as parallel railway tracks appear to meet in the distance so that, from far enough away, they look like a single black line. If you draw one here it splits the page into past and present. Once you've finished, you're free to decide what side of it you're on.

• •

Or perhaps you're not.

There I was. Now here I am.

I am shocked to find myself here.

Here is less than there, one letter less, evidence something has been lost, though I'm not sure exactly what, or when or how.

I get out my phone, click on maps. The pointer says YOU ARE HERE. Well, that's something I suppose. Here I am again, back at the railway station where I started, but I'm not in the same place. I still want to be in love, but find it's nowhere I can stay.

Now that I've crossed that line, come to love's borders, I find I can't go back. I am looking back at something. Was it love? I can no longer tell. Love resists the past tense: *I loved you* points squarely to that state's present absence, but a declaration of love exists in the continuous present, slips from the moment, boundaryless, sends imperfect fingers into the future: *I love you = I will always love you; you* can't say it without a gesture toward forever. Whatever: love's nothing I can hold onto, its abstract never comes to rest in an articled noun. You can have *a* truth, or *a* war, but *a* love? *Be a love* is an injunction to a person to act nicely—to act, yes, but passively, according to instruction. *A love* is not *a lover*, as lovers often do not act nicely, nor do they do as they are told. There's a problem with the noun: it slips towards the verb. Love is an active word, always on the move.

Every love states that it is eternal... a declaration of eternity to be fulfilled or unfurled as best it can be within time.
Alain Badiou, *In Praise of Love*

"You're not even my ex," you told me once. Ex sounds like it should be a suffix, something in the past, but it's a prefix, a beginning. As I am not a satisfactory ex, love is nothing from which I can begin to leave. Unable to exit as to stay, where can I go from here? Nowhere, it seems, not for the moment.

Has something not happened to me? Was the whole thing not an event?
Kierkegaard, *Repetition*

I sit down on one of the benches in the station's concourse outside the Eurostar terminal, where there are bars, and cafés, and shops selling small comforts: cakes, magazines, and makeup, one bookshop, and this moment segues into the last moment I was here.

Time flattens. I scroll through my timeline to prove I got anywhere at all. The awful thing about the Internet is that you can pinpoint the time anything ends. My last message from you was at exactly 12:59 one Saturday, saying you would be late. It is 12:58 now, and it's a Saturday again, for the days come round relentlessly as good weather. It doesn't seem impossible that, at the moment the number flicks over so the time matches exactly, under the spell of the clock, you will appear.

Waiting for you I have wasted so much time like this, breaking down days into hours, crumbling hours into minutes. I've torn off the dates from the day I last saw you, screwing them up, stuffing them into my pockets, hoping to unfold them sometime with you. It's almost a year now since we first met, and soon enough that date will re-cycle, regular as clockwork. How can it have been a year ago? How can the days approach, plain, with no snags? How can those dates continue to exist: surely they were blown off the calendar, leaving nothing but a smoking hole?

The end of love is terrible, but the end of the end of love is sadder. I am sick that time, which does not bring love to an end, also brings love to an end. I know there will be another year, and another year after that, each repeated date papering over the last. And, in the meantime, as time is mean, and as I am not even your ex, I could try to continue to love you, unrequitedly, but—I don't think—unconditionally, or my love would be a gift, like love for a child, not an exchange between adults. Romantic love is a selfish condition. It demands a response, which it always gets, as even the lack of response, turned seamy-side by the lover, is response enough. Love takes place in the conditional which is not even a tense but a mood, twinned with the wishful-thinking subjunctive.

The conditional pulls possibilities back into past, while the subjunctive shunts the sentence forward, still hoping hopelessly for something to arrive: a heavy carriage and a failing engine. Not governed by tenses that find a home in clockwork time, any sentence in this double mood bats back and forth, bypassing the present, restlessly going nowhere.

No surprise: no condition is ever satisfactory for a breakup. Breakup suggests breakdown but the more I break it down, the more I layer up reasons—all those ifs and buts—and they are no resting place. The more it's broken down, the less sense I can make of it, until the whole thing doesn't look like anything at all by the time you sweep up the pieces. How could I ever have tried to build a story out of love, which is all fragments? It takes time to write about moments with their fractal edges, to link them up, and the more insignificant the pieces, the fiddlier it is to put them together into something wide enough to travel across. Writing it down seems such a waste of time.

How much time have I wasted, thinking, writing about you?

For almost the last year I have thought, have written, every day about love. Every day I have a new thought, and it is easy to have new thoughts; the new thoughts never end. My notes sprout notes, but not conclusive ones. The more there are, the further away you get, the more thicknesses of paper I put between us, and the longer it takes to tell even the simplest story. The further apart we are in time, the more I have of you, but the less you are yourself. I have had almost a year to build you. You are now something else, something more mine than yours. Your head has rested beside mine on my pillow for almost a year, no, only the thought of your head, and I have thought about you every day. I still love the *thought* of you. It stays beside me, and it looks almost exactly like you. I've wasted all my time thinking about you, or, rather, I've wasted all my time thinking about my thoughts about you until I'm not sure I can tell the difference between you and them any more. There is so very little to link one thought to another. The art lies in the conjunctions.

All these words, and I still don't know how to make art out of love.

I remember a piece of art where the artist wore a red dress that covered her from neck to beyond her feet, like a lead apron, but was also so red as to make her look as though she might have been skinned. She sat in a bare room on a chair by a table, and the table was bare, and there was space around the table and chair, which were in the middle of the room, with the audience round the edge, standing against the square walls at a safe distance, like at a boxing match. Across the table, opposite the artist, was another chair, and she invited the audience to sit in this chair and look at her. In this piece she was looked at, and she looked back. I say "audience" but I mean one person at a time, so that there were only two of them, the artist and the other, while the looking was going on. Then a photographer took a picture so that the rest of the audience could see what that person looked like when he or she looked at the artist, and maybe this was also a souvenir so the lookers could remember what they looked like when looking, or could prove that they had looked, because no one spoke during the piece, or wrote anything down. It was the kind of art that some people find difficult to call a "piece" of art—as it wasn't something you could keep hold of, or frame and hang in a gallery (maybe that's what the photographer was for)—although the same sort of people are usually happy to call other things that don't last a "piece," like a "piece" of theater, or a "piece" of music.

Marina Abramovic
The Artist is Present, 2010

This piece was a bit like that other piece the artist did years before with a table on which she put 72 objects including a rose a feather honey a whip scissors a scalpel a gun a single bullet, and with them a note that said she would allow the people in the audience to do things to her, which they did: having ripped off her dress, they pushed thorns into her flesh, and threatened to shoot her.

Marina Abramovic
Rhythm 0, 1974

People love to watch pain, until they get bored and go away. Pain is hard to hold onto, but I have held onto mine because it seemed easier to grasp than anything else, or perhaps because it is easier than other things for an artist to represent, or for an audience to notice. You told me once that I should be a cut-up artist, exhibiting my damage. It was one of the destinies you'd painted for me, besides suicide or whore. But, no, I am

Despite the fact that you are an imaginary person, you are in no way a multiplicity, so there is only you and I.
Kierkegaard, *ibid*

not a pain artist: I am a love artist, which is different, though no less ephemeral, no less balanced between active and passive and, like pain art, it needs an observer. One is best but, if not one, then why not many, one by one, like with the artist in the red dress, or like the reader and the writer of a book, as reading, or like love, is a *folie à deux*.

One of the people who came to look at the artist in the red dress was her ex: her ex-lover, ex-collaborator. They had not seen each other for some time, and she had no warning he would appear. He sat down opposite her and looked into her eyes, and his eyes showed an infinity of regret and its inverse: acceptance, or maybe that wasn't what it was—who can tell? In any case, for a moment art stopped and gave way to pure emotion. Then the artist's ex went away and art, which had been present before, once more took love's place. Love stops art because it is love's opposite: art is already finished, while love imperfectly continues. Only one of them can be present at a time. We know it because *They all lived happily ever after*, which only happens when love becomes a story. Only in art do we meet our ends so soon.

The woman in red was an artist and she wanted to stay the whole length of the trip, to make a new kind of art in which the artist remained present, in which art never comes to a (happy) end, but continues in its moment of creation. What was between the artist in red and her ex, I thought could be between us, that thing that spans decades and may change but doesn't leave, that stays, rebounding endlessly between the subjunctive's hope and doubt.

Only he who is really in love, only he is a human being. Only he who can give his love any sort of expression whatever, only he is an artist.
Kierkegaard, *ibid*

It may no longer be love but it *is* something, though I'm not sure what love becomes when it can't be enacted. Sure, we'd have to insert more history between now and that future point in order to get to the same place as the artist in red, and her ex. We haven't earned it yet but we still could. All it would take is time. And I might have to become your ex so we would be able to go beyond an end.

I could never tell if we came to any end because we were always ending. We went straight from all the first times to all the last times. Whenever you told me we were finished, I tried to make a lasting impression, and only a little time passed before you would ask to see me again, always dishing a word when you needed a hook. The closer were got to ending the fewer words we used, until we were shocked to find these words no longer decoration, but that we had come to fulfill them. How horrible to discover ourselves finally at the mercy of what we meant. Still, it all led to nothing, or only to a repeat of the pattern. Our story unrolled like a carpet. Facing forward, I could see only half a foot in front; the rest was behind me. I only understood the pattern looking back at the whole thing from the end. All the time we were not-ending, I couldn't turn to see enough to be able to predict its lines and gaps.

Even now I'm not sure of the edges, whether I've come to them, and if I can distinguish them from the space beyond. But I've never understood this anxiety to neaten up, to finish off. I've forgotten how most books end; I must read one sometime. Everyone remembers the beginnings, all those first lines! And, now I come to think about it, I have stopped reading so many books before the end. They seemed satisfactory just as they were, with the stories keeping going and the characters never reaching any conclusions. I was happy to exist alongside them, just as you do with people you see every day. As for my own story, I've been supplied with enough last lines: *get over it, let it go*, and, again and again, *forget him*. People give me these endings, and so do books and, almost before I can tell, they've taken the place of anything I think, so that it gets hard for me to untangle the stories they've told me from memory.

In the last year I've read everything I could find about love. What did these books tell me? All about what it is to be a lover, next to nothing about the beloved, in any case, nothing that matched your own specific oddness, or maybe I mean my own. But I have found that writing is not a tool that can be turned upon anything: I have not chosen what to write about, I have only decided whether to write about what I have. Writing is not transferrable, perhaps.

One comes to have the disease about which one reads.
Kierkegaard, *ibid*

All love stories end with the letter I. I told you, slyly I suppose, almost nothing about myself, but then there's almost nothing to me. In the short time we were together I tried to make of myself a story that made sense to both of us, but the prompts were always yours, and we worked over what I was until we reached a conclusion I disliked less than some you had proposed. You were wrong about me often, but each statement prompted a question, and I always wanted to reply, until I began to persecute you with answers. Leave him alone, I'd tell myself some

Love has been declared.
Badiou, *In Praise of Love*

days, knowing that whatever my answer, it was bigger than you. If I went looking for love like a punch in the face, is any surprise I found it? But I am still recovering from your words about me, the good ones as much as the bad ones, each of which was mended by the next kind word that always came.

Loving and writing are so close: both involve a little violence. I undertake this effort only for you, though also, and equally, against you. When I end this book I'll extinguish myself but you're coming down with me, or at least my version of you is.

Could it be that to write about love, even to write humbly and responsively, is itself a device to control the topic, to trap and bind it like an animal—so, of necessity, an unloving act?
Nussbaum, *Love's Knowledge*

Writing, I have become willing to be cruel, and I have never been cruel before. (Oh the cruelty of books—inventing people in order to make them suffer!) Breton claimed Nadja was real, but she is untraceable, unphotographed. In his memoir, Breton published her sketches, photos of places they met, as though a space were evidence of a person, and some have read Nadja as pure fantasy, a cut-and-paste job of other lovers. Whoever Nadja was, before the end of the book she disappears. Where does she go? Her author doesn't seem very interested. Breton didn't have the heart to make an end of her. He left her in a limbo of disinformation (rumors of the loony-bin). Was that not an act of cruelty?

Cruelty to whom?

By leaving Nadja's fate unexpectedly open, Breton allows her to be the first to leave. And this may have been an act of love.

The writer is the creation of the word—the word written, which is not the word spoken—which reaches across a gap of space, or time. It was Nadja who created Breton, not the other way around, and you have shown an equal generosity, giving me everything I've written about, which is all I have left of you. Or maybe I have given everything to myself, through the medium of writing to—about—you. It's confusing,

The young girl was not his beloved. She was simply the cause that awakened the poetic in him and thus transformed him into a poet.
Kierkegaard, *ibid*

especially when we were both so quick to make stories. So much of you is left in me. The way I take notes now: small, neat, like you do, the pile of books you told me to read, many of which I have... Look at me now: more you than you are, your leftover. And yet, because we have moved apart in time and space, I find I am not. You peeled off like a paper tattoo. What's left isn't you: a blurry imprint in reverse, transferred to me, no longer your likeness. Am I coming back?

In order to come back I have had to go away. Getting away from you, I've found myself in places where I bumped up against other people: in cities. Moving smoothly through these uncircumscribed spaces where there are no lovers, only strangers, the crowd has shaped me differently. There's not enough contrast. I get fuzzy round the edges, my corners knocked off, never defined so precisely, nor from only one perspective, as in love.

When a scene has little or no apparent structure, we are likely to be confused and frustrated: the eye will roam fruitlessly seeking interest & points of connection, from one fixation to the next, without much success.
Bell, *Landscape Pattern Perception Process*

Cities are made for love, as they are made for loneliness. Because I know it better than it can ever know me, my own city is the easiest place to be lonely, but there are so many different kinds of loneliness in this city, and not all of them can be satisfied by you. I'll bustle against these nothings every day, until I

One sticks his finger in the ground in order to judge where one is. I stick my finger in existence—it feels like nothing.
Kierkegaard, *ibid*

meet another man with his new kind of nothing to fill it. That man I saw across the station bar the day I left—he was ordering, what, a whisky? Looking back, I can see his features clearly, a flash in the forest. And I liked them; he was my type. Seemed like nothing, but now I remember him well. Perhaps he'd do. There is no more beautiful place to look for someone than in a city, but London's so big, and he was leaving too. Will I ever be able to recatch his eye?

We had our cities: one, two, three, plus a ghost city we never got to. No matter: a lover is a tape-recording machine, and I have made a record of all those other cities, have provided myself with scenery to tag my thoughts, to give my mind (my heart, whatever) some landscape. I have recorded the rhythms of the streets, that are written over and under their maps. I have carried them about with me: their noises, the temperature of the air, their smells. I have let my body record them so that, meeting today, I could have told you mouth to mouth.

You have written yourself all over the map of my city until I can no longer distinguish loving you from loving the buildings, the streets. Not that I think of London as anywhere to love now, a dead-end city isolated at the end of the continent, the red and white brickwork, nothing but decoration, the poshed-up villas: nice to see, not anything anyone could ever think about, not really. Priced out of imagination, nothing could go on behind those facades. Unreal city: all swans, dragons, lions—not that they're seen in the flesh, not often: maybe a hedgehog, a fox raiding the bins at dawn and, above, not sparrows, but seagulls. Still, I can't disengage London from love's dis-located headiness. I thought I had walked enough in all the cities in Europe but I find I will have to walk these particular streets again, and many more, before I lose you.

(I saw you once more, a long time after, walking down the Charing Cross Road. There was no home in you.)

I want the world! No I just wanted you and, as I can't have you, I have found it necessary to want everything else. Love has made me greedy, and greed has made me ambitious: that's one more favor you've done me. If *I love you* doesn't mean *I must be near you*, it would be easy for me to keep moving, to continue traveling, writing, in order to defer ending.

There was nothing holding us apart, keeping us together.
    Nothing but words.
    Now there are no more words between us, nothing is happening.
    Nothing.
    Is it possible to *write* that?

I get out my laptop because here, like anywhere else, people will leave you alone if they see you're connected. I open a new email, hit COMPOSE. There are ways of holding on to people, I suppose, and one of them's to keep talking. The more words I type, the more space appears to fill the content. You'd think it'd be the other way round but hit that key—returnreturnreturn—and more page appears. Where there is a gap I put words into it, and there are gaps for stories everywhere. Expand space, and time expands too, the time it takes to write a page, to read it. I could carry on writing to keep time with space, and what I create will continue to loop my story, as though, by putting something into words, I might also make some stay. I could replay the whole thing in words over and over, because I don't want to forget, none of it, not even this. All I want is to remember, endlessly. I know it's not possible. Each loop layers story over experience, which escapes between and through. Writing is a mechanism not for remembering, but for forgetting.

My life is dull now without you to tell it to, and you are the one person who won't allow me to tell it. I could tell my readers everything I could tell my lover. The difference is they can't respond. A book is a one-way process. That's OK. Most people like their pain at one remove and, if they have to get personal, prefer the impersonal: the problem pages, the confessional. To square the public with the private I could join a forum, blog it out, post secrets in public anonymity. Confession dispenses with pain, but the Internet does not forget: its perpetual present makes stories harder to be rid of. There is so little to say, anyway. Or rather, there's so much room online, but there are so few new stories, and mine, which is not, after all, so very unusual, mingles with the stories I have read, until I can hardly tell it from any of the others.

The lesson of so many of these stories is that you get over love. I want to learn nothing from this but, however much I try not to learn, I learn so much—every week, every day. In order to tell my story, I must know little or nothing of what I write until I write it, writing myself out of necessary ignorance, each sentence a performance of inexperience. I must keep on writing to escape knowledge, as knowledge means no more writing. I will not be wise. If I were, how would I ever fall in love again? No knowledge for me, no thank you. What do the wise talk about in the evenings? I won't watch my feet. I'll step in anything that's on the pavement. Messy, yes, and I might be taken for a ride, but at least I'll take a trip and doing so I will preserve something, even if I fall. In love to fall is not to fail (to fail is not to fail! In what, other than love, is failure allowed, expected, embedded the process? In what, other than love, could I fail so well? Where else is failure a sign of success?).

You now begin to see how this lady is: she goes on thinking at all time. She won't simply cry, she will ask what crying consists in. One tear, one argument: that's how her life goes on.
Nussbaum, *ibid*

I am sitting here, at the station, still, because I no longer want to leave this place from which leaving is always an option. Here there are still choices to be made: the endless snack bars, the wine bars, the buffets, their menus affected neither by place nor season. I can even choose not to choose: I've been sitting here all afternoon without going into any of them, and it's getting on for evening, but I can smell the twenty-four-hour coffee and it feels like morning. To stay sitting here, at the station, refusing to make an end, is no kind of wisdom, just a temporary stillness, an absence of pain.

Not that I've suffered all the time; I've even suspected myself, sometimes, of enjoying it. The act of telling has given me a thrill (I've robbed myself of my own suffering! So what?). And, in the meantime I've enjoyed all sorts of other things: eating, and getting drunk, and seeing friends, and brushing my hair until it shone, and reading, and walking through cities, and along canals at sunset, and sitting on hot stone with the wind in my ears. And apart from sometimes having a good time there were other times when I simply didn't have any kind of time at all. I can't mind about everything all the time. It's exhausting. This is only a book. Go off and find some suffering of your own. Let me stay here holding on to what I've got, and suffer while I can. I am ashamed of my weak little pain, that cannot even endure a little space of time.

I get out my phone again. It confirms: YOU HAVE REACHED THE END OF YOUR JOURNEY. I find I don't want to, can't think of a way to end this that won't be with a shrug, a seeyalater, some kind of ironic exit into the wings, which will be revealed as no more than painted card. To leave would be to move on, and, though there has to be some kind of exit, that would not be it. You know already, reader, that I'm not really here, now. The train is long gone and I'm writing all this some time later. I'm only pretending.

I'm a little pretentious, sure, but reading has made you complicit. Stay with me, reader: how can either of us get anywhere unless we pretend?

OK:

Pretend that I walk out of the station. Inside a red bus, lavender seats flower up. A woman frowns past me because I sit down on the steps by the exit, next to one of the many notices that say, CAUTION STEPS. The sun is shining, and in the teeth of the traffic a busker's singing *Every little thing gonna be alright*. And though the old song's blown through creaking lungs, so patently not all right, from one end of that moment to the other, maybe it will be.

Cheer up, darlin', it may never happen!

Well, perhaps it never did. But, like the artist in the red dress, I will keep on sitting and, because I am not ex, nothing will come to an end, though that may mean nothing will rekindle if he ever does sit down opposite me and look into my eyes. I'm beginning to forget whether we ever saw eye-to-eye, but I do remember I tried it once. We were in his old brown car, and I was in the passenger seat. My eyes met his, but I could not look into them any further than I could into the buttons of his coat. Instead, I found myself following the frill of his iris where the blue met the gray until I could have drawn it.

The detailed character of this tale of something which nevertheless didn't happen.
Breton, *Nadja*

Each time I saw you, I stroked you with my eyes until I could sculpt your outsides with my glance and, as I did, I was full of joy. I saw you look at that joy like it was something you could pick up and feel to test its qualities—as you could, because I let you: it was for you—and each time I could tell you were more than half-amused that I'd offered it, or perhaps you were more than half-amused at what I'd offered, but I was happy to have it touched by your gaze, am, oh, happy. It was you who picked it up as if it was something foreign, though it echoed like ringdoves. It was good, good. Good in itself, whatever it was you made of it.

Is there magic in words? Could I influence you subliminally by repeating these liminal words that do no more than trace your limits? If I keep on loving you, saying so, what will happen to us? Probably very little, as very little appears to happen in love, and the less love, the more there is to say about it.

Maybe one day we will see each other again, I mean not across a screen but face-to-face, for what that's worth, and he might even ask me if I wrote this book about him, and I will have to say no. I would have to say *no, I never loved you, not like the person in the book.* Because of this book I will have to deny him In Real Life. People must be protected from words, or more words must be wrapped around to cushion them, until the truth, which words aim at, slips from between the pages, goes somewhere else altogether.

No, words cannot bring anything into being. What's the use in going on? If I keep on writing... but you can't say everything, not in one book. Writing's medium is time, and love's too—and reading!—but love is also the texture of its communication, not just virtual, I mean hair, skin, clothes, touch at close quarters. I dreamt about his coat in Nice, and there was someone else in it. But I could still feel that it was his. Those ghost exteriors were the last things to go. And I'd thought love was noumenal.

What I have learned is very simple. But learning it has been so very complicated. I have traveled this far only so I can say this:

arriving early, I killed time, made myself up in a shop in the station, wiped it off again. It was important that I would not have been sitting for too long, although I knew that I would arrive first, and would be happy for him to find me waiting. Love like hope, though—no—nothing is so like anything else that I can use words to compare one thing to another. *So there they were. She was sitting on stone steps outside a station, reading a book. She was in place. He arrived (late)*, we kissed. Look at us from the outside and we're beautiful.

I refuse to finish this book.

There is no end to love.

Now, where were we?

The author and publishers would like to thank the following for permission to quote:

Notting Hill Editions for Roland Barthes's *Mourning Diary*, translated by Richard Howard (201 1)

Semiotext(e) (2006) and Tuskar Rock (2015) for Chris Kraus's *I Love Dick*

Serpent's Tail (2012) and Flammarion (2009) for Alain Badiou's *In Praise of Love*, translated by Peter Bush

Nebraska Press/Bison Books for Andre Breton's *Mad Love*, Translated by Mary Ann Caws (1988)

Penguin Books for Andre Breton's *Nadja*, Translated by Richard Howard (1999)

Gallimard for *Je suis comme je suis (extraits)*, in *Paroles*, by Jacques Prévert, *Poèmes* (2016)

Semiotext(e) for Chris Kraus's *Aliens & Anorexia* (2000)

Semiotext(e) for Jean Baudrillard's *Simulations*, Translated by Phil Beitchan, Paul Foss, and Paul Patton (1983)

Ginkgo Press for Marshall Macluhan's, *The Medium is the Massage* (2008)

University of Illinois Press for Gayatri Spivak's *Can the Subaltern Speak?* in *Marxism and the Interpretation of Culture* (Cary Nelson and Lawrence Grossberg, 1988)

Bloomsbury Publishing for Anne Carson's Gender and Sound in Audio Culture, Readings in Modern Music, Ed Christoph Cox Daniel Warner (2004)

Writers House for Walter Benjamin's *Illuminations*, translated by Harry Zorn (Pimlico, 1999)

Indiana University Press (2001) and Verlag Klosterman for Martin Heidegger's *Fundamental Concepts of Metaphysics*, Translated by William McNeill and Nicholas Walker

The Dalkey Archive Press for Anne Carson's *Eros The Bittersweet* (2006)

Penguin Books for Susan Sontag's *As Consciousness is Harnessed to Flesh* (2013)

Duke University Press for Denise Riley's *Impersonal Passion: Language as Affect* (2005)

Ishi Press for Albert Speer's *Spandau: The Secret Diaries*, translated by Richard and Clara Winston (2010)

Taylor & Francis and Chicago University Press for Christopher Bell's *Landscape Pattern Perception Process* (Routledge, 2012)

Cambridge University Press for Immanuel Kant's *Analytic of Principles in Critique of Pure Reason*, translated by Paul Guyer and Allen W Wood (1999)

Penguin Books for *Murder, Mourning and Melancholia* by Sigmund Freud, translated by Shaun Whiteside. Original German text copyright © Imago Publishing Co Ltd, 1940, 1946, 1950. Translation and editorial matter copyright © Shaun Whiteside, 2005.

Faber & Faber for Philip Larkin's *Wild Oats* in *The Whitsun Weddings* (2016)

The Adorno Archive for *On Popular Music* (Studies in Philosophy and Social Science, New York Institute of Social Research, 9, 1941)

WW Norton & Company Inc for Jacques Lacan's *Encore* in *The Seminar of Jacques Lacan*, translated by Bruce Fink (1999)

MIT Press for Sherry Turkle's *Evocative Objects* (2007)

The University of Chicago Press for Claude Levi-Strauss's *The Savage Mind* (1968)

Taylor & Francis (2001) and Chicago University Press (1978) for Jacques Derrida's Structure, Sign and Play in Writing and Difference, translated by Alan Bass

GB Agency for Michel Foucault's, *History of Sexuality Vol. 3*, translated by Robert Hurley (Vintage 1988)

Every effort has been made to secure the following permissions:

Basic Books for Sherry Turkle's *Alone together* (2012)

Oxford University Press for Søren Kierkegaard's *Repetition*, translated by M G Piety (2009)

Gallimard for Andre Breton's *Nadja* (1928)

Gerald Duckworth & Co Ltd for Elaine Scarry's *On Beauty and Being Just* (2006)

Penguin Books for Rainer Maria Rilke's *Notebooks of Malte Laurids Brigge*, translated by Michael Hulse (2009)

Random House for Roland Barthes', *A Lover's Discourse*, translated by Richard Howard (2002)

Oxford University Press for Christopher Alexander's *A Timeless Way of Building* (1980)

Penguin Books for Stendhal's *Love*, translated by Gilbert and Suzanne Sale (1975)

Random House, Knopf and Nicole Aragi for *Tag* by Anne Carson, in Float (2016)

Gollancz for Philip K Dick's *Do Androids Dream of Electric Sheep* (2010)

Librarie Plon for Claude Levi-Strauss's, *La Pensée Sauvage* (1962)

Wylie Agency for Italo Calvino's, *Numbers in The Dark*, Translated by Tim Parks (Penguin, 2009)

Oxford University Press for Martha Nussbaum's *Love's Knowledge* (1992)

Early or abridged versions of some chapters have appeared in the following publications:

Ventimiglia and Athens: *Granta Magazine*, 2013 and 2014

Rome: *The Night Museum Guidebook* (Museum of London, 2016)

Vol de Nuit: *Airplane Reading* (Zero Books, 2016)

Amsterdam: *E.R.O.S.* (Eros Press, 2016)

Thanks to Stephen, for the maths, and everything else.

ABOUT THE AUTHOR

Joanna Walsh's work has appeared in *Granta, Narrative, The Stinging Fly* and *Guernica*, amongst others. Her first collection, Fractals, was published by 3:AM Press in 2013, and her non-fiction work *Hotel* was published internationally by Bloomsbury in 2015. This was followed by *Vertigo*, published by And Other Stories in 2016 and shortlisted for the Edge Hill Short Story Prize. Her digitally groundbreaking novella *Seed*, widely praised for its innovation, was released in 2017, and her latest collection of stories *Words from the World's End* is out now.